The TEMPTED SOUL

AN AMISH QUILT NOVEL

ADINA SENFT

Faith Words

New York Boston Nashville

Copyright © 2013 by Shelley Bates

All rights reserved. In accordance with the U.S. Copyright Act of 1976, the scanning, uploading, and electronic sharing of any part of this book without the permission of the publisher is unlawful piracy and theft of the author's intellectual property. If you would like to use material from the book (other than for review purposes), prior written permission must be obtained by contacting the publisher at permissions@hbgusa.com. Thank you for your support of the author's rights.

FaithWords
Hachette Book Group
237 Park Avenue
New York, NY 10017

www.faithwords.com

Printed in the United States of America

RRD-C

First Edition: March 2013
10 9 8 7 6 5 4 3 2 1

FaithWords is a division of Hachette Book Group, Inc.
The FaithWords name and logo are trademarks of Hachette Book Group, Inc.

The Hachette Speakers Bureau provides a wide range of authors for speaking events. To find out more, go to www.hachettespeakersbureau.com or call (866) 376-6591.

The publisher is not responsible for websites (or their content) that are not owned by the publisher.

Library of Congress Cataloging-in-Publication Data

Senft, Adina.
  The tempted soul : an Amish quilt novel / Adina Senft.
    p. cm.
  Summary: "The longing for a child tempts an Amish wife to test the boundaries of her faith in the third installment of the Amish Quilt trilogy." — Provided by publisher.
  ISBN 978-0-89296-849-7 (pbk.) — ISBN 978-1-4555-1793-0 (ebook) 1. Amish—Fiction. 2. Infertility—Fiction. I. Title.
  PS3602.A875T46 2013
  813'.6—dc23
                                2012032115

For my sister Lori

ACKNOWLEDGMENTS

Thanks to Jeff for coming up with ideas that save the day, and to Jackie Yau for constant encouragement and help with getting the facts about IVF right. Thanks also go to Dr. Ronda Wells; neonatal nurse Melissa Maygrove; Dee Stoddard, BSN, RN; and Love Inspired Historicals author Laurie Kingerey for guiding me through Lydia's hospital stay; and to Dr. Manley Clodfelter, with apologies for elevating his heart rate with an ER doc's worst nightmare.

Grateful thanks to Jody Waldrup and the FaithWords art department, whose design of my books and covers is so close to what lives in my head that they constantly amaze me. Lastly, thanks to my editor, Christina Boys, and my agent, Jennifer Jackson, for helping me stitch this series together.

The
TEMPTED
SOUL

There hath no temptation taken you but such as is common to man: but God [is] faithful, who will not suffer you to be tempted above that ye are able; but will with the temptation also make a way to escape, that ye may be able to bear [it].

—I Cor. 10:13, KJV

CHAPTER 1

Chickens and babies had a number of things in common. They needed food and protection. They made their needs known with a variety of sounds. And they loved to be loved.

Carrie Miller buttoned her jacket and sat on the top step of the porch, and within a few moments, Dinah, one of her six Buff Orpington hens, had climbed into her lap and settled there with a contented sigh. If ever a woman was rich in love, Carrie was that woman. She had a husband who loved her and wasn't afraid to show it. She had a home to care for, and friends she could count on no matter what. And now, three quarters of her flock had seen her sitting, so they hopped up the wooden steps and clustered around her, some lying on their sides to soak up the early October sun, some preening their feathers, and some circling and waiting for Dinah to leave her lap so they could have their turn.

Her best friends, Amelia Fischer and Emma Stolzfus, would laugh and ask if the chickens also had their own chairs at the kitchen table with her and Melvin. Or worse, make pointed comments about the intended use of barnyard animals, which God had said were for food. But Carrie just smiled and let them have their fun.

Most days, she enjoyed the chickens as comforting, affectionate companions who would never see the inside of a soup pot if Carrie had anything to say about it.

But on some days...

Days like today, when her monthly had made its scheduled appearance.

On days like these, she teetered on the edge of grief and despair, knowing she must not fall in, and yet finding it impossible not to. On days like today, even the chickens couldn't help. Her left arm tightened around Dinah's fluffy golden body, making the shape of a cradle that in almost eleven years of marriage, had never been filled with what she wanted most—a child of her own.

In their district in Whinburg Township, Pennsylvania—in every district, every Amish community, no matter where you were in the country—the *Kinner* were celebrated as a blessing from God. Some women had families of eight or ten, a miracle Carrie could hardly comprehend. In Whinburg, five or six was the average number, and if you weren't expecting by the end of your first year of marriage, why, the married women would start asking gentle questions.

Some were more sensitive than others when it became obvious their humor and concern caused her pain. Some, like her mother-in-law, Aleta Miller, saw it as their duty to act as a kind of coach, blissfully unaware that their remarks and hints and general helpfulness on the subject were enough to make a person run for the chicken coop, where she could find acceptance and blessed, blessed silence.

And some, like Amelia and Emma, had stopped asking at all.

This was only one of the reasons why Tuesday afternoons meant everything to her. The three of them met every week, in the two hours before Amelia's two boys got home from school, ostensibly to work on a quilt, but really to refresh themselves at the wells of one another's friendship. There were some weeks, when Melvin's work on the farm had not produced as well as it might have, that their time together literally saved Carrie from physical hunger. Certainly it saved her from a kind of hunger of the heart—the kind that a husband, no matter how beloved and caring—might not even know existed.

And today was Tuesday.

Emma had an eye for the little gifts that the *gut Gott* sprinkled upon His children from the largesse of His hands. For Carrie, Tuesdays were among those gifts.

"All right, you," she said to Dinah, sliding her hand under the bird's feet and gently setting her on the warm planks of the porch, "it is time for both of us to give up our idle ways. I'll be back in time to put you in the coop, and the pork roast will be cooked and ready for Melvin's supper."

Dinah stalked away to inspect the flowerbeds, the rest of the flock scrambling to their feet to follow her, just in case they missed out on something.

The quilting frolic was to be at the *Daadi Haus,* where Emma lived with her elderly mother, Lena. The Stolzfus place being way over on the other side of the highway, it meant that either Carrie planned forty-five minutes' walk or simply hitched up and drove. But today, as on most days, Melvin had the buggy to go to the industrial area on the fringes of Lancaster to talk to the businesses there about building shipping pallets. She could take the spring wagon, which was their only other vehicle, but decided against it. Walking was good for her, and she often observed more on foot than she might when she was watching traffic and keeping an eye out for hazards that might spook Jimsy, their gelding.

Besides, she knew a shortcut or two that Jimsy couldn't manage, and that included a walk along the creek that ran through the settlement. It was a good place to watch birds and see the occasional fox or raccoon, and an equally good place to pick flowers and leaves to make things with.

By the time she let herself in through the back gate of the Stolzfus place, she had spotted out a loop of autumn-red Virginia creeper and some wild grape that would make the perfect base for an autumn harvest wreath. Her sister Susan's birthday was coming up, and she knew just the place in her house where it would fit perfectly.

Emma waved from the back porch of the *Daadi Haus*. "You're early! Amelia isn't even here yet, and she's only ten minutes over the field."

"I didn't want to rush the walk on such a pretty day, so I left a little sooner." Carrie hugged Emma, then held her at arm's length. "You look so happy, *Liewi*. Wedding plans must agree with you."

If you wanted to transform a plain, workaday woman into a beautiful one, just apply happiness. It worked so much better than face paint.

Emma's smile flashed and her green eyes sparkled. "They do indeed. Every job I finish, every jar of tomatoes I can, every quart of beans I put up brings me closer to November first. I'm canning my way through the calendar, vegetable by vegetable. By the time we get to potatoes, I'll be married."

Carrie laughed. "That's a good way to look at all this work." In the kitchen, she could see that Emma had only just stopped for the day. Rows of beans and carrots in glass jars sat cooling on towels laid out on the counter, and clean ones filled the drain rack for tomorrow. "I don't know about you, but my garden has been huge this year. I suppose it was because we had such a wet spring."

"God has been very good." Emma put the kettle on the stove, but didn't light the gas burner. It was better to have tea and a snack after you got your work done, not before. Otherwise, you might never get to it. "Lots of vegetables means we can begin married life with a full pantry, and leave plenty for Mamm to take with her when she goes to my sister Katherine's to live. And with your big garden, you will have enough to feed Melvin until April at least."

"Longer if he travels to the auctions to talk to people about buying pallets. I'll be on my own for those weeks."

Emma's gaze settled on her, and Carrie resisted the urge to look away. A gaze like that commanded honesty—and of course they were honest with each other. You couldn't very well offer counsel to a friend if she hid her true feelings and thoughts from you. But some things lay so close to the heart that it was all too easy for words to bruise them.

"Does he have to go?" Emma asked quietly.

"It...it's what he's good at." Melvin had worked so hard at being a farmer, which he was not good at. He'd sunk money they didn't have into the soil, where seed seemed to rot and plows churned up more rocks than crops. In a good year, when something actually grew, then the market would be down and the price of corn or soybeans would be poor, and they would face an oncoming winter with a feeling akin to panic.

God had always provided, but in those moments before He did, Carrie had gazed into her empty cupboards and resigned herself to another supper of eggs on toast instead of the creamed potatoes, pork chops and gravy, and buttered beans she knew other women in the settlement were preparing for their families.

Thank heaven for the chickens. They had sustained her and Melvin through some thin times. And not once had he forced her to put one of them on the table.

He was a good man. Things were looking up for them, now that he had leased his fields out, bought into the pallet shop, and found his calling as one who could bring in business simply by talking to people. Carrie had even put on a little weight, and was now pinning her belt apron closer to the center of her back, as was normal. She needed to eat good things and get her strength up, and then maybe a tiny seed would sprout in a more fertile environment.

She must take a page from Emma's book and look at all the gifts God was providing. Then maybe she could get her mind off those that He was not.

Not yet, anyway.

A few minutes later, they heard Amelia's footsteps on the porch. "Hallo, where is everyone?"

"We're in the kitchen," Emma called.

Carrie met her on the threshold in a flurry of hugs and sorting of carry bags. "Where is Lena today?" she asked Emma as they trooped into the front room, the largest in the house. It gleamed with polish, and in the middle was the dining room table, all its leaves inserted, waiting for the quilt.

"Katherine came up yesterday to get some of her things, and Mamm decided to go along for a visit. She'll be back tomorrow."

"It seems strange to be here without her," Amelia said. "Take a corner of this, will you?"

They shook out the quilt and spread it over the tabletop, its three layers pinned together, the white lines looking like ghosts of the patterns they would quilt on it over the next several weeks.

"It is strange," Emma said, smoothing the fabric with something almost like affection. It was, after all, to be her wedding quilt, made by the three of them over the last year. Their confidences, tears, and laughter had all been stitched into it, square by square. The tiny stitches of their quilting patterns would secure it all, like a protective blanket of friendship that Emma would take into her new life.

Carrie wondered what more the quilt could hold. Until the moment they finished stitching down the binding, she supposed, it would always be able to take just a little more.

But Emma was still speaking. Carrie snapped her wandering thoughts back into order.

"I haven't stayed here alone much since Mamm and I moved in here. I used to chafe at my lack of freedom, but now I see what a gift it has been, being with her all this time." She straightened, her generous mouth a little rueful. "For her seventy-ninth birthday, she'll be down at Katherine's. I wonder if it will seem strange to her, not to celebrate a birthday on the home place. I know it will seem awfully strange to me."

Carrie found her marking chalk and located the place on the twined-feathers border where she'd left off the Tuesday before. "Who will be moving in here after November?" Since Emma's oldest sister, Karen, and her husband owned the farm now, the tenants of the *Daadi Haus* were their decision.

"I haven't been officially informed," said Emma dryly, "but I have a feeling that John's folks will be moving in. His younger brothers are planning to sell that big place they've been farming on the other side of Intercourse, and move to the new settlement in upstate New York. If they do that, the old folks will need somewhere to live."

"Does Karen get along with her in-laws?" Amelia asked almost absently, focused on the pattern she was marking.

Emma thought for a moment. "Well, if you take Carrie's mother-in-law, mix in two cups of your mother, sprinkle with a bit of Mamm—not too much, mind—and a few teaspoons of Mary Lapp, and then whip it all up with some cider vinegar, you'd have an approximation of Ada Stolzfus."

Amelia snorted through her nose, and Carrie let out a whoop of laughter that surprised even her. "Emma!"

"What? It's true." Emma smiled the kind of smile that sees the end of great tribulation and the blessings on the other side. "After all these years of ruling the roost, my sister is going to meet her match—right next door."

"God's plans for us are truly *wunderbaar*," Amelia said, her face not only straight but positively beatific.

"Amen," Carrie said on an equally solemn note, and got back to work before the look on Emma's face made them all burst into unseemly laughter. Only they knew what a trial Karen was to Emma, and how everyone on the farm had chafed under the reins of her control.

When she reached the end of one of the long sides of the quilt, Carrie had to do a little adjusting of the width of the feathers to make them meet the corner pattern properly. "If you had told me in third grade that I'd be using arithmetic every time I picked up a quilting needle, I might have paid more attention."

Emma nodded. "I was explaining to MaryAnn not too long ago that it's vital to learn fractions, otherwise you'll have a lot of *Druwwel* in the kitchen. Being Karen's daughter, she has a very practical view of that kind of thing."

"Nothing more practical than fractions," Amelia said, eyeballing her own corner and clearly doing the same calculations in her head. "She'll need them when she's older and running her own home. Speaking of children getting older, I saw Lydia Zook riding in a courting buggy on Sunday evening. How can that child be sixteen already?"

Carrie nodded sadly. "I know what you mean. I worked as a *Maud* for poor Rachel when Lydia was born—which was only last week, wasn't it?"

"Listen to us," Emma said. "We sound just like the old ladies we were determined never to be. And in case you were wondering, yes, time does go faster the less of it you have left."

"I had never wondered that, but thank you for telling me," Carrie said wryly. "How does anyone know how much they have left, anyway? That's in God's hands."

"Look at Mamm," Emma said. "She's seventy-eight and doesn't seem to mind how fast it goes, only that she gets as much accomplished in a day as she can."

"And then you have someone like poor Lavina Weaver, whose time was cut off in her twenties."

A little silence fell. It hadn't been so long ago that the community had buried Grant Weaver's runaway first wife, who had chosen an *Englisch* man over her husband and family. Carrie risked a glance at Emma, who merely nodded in agreement and whisked chalk along the guides without so much as a hitch in her pace.

"Anyway," Carrie went on, "Look at the Grohl girls. With none of them spoken for yet, even Esther at twenty-eight, the passing of time has to be pretty worrisome for their mother."

"Speaking as someone who waited two years past that, I think you're rushing things," Emma said. "There's time enough yet for all those girls."

Time enough yet.

Time plodded by, as predictable as a plow horse you'd used all your life. Or raced by, like a trotter driven by a teenage boy down the straightaway on Camas Creek Road. But in the end, it passed, leaving you standing on the wayside wondering how you'd been left behind.

CHAPTER 2

When she got home at close to five o'clock, the barn door was standing open. How had Melvin beat her home when he'd have had all that traffic coming out of Lancaster to contend with? Carrie hurried into the bedroom and exchanged her cape and apron for a bib apron, then got to work with final preparations for dinner.

The nice pork roast from the hog they'd butchered last fall, the last of the tomatoes on the sunny side of the house in a salad with basil and chunks of mozzarella cheese, creamed corn, and the little red potatoes that Melvin loved roasted in with the meat. It was the kind of meal that, two years ago, she could only have dreamed about.

Literally. She'd dreamed about food a lot. Endless tables of it—main courses, side dishes, desserts—she'd sat down to many a feast and then awakened in the morning to the cold reality of empty cupboards and a cellar that didn't contain much more than potatoes and onions. Carrie shuddered at the memory and checked the gas oven to make sure the roast had not browned too much on the top.

God sent tribulation to try the soul and refine it as gold, but she couldn't see what good had come of those years other than the fat section of cards in her recipe box, all featuring potatoes and onions. And eggs. She could make more things out of eggs than anyone else she knew.

The sound of heavy steps on the stairs meant Melvin had finished putting the horse away. He sat on the bench in the mudroom and took off his work boots. "It smells *gut* in here, Carrie. I've had a hungry day."

"A short one, too." She maneuvered the roasting pan onto the counter so the roast could sit for ten minutes, then crossed the kitchen. She framed his upturned face with her patchwork potholders and kissed him, whereupon he grabbed her around the waist.

"Come here, *Fraa*, and do that properly." She dropped into his lap with a squeal. It was hard to kiss and laugh at the same time, but somehow they managed it.

When he set her on her feet again, and she returned to the stove to stir the corn, she was still smiling. "I thought sure I'd beat you home. Did you decide not to go to Lancaster and all you boys go fishing instead? It was a beautiful afternoon for it."

"*Nei*, not at all. Brian Steiner would never leave the shop on a work day. The only things he closes for are Thanksgiving, Old Christmas, and the Lord's Day. No, he told me before I left this morning to start packing."

Carrie stopped stirring. "Packing for what?" Oh, surely not. Not another trip, so soon after the last one.

"Apparently there's some kind of wood-industry trade show down in Philadelphia this weekend. He's gone in on a booth with his cousins, who are also in the cabinetmaking business, and he wants me to go."

"If he's gone in on it with his family, then he should go." Oh dear. That had come out a little sharper than she'd meant it to. She remembered she was stirring creamed corn, and turned the flame down to barely a sputter.

"Oh, he's going, all right. But he's not much of a talker. That's why he wants me."

Melvin sounded so happy that at last he had a skill someone needed that she didn't have the heart to let him see how much the news had upset her. "How long will you be gone? Just the weekend?" Two days. She could live with two days. She had before.

"He wants us to go down on the train tomorrow and spend Thursday setting up. The show runs Friday through Monday, but of course our booth will be closed Sunday. With teardown and working up any orders, we'll miss the Tuesday train, so I suppose we'll be back Wednesday sometime."

"A week." She schooled her face to calmness, though she felt anything but.

"I know what you're thinking, *Liebschdi*. And I don't like it either, leaving you alone to manage everything. But this time it will be different."

"Different how? Am I to go with you?"

He actually laughed, as if this idea were absurd. It wasn't absurd at all. She would love to go to Philadelphia, even if it was to spend a day in some big *Englisch* convention center, surrounded by machinery and wood products and goodness knows what. At least they would be together.

"I don't think there would be much to interest you there. Besides, I might not even come back Wednesday. If I don't run down there Sunday, I might stop off at the home place and see Mamm and my brothers."

"I could do that, too." Only Emma, Amelia, and the good *Gott* knew what it cost her to say so. Even a day in her mother-in-law's company was twelve hours too long—but she would do it if it meant she and Melvin could share the rest of the adventure.

"I don't think so, Carrie," he said gently, wrapping his arms around her waist from behind and resting his chin on her shoulder. "If you came, we would have to arrange a motel room just for us, instead of all the men bunking in together to save money. And I would really worry about you, wandering around that place once you got bored at the booth. I wouldn't be able to concentrate on what Brian wants me there for."

"I know," she said softly, poking at the corn now with the tip of the spoon. "But I miss you so much when you're gone. I was hoping this week we might finish picking the apples together, and there's the two sheds to be painted before the rain starts, and—"

"And I have all that taken care of." He released her. "Joshua Steiner is going to help us out while I'm gone."

"He is?" Joshua Steiner had leased one of their fields, and had it planted in beans practically before he'd finished shaking Melvin's hand. He also had his fingers in several other pies in an effort to make a living, since at the moment he didn't have a place of his own. "How will he have time to do that when he's the hired man at that big *Englisch* place down the highway?"

"Apparently it's run pretty well, and he can take time off when he wants to. He came the other day and asked us if we had any work at the shop, of all things. Of course Brian told him no."

Of course he had. Carrie seemed to remember a little history involving a female cousin, back before Bishop Daniel had politely asked Joshua to leave town on an extended visit that had wound up lasting ten years. The fact that the cousin was now happily married and living in another settlement obviously didn't hold any water with Brian Steiner. Cousins or not, he didn't have much use for Joshua.

She wondered if Melvin knew. Or if it would make any difference if he did. He hated gossip like poison, and would probably see any attempts to pass on the reasons for Brian's dislike as just that.

What some called information or history, he called gossip.

Melvin went on, "But I caught up to him out in the parking lot before he got into his buggy, and floated the idea that maybe he could look in on you once or twice while I'm gone. To see if you need anything."

"I don't need anyone besides you looking in on me." Carrie smoothed his hair away from his face. "Someone needs a haircut before he goes to the big city."

"Then someone had better get it done tonight." He kissed her again. "I know you don't need to be looked in on, Carrie. Goodness knows you've been on your own plenty of times before. But like you say, Joshua can do those things you had planned. He can even get started painting the sheds, and I'll finish up when I get home next week. And I'd like to talk with him about putting a second floor in the barn, too, so I can use the ground floor for a workshop."

He wasn't about to be talked out of a plan he'd obviously given some thought to, and Joshua had already agreed to. It wasn't her place to argue and insist on having things her way.

She had to look beyond the inconvenience of having to give someone unfamiliar with their place instructions when it would probably be faster to do some of those things herself. She had to look at Melvin's good heart. He cared about her, cared that she was looked after.

So she kept her unwillingness to herself, and instead, handed him the carving knife. "I think the roast has sat long enough. Would you carve it?"

She could do it herself, and had done it before.

But that wasn't the point, was it?

* * *

Since the train left Lancaster at noon, that meant Melvin had to meet Brian at the shop at seven to catch the eight o'clock bus. It only came through Whinburg twice a day, so if he missed it, Carrie would have to drive him to the Lancaster city limits to catch a city bus, and she'd do anything she had to in order to avoid that. She hated going anywhere near the city; even the tourist area where the edges of it petered out on Highway 30 made her so nervous in traffic she could hardly concentrate. The *Englisch* cars went too fast, and sometimes the drivers even leaned on their horns as they zipped by on the left, frightening the horse practically into the ditch.

She had no difficulties with the *Englisch* as a rule—she counted many in the community as friends, in fact—but even the nice tourists who drove slowly and respectfully had a bad habit of staring. In their rearview mirrors, in their side mirrors, sometimes in no mirrors at all, simply craning their heads around to look. Even in a closed buggy with the storm front up, she felt like a mannequin on display.

The Amish looked the way they did to convey a spirit of *Gelassenheit*, of humility and conformity untainted by the worldly fashions of the day. But Carrie had a feeling that the only thing she managed to convey was anxiety and impatience at the driver who, staring, swerved much too close to the buggy for comfort.

At least the drive home from Whinburg would be along familiar roads, with the mist rising off the fields and the sun beginning to warm the air. She looked forward to it.

"Good-bye, *Liebschdi*. I'll see you in a week." Melvin hugged her before he jumped down from the buggy. He could have shown his affection in the parking lot, but it wouldn't be seemly, since there were Brian and his brother Boyd already, standing by the big family buggy and dressed in their away coats and dark pants, small suitcases on the ground beside them.

She got out and waved at them. "A safe and prosperous journey," she called, and took Jimsy's halter to back him around.

"Let me do that." Startled, she turned to see Joshua Steiner crossing the yard, a hand held out. Melvin shook it and turned to her.

"I told Joshua he might come over today. It seemed like a good idea for him to meet us here, and catch a ride home with you."

Over his shoulder, she saw Brian turn away and say something to Boyd.

Joshua's quick eye didn't miss the direction of her gaze. He patted the horse's nose and his lopsided grin held ruefulness. "Don't mind my cousin's bad manners. He's just glad he doesn't have to put up with me all the way to Philadelphia."

"Were you to have gone?" Carrie asked. "I didn't know you were interested in cabinetmaking."

He laughed. "I'm not. And *nei*, I have nothing to do with this trip. It's just that I don't get a chance to see this side of the Steiner family much. Meeting you and Melvin here was a good opportunity."

Not good enough to shake hands and make up an ages-old quarrel, it seemed, but plenty good enough to rile somebody up.

Men. Honestly.

David Yoder stepped out of the back of the adjoining pallet shop, followed by Eli Fischer, Amelia's husband of two months. Seeing her, Eli waved. "*Guder Mariye*, Carrie. I didn't expect to see you here."

"She's dropping me off," Melvin said. "I'm going to Philadelphia with the boys, here."

"Ah." Eli took in Joshua on one side of the yard and Brian and Boyd on the other, but it was clear he thought nothing of it. He was from Lebanon County, and had only recently moved here for Amelia's sake. What with having important things like courting and marrying her best friend on his mind, clearly there hadn't been enough time to learn all the family business in the shop next door.

"Time to go," Brian said, "or we won't get to that bus in time."

In the flurry of activity in the yard, somehow Carrie found herself in the passenger seat once again and Joshua driving away at a brisk pace, barely stopping to look for oncoming traffic as he guided Jimsy into the right turn at the light.

She was perfectly capable of driving her own buggy. It wasn't like they were in the middle of downtown Lancaster. But to say so would be forward, not to mention ungracious, after he'd agreed to give them the gift of his hands and his time.

How strange it felt, him sitting there on her right with the reins in his hands. She hadn't driven next to a man other than Melvin or her *Daed* in ten years. The strangeness of it made her aware that she needed to keep a couple of inches of space between them. It made her body feel stiff, without its usual easiness with the bumps and turns of the road.

"Everything all right over there?" Joshua asked, glancing at her. "You're awfully quiet."

"I'm not much of a talker."

"No? I've seen you at church at potlucks and things, chattering away with everyone from old Sarah Yoder to the *Youngie*."

"Both Sarah and the *Youngie* tend to do all the talking," she pointed out. "I just listen."

"Oh, I see." Silence fell, in which the clopping of Jimsy's hooves seemed unnaturally loud. "What's the horse's name?" he asked as though he'd thought the same thing, and it had reminded him to ask.

"Jimsy." One of the gelding's ears swiveled back, as though inquiring as to why his name had come up.

"That's a funny name for a horse. Don't the people around here call their animals things like Ajax and Caesar and Hero?"

The people around here? Didn't he consider himself one of them? "He's a retired racehorse. His real name is Jamieson's Victory Dance. We thought of calling him Vic, but Jimsy seemed to suit him better."

"A racehorse, huh? Have you ever taken him out on Camas Creek Road and put him through his paces?"

"*Nei*. What would be the point? We don't want him racing, we want him to take us to town and to church and to visit."

"Poor Jamieson's Victory Dance. I bet he wants to race, don't you, boy?"

For a moment Carrie thought he would actually flap the reins over poor Jimsy's back and make him do it, traffic and curves notwithstanding. "Joshua—"

"What?"

"I thought you—" She swallowed and subsided. "Never mind."

He shook his head. "Carrie. What a low opinion you must have of me if you'd think I would race a horse that doesn't belong to me, while I was driving a buggy that doesn't belong to me, next to a woman who doesn't belong to me."

"I don't—"

"Your husband has entrusted you to my care for a week, and believe me, I take that seriously."

"I'm not in your care." It bothered her to hear him say such a thing—wasn't he just looking in now and again? She wasn't in anyone's care except for Melvin's and God's, and that's exactly the way she wanted it.

And now she sounded like a sulky child. "But I do appreciate your helping us," she said in a gentler tone.

To her enormous relief, he said nothing more, only slowed the horse as they approached the highway junction. "Have you and Melvin worked out a schedule for the things he wants done?" she asked. And did he mean to start today? If he did, they would stay on the highway and go home. If not, they would make another right turn, and she would drop him at his parents' place, where he was staying.

He nodded. "I have to go to work at Hill's today, but I can come by tomorrow afternoon if that suits."

"That would be fine. It's baking day, so there will be cake to eat with your coffee, if you want."

"That's the second best offer I've had all day." He flapped the reins and made the turn toward his folks' farm, leaving her to wonder what the best offer had been.

And then deciding she really didn't want to know.

CHAPTER 3

After lunch the following day, Carrie had barely got the first of her pans of oatmeal chocolate chip cookies in the oven, when she heard the crunch of wheels in the lane through the open window.

"Sorry I'm late," Joshua called as she walked onto the porch. He jumped out and tied the horse to their rail, where he began cropping the grass. The first of her flowerbeds had been strategically located just out of reins' reach, but the grass was fair game to visiting horses.

"I thought you were going to Hill's first." Her tone was friendly, but really, when a man said he was coming by in the afternoon, he didn't usually mean one o'clock. She had cake batter waiting for when the cookies were finished, and then there was all the cleanup to do before anyone could sit at the table.

"I did," he said. "I had to wait for the vet, or I'd have been here sooner."

"I wouldn't have been ready sooner," she told him. "I'm not ready now."

"We can talk while you work. I don't mind."

She did, but she tamped it down and tried to be gracious. He was here to find out how he could help. She'd better be careful, or he'd get offended and go away, and then she'd have to explain to Melvin what she'd done. He deserved a nicer homecoming next week than that.

Her timer pinged. While she took the tray of cookies out and set them on the racks on the counter, he settled himself at the table. After she slid another tray of cookies in, she got down a mug and poured a cup of coffee from the pot on the stove.

"Thanks. Those look good."

"They're too hot to eat yet."

"What else are you making?" He looked as though he was about to scoop a fingerful of cake batter out of the bowl.

"A carrot cake and a lemon–poppy seed cake. I'm invited to Emma and Lena's tomorrow night, and I told them I'd bring dessert. Lemon–poppy seed is Emma's favorite."

"I remember. When we were kids, she used to get in trouble for cutting a slice out of the cake before dinner, especially when she'd made it."

That didn't sound like Emma. "More likely a certain person egged her on until she did it."

He grinned, an easy smile that took credit for the bad behavior as much as it enjoyed the memory. "Maybe. Once or twice." He gazed into the distance, in the direction of the window over the sink. "I miss those days."

"I think Emma prefers now to then."

His attention snapped back to the table and the present. "I suppose she does. When's the wedding?"

"November first. Her sister Katherine and I are going to be *Neuwesitzern*."

"Not Amelia? I thought you three were tight."

She frowned at the *Englisch* expression, which didn't seem so complimentary to her Amish ears. "Amelia has her boys and her husband to think of, but of course she'll still be there. Emma and Katherine are close, and she and I are close, so I think it's very appropriate."

"Lucky thing you're already married. All these weddings. What do the *Englisch* say? Three times a bridesmaid, never a bride?"

The timer pinged again, thank goodness, and she got up. As she transferred cookies from pan to rack and dropped raw dough onto new pans, she cudgeled her brain for something else to talk about. The subject of weddings would inevitably lead to the subject of children, which she would not discuss with someone she didn't know very well. Or with those she did, for that matter.

"So what's the book on the windowsill?"

He'd gotten up, coffee mug in hand, and was ranging around the room as though he'd grown up in it. She had no doubt that at some point he would circle in on the coolest of the cookies.

She resisted the urge to snatch up the book and stuff it in a drawer. "My songbook."

"You play an instrument?" He sounded surprised, as well he might. The Amish didn't play instruments—they were showy, made an individual person stand out in a crowd, and drew the kind of attention that could all too easily become a source of pride.

"Of course not."

"Sing, then?"

"We all sing, Joshua."

"But this does not look like *die Ausbund*, Carrie Miller. What songs are you singing in your own house that you wouldn't sing in church?"

"Oh, don't look so shocked. Lots of people make song-books." He leaned over the sink to pick it up, and she fought down a ridiculous panic. There was nothing in that book to be ashamed of. It was just private, that was all. "*Gibts mir.*"

"In a minute. I want to look." He held it out of her reach, holding it over his head and looking up into it as he flipped from page to page.

"Joshua. Stop it." She would not jump and snatch; that was clearly what he wanted. It was just like with the chickens—the more a bird showed she wanted someone else's worm, the harder they'd try to keep it away from her. So Carrie poured herself a cup of coffee and began to arrange the warm cookies on a plate.

He came back to the table, looking interested. "So you collect songs. Where do they come from?"

She shrugged, and offered him the plate. When both hands were busy with the cookies, she whipped the book off the table and slid it into the nearest drawer, among the clean dish towels. "Most of these are from when I was on *Rumspringe.*"

"And you remember the tunes after all this time?"

He made it sound as though she were as old as Lena Stolzfus. "I've been singing them for years. When I do the dishes. When I feed the hens. They're like old friends."

They held precious memories, too, of going to Singing on Sunday nights and being the one who dared to suggest a song in the little hymnbook, or one that the Mennonite kids sang—even, that one time, a Psalm set to music that she'd heard the *Englisch* young folks singing at a tent revival meeting at the park in town. It had a jazzy syncopated beat that was irresistible, and she'd come home and written it down.

Unto Thee, O Lord, do I lift up my soul.

And then the boys and girls would split, the girls singing the echo.

O my God
I trust in thee:
Let me not be ashamed, let not mine enemies triumph over me.

"So," Joshua said, evidently looking for another subject now that he'd failed to rile her with this one, "Melvin gave me a general idea of what to do around your place. Paint the sheds, clean out the barn and organize it, that kind of thing. But I want to know what you'd like me to do."

She waved in the general direction of the back part of their acreage. "I have a dozen apple trees out there whose fruit is going to the birds if I don't finish picking them. That's the first thing on my list."

"Sounds like the first priority," he agreed, nodding. "I never objected to leaving painting for another day."

"That's not true. I saw you helping out at Amelia and Eli's not so long ago. They painted everything that was nailed down, just before their wedding."

"Ah, but that was different. Everyone who could swing a brush was there, including that *Englisch* man who turned up from New York City and embarrassed Emma so bad."

"He'll turn up again," Carrie informed him. "His name is Tyler West and he's invited to her wedding."

"Maybe he'll come early and paint."

Now, there was a sarcastic tone. "What's the matter? Don't you like him?"

"Whether I like him or not isn't the point. He's an *Englisch* man and he has no business here, especially at our weddings."

Carrie gazed at him curiously. He sounded so emphatic, and his face had darkened with displeasure. He really meant it. The joker and tease of a few minutes ago had disappeared completely.

"That's for Emma to decide," she said mildly, "and he is representing her book. In a way, he's her business partner."

Joshua pushed away from the table. "I'll go look over those sheds. I'll need to know how much paint to buy."

The door had swung shut behind him before Carrie found the wits to open her mouth. "All right," she said to the empty room. "Remind me not to bring up Tyler West again."

It was no secret that Joshua had wanted to court Emma earlier in the summer. He hadn't been the only one. But Carrie had never seen Joshua react this way to the mention of Calvin King's name, or of Grant Weaver's, either. Did he have some kind of problem with the *Englisch*? Or just with Emma's agent in particular? Or maybe the subject of weddings was as sore with him as it had once been for Emma. He was long past the age when a man usually settled down.

Shaking her head, Carrie turned at the timer's ping and took the next tray of cookies out of the oven. She would have to ask Emma about it when she saw her tomorrow night.

* * *

"I have no idea," Emma said when Carrie told her and Lena the story over spareribs and macaroni and cheese the next evening. Emma never served chicken when she knew Carrie was coming. "To my knowledge, Joshua has never even spoken to Tyler West."

"Maybe it was something else, then. Maybe he just has a problem with *Englisch* folks."

"I wouldn't say that," Lena put in, a little dryly. "Not the female half, anyway."

"Mamm!" Emma sounded shocked.

"That boy has a bad reputation, and you know it. I'm a little surprised at Melvin, if the truth be told. Not every man would let Joshua Steiner hang around his place when he was away."

It was a good thing that Carrie had known Lena all her life—and what's more, loved her nearly as much as Emma did. Otherwise, she might take this as a slight on her own morals, and get offended. Taking offense was a sin, because it meant you had too high an opinion of yourself. "I'm sure those rumors aren't true."

"They aren't," Emma said steadily. "Joshua told me so himself. That girl he was supposed to have gotten in the family way up in Indiana turned out to have been playing around with an *Englisch* man, too. And she went outside and married him."

Every Amish woman faced that choice once in her life— the opportunity to discover the world outside the church. That was what *Rumspringe* was for, after all: to give a person the experience to make an informed decision.

Carrie had had her share of running around until she met Melvin, and then the choice wasn't a choice at all. Joining church was the most natural thing in the world when it meant having the life she knew with the man she loved.

"Even if he had the worst reputation in the world, he has still leased one of our fields," she said. "And Melvin trusts both me and him."

"Of course he does," Emma said. "You probably won't see much of Joshua anyway if he's doing the outside work."

"That's true," she said. "And it's good. He makes me nervous."

"Nervous how?" Lena looked up from her plate.

"Oh, I don't know. He's nosy. He was in the kitchen yesterday, supposedly finding out what we needed done, and he spent nearly the whole time needling me about my songbook."

"Your songbook." Now Lena put down her fork. "Why?"

Carrie shrugged. "Maybe he's never seen one before, and there it was, lying on the windowsill by the sink, where I'd been doing the dishes."

Even Emma looked perplexed. "Well, I never. You've had that book practically since you were a girl. Didn't we used to copy out songs in it in the days before the *Youngie* would let us come to Singing?"

"That's the one. We'd sit up in the tree in the orchard here and practice, like so many birds on a branch."

"Is that how my Pink Lady got broken that one summer?" Lena raised her eyebrows. "You girls up in it singing?" Carrie and Emma made identical *uh-oh* faces at each other, and Lena laughed. "That poor tree. It made the best pie apples, and it died that winter."

"The price we paid for our reckless ways," Carrie told her. "I've always been sorry, and did my singing at the sink after that."

"It was hard, though, being fourteen and fifteen," Emma said, gazing into the distance at the memory of the girls they had been. Girls who had graduated from eighth grade but who would not go on to high school, like *Englisch* students. Hardly any Amish scholars went on—an *Englisch* education promoted self-sufficiency, pride, and a tendency to criticize and challenge the way things were always done. Amish parents spent a whole childhood training those things out of their offspring. Nobody wanted them to go where they would be put back in. "Too old to be in school, and too young to go to Singing. Even the sixteen-year-olds looked mature and experienced to us."

"Now we look at someone like Lydia Zook and think, oh, she's so young."

"You two are still young," Lena said, her eyes misting. "And now my youngest will be married and have a home and family of her own."

Emma smiled at her with such love that Carrie's own eyes filled. "I wish everyone could find the one that God means for them. Even Joshua. He's always at home in a crowd, always has something amusing to say…but he just seems so lonely."

"Is that why you let him court you?" Carrie asked.

Emma snorted and stood to collect their plates. "The world's briefest courtship. I think it lasted one evening."

"I wouldn't have called it even that," Lena said, attempting to get up.

"Mamm, sit and let me do it. I only have a few weeks left to do things for you. What would you have called it?"

"Oh, I think you and your friends probably came to the same conclusion I did. That boy was using you for a cloak of respectability, and every time I see him, I want to take him to task for it."

"It's over and done, Mamm, and it doesn't matter."

"Maybe not. I suppose once you're married, I'll have to forgive him."

"I hope you'll forgive him before then." Emma's eyes laughed at her, though her mouth remained solemn. "Your being mad at him won't bother him a bit, and it will just put a hard spot in your heart that God will have to soften."

"I won't put God to that trouble," Lena said. "Is that lemon–poppy seed cake?"

"Carrie brought it. She's trying to fatten me up so I can't get into my wedding clothes."

"I am not!" Carrie protested, laughing. "It's not often I get to do something for you, so I'm taking my opportunities while I have them. And I know how much you like this kind."

And in the simple pleasure of cake for dessert, the subject of Joshua Steiner was dropped. But deep in her heart, Carrie wondered if maybe Emma was right. Maybe he was lonely. She resolved to be a little more patient with him the next time she saw him. After all, Melvin would not have asked him to help them if he didn't think Joshua was a good man.

And only a good man would have agreed to help, especially since they couldn't afford to pay him a cent. If he came tomorrow, she would have her own work done and be ready to help him if he needed it. After all, as her *Daed* used to say, "No one is useless in this world if he lightens someone else's burden."

Joshua was lightening hers, so it seemed only fair.

CHAPTER 4

On Saturdays, Joshua explained as he stood in the kitchen door watching her, he only needed to look after the Hill cows in the morning, and the family dealt with them during the rest of the day and on Sundays.

Carrie plunged her mop into the bucket and leaned on it like a warrior might have leaned on his spear. "I was going to have everything finished so I could help you in the orchard this afternoon."

"Don't worry." He grinned as though he'd caught her shirking. "I'll leave enough for you."

She felt out of sorts, partly because of her time of the month and partly because he always seemed to turn up when she wasn't expecting him, and it was beginning to jangle her nerves. "There are baskets in the cellar, but to get there, you'd have to cross my wet floor. Just wait there and I'll get them."

She had to cross it herself, since she was backing across the floor toward the bedrooms so that she could sweep them. However, she'd rather mop up her own footprints than his, especially since his boots probably hadn't seen a scraper since they'd visited the cows this morning.

She balanced the stack of apple baskets—made by Amelia's

father, Isaac Lehman, who took a craftsman's quiet satisfaction in making even the humblest household item fulfill its purpose for years—in both arms as she emerged from the cellar. "I left off on the Gravenstein. By the time you fill one of these, I'll have the drying boxes ready outside."

"Not going to rig the generator to a dehydrator?"

She pushed the baskets into his arms. "The drying boxes worked for Mamm, and they work just fine for me." Lined with black paper and with air holes for good circulation, the boxes came up to her shoulder and could dry twelve racks of apple slices at a time.

"Where are they? Do you need help setting them up?"

"*Nei*. What I need is to finish my inside work." And for him to stop talking and get himself out to the orchard to do something useful.

Too late, she remembered her resolve to be patient with him.

Laughing, apparently at her little show of temper, he finally left, and Carrie could focus on wiping up her footprints and getting the floor done. By the time she'd swept the other rooms, the kitchen was dry. It didn't take long to get the worktable ready for that first basket of fruit—paring knives and the big cooling racks originally meant for bakery cakes that Daed had measured carefully before he built the drying boxes to accommodate them.

Carrie sat for a moment on a kitchen chair. Seemed like Joshua should be back by now with the first basket. Even she could pick a bushel of apples faster than this.

With a sigh, she got up and left the house. The chickens, sensing there might be food somewhere in this change in routine, fell in behind her like a string of train cars.

She found Joshua up in the Gravenstein on a ladder, picking steadily, two full baskets in the grass at the base of the tree. "I thought you might have brought these in so I could get started," she said, tilting her head up and shading her eyes against a sun that arced lower in the sky every day.

He looked down at her. "What are those *Hinkel* doing here?"

She picked Dinah up and felt her settle into her arms. "They come with me wherever I go on the place. I think they're looking for a change from worms and bugs." Two of the hens had already found a drift of windfalls and were attacking them with happy ferocity. "I see you found the wagon. I'll take these and bring it back to you."

"How many apples can you do in one afternoon?"

"Enough to fill the boxes, and I make applesauce out of whatever is left over. It takes a couple of days to dry them— maybe less if the weather stays fine like this."

"I'll come with you."

He began to climb down before she could say no, and there she was, in the very situation she'd been trying to avoid. She put Dinah down and caught up the handle of the wagon. What was the matter with him? The wagon, a child's red one that had once belonged to her youngest brother Orval, bumped along behind her with its burden of bushels. Did the man not think of the most efficient way of doing something?

"Wait up." Joshua jogged up beside her and took the handle. "You look mad."

"I'm not. It's just that I could have had a dozen apples peeled by now if you'd brought me a bushel to start with. Now I've lost all that time, and the sun is over the oak tree already."

He laughed. "Relax, Carrie. You have days to peel apples

in, and the weather forecast is clear and sunny into the middle of next week."

"How do you know?"

"The Hills have a radio in the barn. It's on all the time.
You'd be surprised at all the things I know about politics,
economics, and movie stars."

"I hope you're as well acquainted with your Bible."

"You sound like Mary Lapp."

"I'm related to Mary Lapp. Melvin's mother is her sister."

"Still. You'd better be careful. A virtuous woman like that
can't be duplicated."

Carrie had the feeling that Mary would find nothing to be
puffed up about in that remark.

She hefted one of the bushel baskets and took it in to the
kitchen counter. Joshua brought the other one, and she'd begun to run water into the sink to wash the fruit when she
realized he hadn't left. Instead, he'd parked himself at the
table.

"Would you like an afternoon snack?" Hospitality demanded that she make the offer, even though he'd done
hardly anything yet and she had her hands full—literally.

"Nope. If you're that far behind, I'll give you a hand here.
Seems to me the picking goes faster than the preparing."

"That's not necessary. Melvin hired you to do the outside
work, not mine."

"Many hands make light work, isn't that what they say?"

There was no point in fighting him. He was obviously
going to do what he wanted in her kitchen, and she didn't
have the time to argue. "Fine. Here. Start with these. Do you
know how to pare an apple?"

"I've seen it often enough." He picked up one of the paring knives and sliced a chunk out of the fruit in his hand. She

bit back the urge to scold, then to instruct. "Don't you have one of those paring devices that spin the apple around and the skin comes off in one long curl?"

"I do that with these devices here." She waggled her hands at him. "Watch."

Many years of practice had her turning the apple and the skin furling away from it in a long ribbon. Then she quartered it, sliced it, and laid the pieces on the drying racks. The whole operation was done before he'd got halfway around his own apple.

"By the time I get through those bushels, I might be one twentieth as good as you." His curl broke, and sighing, he kept going.

"This is why you need a wife. If you like *Schnitz* pie and applesauce, she would be doing this for you."

"I do like them, and it's not for lack of trying that I haven't found a girl who will have me."

"I don't think you're trying very hard. Who are you taking home from Singing on Sunday night?"

"An old man like me doesn't belong at Singing with all the *Youngie*."

"That's where you'll find the single girls—young women like Esther Grohl, who's close to your age and who would make a wonderful wife." Carrie was on her third apple as he quartered his first one. "You can't go looking for corn in a bean field."

"Apparently I can find chicken in an apple orchard, though."

"Not by now, you won't. They'll all be back on the lawn."

"But you see my point. I'm not looking for an eighteen-year-old."

Which was why she'd mentioned Esther. "You're not

much older than that." She calculated for a second. He and her next youngest brother, Kenneth, had been in the same class at school. "You're only twenty-eight, aren't you?"

"Soon twenty-nine." He glanced up at her. "You don't know any girls like you, do you? Pretty, good in the kitchen, like to laugh?"

"I know at least a dozen with one or more of those qualifications." She would not react. He had no business calling a married woman anything but her name, never mind things that would only make her too fond of her bathroom mirror. "And most of them go to Singing. It doesn't matter how old you are, Joshua."

"Feels out of place," he mumbled, partially covered by his interest in choosing the perfect apple to pare next.

"Do you mean Singing feels out of place, or you do?" There was nothing wrong with her hearing.

"I do, I suppose. These kids have never been outside Lancaster County. Never done anything or seen anything."

"How can you say that? Look at Esther. She and her sister, Marianne, and two other girls just came back from a tour of twelve different national parks, from here to Montana to California."

"I don't want to look at Esther."

"She may not be as pretty as some, but you can't say she's never been anywhere or done anything. And goodness knows, she can cook."

"All the Grohl girls can. They're worth their weight in rubies. But I've decided I need to catch a young one and train her up proper. Like that Zook girl. What's her name?"

"Lydia."

"That's right. I wonder if she sells purple? You know, like that woman in the Bible."

"I imagine she does. I heard last church Sunday that she's working in the fabric shop in Whinburg."

He threw back his head and laughed. "There's no putting one over on you, is there, Fraa Miller?"

She dropped her chin and concentrated on the perfect peel curling off her knife.

"Aw, now I've made you blush. Look, this is hopeless. I guess skill at peeling is one of those things you're born with, like a good singing voice or the ability to dowse water with a forked stick."

"I think it's more a matter of practice," she said dryly. "And if you're not in the habit of being in the kitchen, you can't be expected to do it perfectly the first time."

"You're kind to excuse my clumsiness. But it's back to the trees for me."

He dumped the remaining apples into the deep water in the sink, picked up the baskets, and took himself off, whistling.

Carrie let out a long breath and rolled her shoulders. Thank goodness. What a trying conversation.

The only good part about it was his joke about Lydia. How strange that she had come up in conversation so many times this week. The poor thing. Her mother had died of an untreated infection when Lydia was six, and she'd been keeping house the best she could ever since, with occasional help from the women of the community. Tall, gangly Abe Zook was probably not going to win any prizes for his skills as a father ("He's got a face like barbed wire, all sharp and hooked," Emma had whispered once, when they'd seen him out in his field whipping up his plow mule), but he was a member of the church, and once a year the whole *Gmee* got together to put a shine on his ramshackle place when it was his turn to host the service.

As the years passed, people realized that all the best of Abe and Rachel had been distilled into their only living daughter, with her red hair and pretty face. But as Carrie's *Mammi* used to say, "Handsome is as handsome does." It was a person's works in God's service and their kindness toward others that counted, not what they looked like, and Lydia had a feisty spirit that would get her into *Druwwel* one of these days.

Carrie picked up the next apple and began to hum.

Let me not be ashamed, let not mine enemies triumph over me.

* * *

Dear Carrie,

We've arrived safely and I thought you'd like this postcard of chickens. Hope you are well and that Joshua is working out. Despite what people say about him, I know you will show him Christian kindness and I'm sure he'll like your cooking as much as I do. I miss it already, and you too.

Your husband,
Melvin

P.S. I'm thinking gossip is like a plague. You get two people together and they pass it on, and pretty soon everyone is infected.

Carrie read the postcard again and took it upstairs to their bedroom, where she tucked it in the top drawer of her dresser. There were a few letters there already from Melvin, as he'd traveled around over the last year. The two of them had written back and forth when they'd been courting, of course, since she'd met him at a band hop fifty miles away from Whinburg, in his district. But those youthful letters had been thrown away through some accident of spring cleaning. She was determined that the letters he'd written as her husband wouldn't suffer the same fate. He wasn't as eloquent on paper as he was in person, but every word was precious.

Downstairs, she smiled as she thought of him coming to a halt at the picture of the mother hen. Under her were a lot of tiny legs, so that she looked like a puffy tree with a dozen tiny trunks. Buried in those feathers, safe and warm, were her chicks.

Unaccountably, Carrie's throat closed up.

Maybe Melvin was trying to tell her that he still had hope they'd have lots of chicks of their own yet. Or maybe that they should be satisfied with feathery children rather than real ones. Or maybe he just liked the humor in it and wasn't trying to say anything at all.

"Back to work, Carrie." Her own voice sounded loud in the kitchen, and she set to work with the apples once again.

It was Saturday, when she usually dusted and did light housework, with the evening sacred to preparing her spirit for church the next day. Today she'd abandoned those tasks and turned to the more urgent one—apples. She'd filled the two drying boxes and turned them to the sun, and now the kitchen was soft with the scent of apples and cinnamon as a big kettle of them cooked down on the stove.

Three successive thuds on the porch outside told her Joshua and the baskets were back. "Should I just leave these out here?" he called through the open door.

"*Ja*. They'll keep cool overnight and I'll get started on them early Monday."

He came through the door dusting off his hands. "It smells good in here."

"I've made dinner, if you want to stay."

He raised his eyebrows in a comical way that told her the next words out of his mouth would probably be outrageous. "Fraa Miller, asking a single man to dinner?"

"*Ja*," she said. "You've put in a day's work. A meal is included, and you didn't eat lunch." His lips twitched at her schoolmarm tone, but what else was she to say?

"*Denki*, but Mamm will have dinner for me when I get back."

"There's enough for two or three here. I'm so used to cooking for two I didn't think to cut it down." She'd made pork hash from the roast the other day, and rice and baked squash, plus the usual accompaniments of beet pickles, bread and jam, and a taste of the fresh applesauce.

"Then maybe we can have the leftovers for lunch tomorrow."

She nearly took a step backward in shock. "Tomorrow is Sunday."

Lifting his hat with the back of one hand, he scratched his head. "Is it? So it is. Time flies."

Goodness. How could he forget? Church Sunday was the lynchpin around which their days revolved. On Saturdays you got ready for it, on Mondays you washed clothes after it, and the other days you sewed and baked so you wouldn't have to do those things on Saturday, Sunday, and Monday.

Maybe men thought of time differently. This one did, at least.

"Monday, then," he said easily.

"Monday is wash day."

"You can't dry apples on wash day?"

"I can take them in out of the drying boxes in the evening if I have time, but doing the wash takes a woman all day. There are sheets and towels and the clothes from Sunday, and aprons from during the week, and—"

"All right, all right." He held up his hands, grinning, as though he were warding off a dozen tasks flying at him.

Hmph. They were her tasks, and did he see her flinching?

"I'll come Tuesday, then, after I get my chores done at Hill's."

"Fine." Tuesday was sewing day, and she had hardly any of it to do. "Apple day it is, then. See you at church, Joshua."

"Oh, you will." Settling his hat, he left, and a few minutes later she heard the crunch and jingle of wagon and harness in the lane.

At last.

Carrie pulled her oldest bib apron off the hook on the back of the door. Now that the sun had gone down, the chickens had mostly put themselves to bed in the coop. This was her favorite time of the day. She didn't get the opportunity very often, because meals often interfered, but when Melvin was away, she indulged herself.

A rickety wooden chair too shabby to leave where company could see it stood inside the coop near the roosts. When she sat, Dinah jumped up in her lap and settled there. Carrie was sure she would just sleep the whole night through with the happy certainty that her human would act as her pillow all night. It never happened, of course, but the hen would cuddle down as though this time it might.

Carrie held her, and before long Lizzie-bit jumped on her shoulder. Then Rhoda jumped up to occupy the other knee.

Lizzie's feathers warmed her neck, and the relaxed feet of the two in her lap told her they were content and secure.

Such a gift.

She was often happy, but contentment—complete acceptance of God's will for her and satisfaction in her place—often seemed as far out of her reach as a straw hat snatched away by the wind.

Inwardly, she shook her head at herself, but her heart didn't seem to be paying attention.

Why me, Lord? Why are some women given children by the dozen, and I must make do with my birds? I love my birds, and I thank You for them, but please, might I not have even one child to bring up in Your ways and Your love?

Her prayer winged its way through the ceiling and up into the sky, but there was no answer, only the gentle breathing all around her.

CHAPTER 5

Church the next day was held at Carrie's parents' place, which meant a drive of four miles. Melvin's weekend away with Brian and Boyd had been carefully scheduled, taking into account the fact that church could have been at the farm of any one of them. She had a feeling that, once they knew of the cabinet show's date, a discreet word may have been dropped in Bishop Daniel's ear so that he would not announce any of their places as being next in the rotation.

With two dozen families in the district, everyone came up at least once a year, but that didn't mean a little jiggling of the bimonthly schedule didn't happen now and again. Twice a year was Communion Sunday, the most important day of the church year, when the service lasted all day and included the passing of the bread and the cup, and the foot washing in the afternoon. Leading up to that were several weeks of preparation. Two weeks from now was New Birth Sunday, when baptisms were performed, and two weeks after that would be Council Meeting. This was the time to prepare for Communion Sunday two weeks later. It was important for the unity of the church that everyone made sure they were in harmony with their neighbors, to the point that if you had a problem with someone, you had better get it straightened out before you confessed in public that you were ready to take Communion.

After the sermon on the shepherd was over and everyone was filing out of the big shed where Daed kept the farming equipment during every other week of the year, Carrie made her way into the kitchen to give her mother and sisters a hand with the lunch.

Miriam King gave her a quick hug and waved at the food on the counters. "The boys will have set up the tables in the shed by now. Can you carry those loaves of bread over? One to a table, and jam and peanut-butter spread too."

Mamm had been serving exactly this lunch for as long as Carrie had been alive. It varied some with the seasons, but the cold cuts for making sandwiches were as predictable as daylight.

She took the basket of loaves and went back to the shed. There, the boys had rearranged the benches and set up tables, and from cubbyholes in the wagon, taken out the eating utensils. All three of the Grohl girls—Esther, Marianne, and Sarah—paced the rows of tables, with knives, forks, and spoons going down first, then plates. Lydia Zook, who was in the same buddy bunch as Sarah, brought up the rear with the cups. With everyone working together, it took less than ten minutes to set the tables for sixty people.

Then Carrie was free to begin slicing bread at each table so that people could make sandwiches. Platters of cold cuts bloomed around her as her sisters brought in food, and the single girls arranged the potluck offerings around the main part of the meal.

In less than half an hour after Bishop Daniel had blessed and dismissed them from the service, he was standing at the front of the room again, looking out over the tables of the seated congregation and raising his hand for silence so that they might say grace.

Afterward, as they began to eat, Carrie's sister Naomi leaned back over the aisle and nudged her so that she looked over her shoulder. "Mamm wants to talk to you after cleanup."

"What about?" Her mother was a pretty easygoing person. Nothing seemed to faze her, whether it was getting the place ready for a wedding or giving an unexpected guest their supper.

"I don't know. She just said that if I saw you, to tell you."

Carrie nodded and let herself be drawn back into conversation with the women on either side of her, both of whom wanted to know the same thing. "Where is Melvin today? Is he sick?"

Illness and absence were the only two reasons a person might miss church—and even then, he would do everything he could to avoid the latter. If it was your week for church, it was absolutely unthinkable for you or any member of your family to be away. It simply didn't happen. The Kingdom came first, no matter what your other plans might be—unless you were in the hospital and couldn't help it.

"He and Brian and Boyd have gone down to Philadelphia for a cabinetmaker's trade show," she answered. She didn't mind saying so to Ellie King Byler—she was one of her cousins and the pragmatic sort. She took what you said at face value and didn't go adding to or subtracting from it like some. "They'll be back by Wednesday, late."

Ellie nodded, satisfied. "Melvin will enjoy talking to folks down there."

"And maybe selling the pallet shop's services."

"It takes a special person to be able to do that." Ellie shook her head. "I have enough trouble asking for the right size at the shoe store."

"You should go to the shoe warehouse on the county highway," Carrie advised her. "The Mennonite girls there know exactly what we're looking for, and don't make you feel funny for wanting black lace-up oxfords instead of pink stilettos with butterflies on them."

Ellie snickered into her glass of water. Carrie figured that would tickle her. She'd married into a real conservative family whose idea of a radical change was making a dress out of blue fabric instead of dark green.

Cleanup always seemed to take longer than the preparation and eating of the meal . . . much like canning and drying food, she supposed. But eventually the hubbub of clattering dishes and packing up leftovers was done, the bench wagon loaded up with its burden, and its driver rolled out of the yard to take it to the farm of one of Old Joe Yoder's grandsons, whose turn it would be two weeks from now.

Mamm met Carrie in the kitchen doorway. "Let's go for a walk, *Liewi*."

She hesitated for half a second, then fell in step with her mother as they crossed the yard, heading for the same place they'd been walking since Carrie was a toddler—the copse of shady maples and elms tucked into a fold of the fields.

"I suppose this is where I learned to like my nature rambles," she said, lifting her face to the autumn sun. "I always liked going on walks with you."

"I should be back at the house being a good hostess," Mamm said. "But Naomi knows where everything is, so if someone needs something, she can find it. Besides, that girl likes nothing more than to chatter with folks, and with all the young girls around to look after her *Kinner*, she doesn't have to keep after them every minute of the afternoon."

Carrie looked away. Five *Kinner*. Naomi was the perfect Amish wife and mother. If Carrie didn't love her so dearly, she would look at her and despair.

"So what would make you come out with me and abandon the ladies in the sitting room?"

Mamm gave her a sideways look and chewed on the inside of her cheek. Carrie felt the first stirrings of alarm.

"Mamm? What's wrong? What news have you had?"

Her mother snorted. "News. That's one way of putting it, when your bishop's wife stops in to tell you that a single man has been seen calling on her married daughter not once, but twice in the same week. That was news, let me tell you."

A giggle burst out of Carrie's mouth before she could stop it. "Is that all? Mamm, Melvin hired Joshua Steiner to help around the place while he's away. Everything is fine."

"Is it?" It was less a question than a statement.

"He's been out in the orchard picking apples. I'm using the drying racks Daed made you. We've done nearly a hundred pounds already."

"I don't like you using the word 'we' about someone who isn't Melvin, *Liewi*."

"All right, then. The hired man and I did nearly a hundred pounds."

"Does he have to help while Melvin's gone?"

"It wouldn't make much sense to have his help while Melvin is there to do it." She sounded as puzzled as she felt. "What's wrong, Mamm?"

Miriam kicked a stone, then headed down the slope toward the thick stand of trees as though it were a refuge. Carrie had to pick up her pace to keep up with her. "It's just that…I suppose I don't much like having to explain my daughter's business to Mary Lapp, especially when I don't know anything about it."

Gossip is a plague. "I'm sure she thought she was doing the right thing, looking out for me. She is Melvin's aunt, after all."

"Aunt or not, if it had been any man but Joshua Steiner, she would have driven on by and never thought to mention it."

That was true, and there was no saying it wasn't. "Joshua is interested in someone else, Mamm." Otherwise, why would he have brought up Lydia Zook's name? She was awfully young, but stranger matches had been made. "In any case, he's changed."

"Not according to the rest of the Steiners."

"They shouldn't be holding grudges."

"I agree with you. But maybe it's less a grudge than a kind of watchful caution."

"So is that what you're asking me out for a walk for? To urge me to watchful caution?"

"I don't know." Miriam leaned on an elm and crossed her arms. "I suppose I just wanted to find out what was going on. I know full well no man in the world can compete with Melvin in your eyes."

Carrie wrapped her in a hug, crossed arms and all, then released her. "You're right. My man hired Joshua to help me, and that's all there is to it. Anyone who thinks anything else is going on needs to do a bit of praying, that's all."

"I don't know if Mary actually thinks that. She was more concerned about how it looked."

"It looks as innocent as it is, Mamm, and you can tell her so the next time she drives by."

"You might need to tell her yourself. I don't think she and Daniel have left yet."

"I'd rather behave as though the thought would never occur to me. It should never have occurred to her, either."

"Don't go getting offended, *Docher*."

"I'm not." And she wasn't. There was nothing for gossip to get its teeth into. "Mamm, look. The penny plants have dried. Help me pick some for the wreath I'm making for Susan's birthday."

They spent a peaceful few minutes gathering up the stalks of flat, dry seedpods that shivered on their stems like coins.

But Miriam wasn't finished yet. As they walked back to the home place over the hill, she said, as though their conversation had not been interrupted, "It's good he's doing the outside work, then. That's where he belongs."

Not inside with you, Carrie heard as clearly as though she'd said it.

If she said once more that Miriam didn't have to worry, she would sound like she was protesting too much. So Carrie said nothing.

Actions spoke louder than words. Everyone knew that.

* * *

Dear Melvin and Carrie,

I just finished baking ten pumpkin pies for Simon to take to the girls' stall at the farmers' market. Who would have thought I'd still be getting up at three to do the baking? Lucky thing it's only once a month, and they always sell out of my pies, even at ten dollars apiece. Imagine paying that much for something you could do so easily yourself!

I hope you two are well. Everyone is fine down here. Simon says you'll be coming for a visit, Melvin. That will be nice, though I'm not so sure being apart from your wife is a good idea. I'm not going to get grandchildren that way unless you plan to do it by mail.

Time to get busy with the washing.

Love from your
Mamm Miller

At one thirty on Tuesday, Carrie put the finishing touches on a whimsical cake she'd made for the quilting frolic. She'd rolled out royal frosting so that the surface was smooth, and then cut out shapes of birds and leaves for the top. A few brushes of food coloring and beet juice, and she had a funny little picture of a bird family in the red leaves of a maple tree—a father bird, a mother, two little birds, and a baby. She hoped Emma would like it, even if birds didn't hatch babies in the fall.

She deserved a little whimsy. It would take the sting out of the letter from Melvin's mother, who never failed to bring up the subject of children. She could be writing about a train trip to Timbuktu and would still manage to work it in somewhere.

The crunch of wheels on the gravel in the lane told her one of them was here much earlier than usual. Maybe she had news and couldn't wait to share it. Carrie dashed out onto the porch and pulled up as though someone had yanked hard on her reins.

Joshua climbed down from his buggy and raised his eyebrows in surprise when he saw her. "Going somewhere?"

"*Nei*, I thought you were someone else. Amelia and Emma

and I meet every Tuesday afternoon for quilting. Today we're meeting here."

"What about the apples?"

She sucked in a long breath. How *vergesslich* she was! She'd told him to come Tuesday and then promptly forgotten all about it, what with Melvin away, the letter, and the anticipation of being with her friends again. Since her household was the quietest, they would use the big frame she had set up in the spare room, and every frolic would be here until they finished the stitching. She couldn't miss stretching out their quilt on the frame and taking those first few stitches this afternoon for the sake of a few dried apples.

"You can still pick the apples," she said. "The two Spartans are next—they're loaded. I can start peeling and slicing when the girls leave. Amelia has to be home at four when her boys come in from school."

"Oh, I see," he said in a tone that many would have mistaken for jovial. "I'll be working while you're inside having fun with your friends?"

The fourth of five children, Carrie had always been sensitive to tones of voice that might tell her what actions or words would not. "My husband did hire you to work," she said finally, hoping she didn't sound too ungracious.

"I know that." His tone told her he didn't much appreciate having the obvious pointed out to him. "I was looking forward to seeing you. You're like the gravy that helps both the liver and the onions go down."

"Thanks a lot," she said before she thought. "Which is this job, the liver or the onions?"

"Definitely the onions. The liver keeps body and soul together, over there at Hill's. I'm doing this because a man asked me for help and I had it in my power to give it to him."

Carrie could recognize the guilt treatment when she saw it. Aleta Miller only had an eighth-grade education like the rest of them, but she had a college degree in guilt.

"And we appreciate it," she said. "If you'd rather not pick apples, the paint for the sheds is in the barn. The brushes, too, and some drop cloths."

"*Denki.*" Then he grinned, as though it was all water off a duck's back. "I'll manage with no company and nothing to eat."

If she went in to fix him something, the girls would be here before she was finished—and he might cut into the cake before Emma could see her happy little message. "You haven't eaten anything I've offered you so far. I didn't think of it."

"That seems to be my fate with women," he said, dropping his smile and his gaze to fiddle with his horse's reins as though he didn't know whether to tie up or not.

"Oh, for goodness' sake, Joshua. Stop feeling sorry for yourself. If you want something to eat, I have bread and jam and...and apples. Just don't touch the cake. That's for Emma."

"And what is Emma doing for you that she deserves a cake?"

"It's not what she can do for me, it's what I can do for her."

"A *gut* Amish woman, doing for her friends." The needle of sarcasm was back under the smile. "I told Mamm you'd invited me last time, that you expected me to eat here."

Could anyone be more aggravating? "I don't have a company dinner planned. You'll have to take—" She stopped.

It's good he's doing the outside work. That's where he belongs. "Take what?"

She was the one at fault here. She'd asked him to come and then forgotten about it. The least she could do was feed him for an afternoon's work. "Take potluck. I can make a sausage-and-green-bean casserole. And we'll have the rest of the cake. I won't send it home with Emma if you're staying."

"I'll look forward to that. I'll just put my animal in the barn, then, and get started on those sheds. We'll do apples tomorrow."

He unhitched his horse and led it into the barn while Carrie went inside, her pleasure in her cake a little flattened now. It didn't matter what it looked like with him here. Everything was open and honest, and every woman in the settlement had cooked for a cleaning frolic or a work party at some time or another. This was no different.

Emma and Amelia came together in the latter's buggy, looking curiously at the extra buggy in the yard with its empty rails propped on the ground in front of it. Carrie said, "That's Joshua Steiner's. He's painting the sheds today."

As though he'd been waiting to be introduced, he came out of the barn with a can of paint, and waved a brush at them before rounding the corner. The two women followed Carrie into the house, the quilt rolled up like a carpet between them.

"Just leave it rolled up until you get your shawls off," Carrie suggested. "I have a surprise for you in the kitchen."

"Oh, look at this!" Emma clasped her hands to her chest in delight when she saw the cake, bending over it to take in every detail. "Did you do all this yourself?"

Carrie practically hugged herself. The light in Emma's face was worth an early start this morning on all that icing. "Yes. It's a family of *weaver*birds, you see?"

Amelia laughed, her eyes sparkling as she leaned over the cake. "Only you would think of something like this. Surely you don't mean for us to eat it, do you?"

"I sure hope you will. Most of it, anyway. I told Joshua he could have some for dessert tonight."

"Carrie," Emma said suddenly, "I want to ask you something."

Oh dear. She shouldn't have brought Joshua's name into the conversation. Maybe Emma had been talking to Mary Lapp, too. "What?"

"Don't look so dismayed. Though you might after I— what I mean to say is, will you make my wedding cake? I want one just like this, with the birds and the babies and leaves and everything. Grant will love it."

"You make far nicer cakes than the bakery in town, *Liewi*," Amelia said. "The one you made for my wedding was so pretty I wished I hadn't wasted the money on a store-bought one."

"I'll buy you all the ingredients," Emma went on. "All you'd have to do is make it."

"Never mind," Carrie said, touched to the core. "It will be my wedding gift to you. I'll make the one for the *Eck*, and then plain sheet cakes for cutting in the kitchen."

"I'll help you," Amelia said. "You'll be baking for days otherwise."

"We'll all be baking for days," Emma said. "I'm trying to keep it small, but with inviting the whole *Gmee* and our family, two hundred seems like just a starting point."

"Getting nervous?" Amelia nudged her.

Emma bumped her back. "Not about getting married, not after waiting all this time. Just about planning the whole thing, and making sure it all gets done in time."

Amelia slid an arm around her shoulders. "That's what we're here for. There's no substitute for experience, and of course, you've got Karen."

"Thank goodness," Emma said seriously over Carrie's giggle. "I mean it. She's taking this on like Jonas Yoder takes on building a barn—everyone has their jobs to do, when to do them by, and what they'll need to do them with. I've just dropped the reins and given her her head, because I'll exhaust myself if I don't."

"Grant wouldn't want that," Carrie said slyly.

Now it was Emma's turn to poke her. "None of that, you. I'm beginning to think I've been wrong all this time to overlook her gift for organization. The next time I get impatient with her, I'll just remember her lists of what she's going to need in the kitchen to feed my crowd, and button my lips."

"Come on. Let's get our quilt on its frame." They trooped upstairs and, with the ends of the quilt secured, rolled them into the frame until the center section was the only part exposed as a work surface.

"Should we do the flower medallions first?" Amelia asked, tactfully giving Emma the choice of the first stitches.

"I think so," Emma said. "If we do that, it will anchor the layers together evenly. Then we can stitch the diamonds in the plain squares, and leave the feathers on the borders for last, in case things shift around a little."

"I'll take this rose, then." Carrie seated herself on one side, Emma the other, and Amelia took the middle, where the markings indicated a day lily would soon bloom.

Amelia threaded her needle with the accuracy of long experience, and began to load stitches on it. "What was that you said about Joshua having some of Emma's cake, Carrie?"

She might have known that wouldn't pass unnoticed. "He told his mother he'd be eating here today. I've invited him to stay before, but he didn't want to worry her."

"Just the two of you?" Emma's tone was conversational as she stitched the long side of a daisy petal.

"*Ja*. And before you say anything, save your breath. Mamm has already said it."

"I wasn't going to say a word." Emma kept her eyes on her work. "Especially if Miriam has already seeded that ground."

"I don't know what everyone is getting so worked up about," Carrie said, her own frustration bubbling to the surface. "Melvin hired the man to do chores while he was gone. That's it. From the way Mamm talked to me, you'd think I was in some kind of danger from him. But I'm not. I think he's got eyes for someone else."

"We all know you're not," Amelia said, her voice as soothing as lotion on a sunburn. "But you know how people are. The appearance of evil can be as damaging as the evil itself."

"There is no evil. Or appearance. Or anything. There's just dried apples and paint!"

"Did you have a lot of apples this year?" Emma nudged the topic in a different direction, and Carrie grasped the opportunity to get her emotions under control.

"Yes, the trees were loaded. It will be all I can do to finish picking before the first frost. And now the beets are ready to be pulled up, and I have to start on pickles soon."

"If you like, I'll stay tonight and give you a hand," Emma said. "I can catch a ride home with Joshua afterward. We haven't really talked much since the summer. It will be *gut* to catch up."

Carrie wasn't stupid—as the old folks might say, she could see through a grindstone when there was a hole in it. It was completely unnecessary for her friend to give up an evening playing Scrabble with Grant and his girls in order to stay and play chaperone for two people who hardly knew each other outside of Sundays.

On the other hand, there were all those apples and she only had one pair of hands. The thought of them made her happy, because she would have fruit through the winter.

"That would be wonderful *gut*," she told Emma. "I would love the help, and as you say, Joshua goes right past your place on his way home."

"Perfect. That's settled, then."

"I'll drop in on Lena and let her know you're staying for supper," Amelia said.

It was unnecessary. Silly, even. But at the same time, Carrie couldn't help but remember her Bible. *A true friend sticketh closer than a brother.*

Or a sister, as the case may be.

Chapter 6

Joshua looked a little taken aback when he came into the kitchen, shaking off his hands after washing them at the vegetable sink outside. "Emma," he greeted her. "Waiting for Grant to pick you up?"

"*Nei*." She turned from the counter, where she was slicing bread for supper. "Carrie needs a hand with those apples out on the porch, so I thought I'd stay and help this evening."

"Is that so? Won't Lena miss you?"

"When I'm out, Karen sends Maryann or Nathaniel to bring her to the big house for dinner. We eat over there a couple of times a week anyway. It's nothing unusual."

"What a *gut* friend you are." He settled himself at the table, being careful not to take Melvin's chair. Emma said nothing to this superfluous compliment, while the bread fell to the board in even slices.

"How are the sheds coming?" Carrie asked, setting two dishes of pickles on the table—dilly beans and tiny pearl onions.

"The equipment shed is scraped and ready for the first coat. The chicken house will have to wait, and I'll alternate between apples and painting."

"Melvin will appreciate your help on the barn." Emma

brought the bread to the table, and added the butter dish and a jar of plum jelly. "You might put out the word and make a work frolic of it."

"Are you telling me how to do my job, Emma?" Joshua settled back in his chair, toying with the fork in front of him. "Does Grant put up with that?"

"Grant has been married before, and knows that a wife's help includes sensible suggestions."

Carrie wished she could speak so calmly when it was clear that Joshua—for some reason that eluded her—was itching to stir someone up. And the little dig about his single state hadn't got past her, either.

"But you're not his wife yet," Joshua said.

"You're right. I should have said a *fiancée's* help."

Unexpectedly, he grinned at her. "I can't get under your skin, can I?"

"I don't know why you'd want to." Emma poured a glass of water and set it in front of him. "The thing about mosquitoes getting under your skin is that nine times out of ten, they get slapped."

He threw back his head and laughed. "Now, you see? This is what I miss about the old times. No matter what I did, you always had an answer for me—whether I liked it or not." He sobered a little. "Sure you won't change your mind?"

Good heavens. Carrie hoped she didn't look as shocked as she felt. And with the invitations already going out!

"My mind was made up long before you ever had a chance to change it," Emma told him. A smile of perfect contentment made her face glow. "So never mind your teasing."

That's all it was—teasing between two childhood friends. Carrie shook her head at herself for being so gullible. Of course she knew that Emma had had a talk with Joshua and told him there could never be anything between them. And now that wedding plans were in motion, the idea that anyone could come between her and Grant was ludicrous.

Especially Joshua...who was not the best marital prospect to begin with.

Carrie bent to check the casserole. It was bubbling hot and nicely browned, so she pulled it out and set it on the table. Joshua seemed to have recovered his good humor, and told stories of his life in Indiana that had them laughing and joking—as though all three of them had been childhood friends.

At length he pushed his dessert plate away and waved off her offer of another cup of coffee. "No, thanks, Carrie. That was a fine piece of cake."

"Carrie is going to make me a wedding cake just like it," Emma said. "She has a talent for them."

"Why don't you work in a bakery, then?" he asked Carrie.

It had honestly never occurred to her. "I don't know. When would I have the time?"

"If you found a couple of hours a day, you could put a little money by."

"Cakes like this take more than a couple of hours, Joshua," Emma reminded him. "A wedding cake takes a couple of days."

"Besides," Carrie said, "the bakeries around here already have enough people. Most of them are family operations. If they needed an extra person, they would hire a sister or a cousin, not me."

Emma began to stack the plates, and Carrie ran hot water into the sink.

"Joshua, are you going out to the orchard to pick?" Carrie asked. "I know it's nearly dark, but there's time enough to get in a bushel, I think. Emma and I have a good two or three hours of work here."

"No, I think I'd best be getting home."

"I was hoping to catch a ride with you," Emma said.

"You're welcome to come. I'd be glad of the company."

"I didn't mean now, Joshua, I meant later, when we had these apples done. You could pick another couple of baskets—it won't be dark for a while yet."

"I have some things to do. Sorry about that, Emma. Thanks for dinner, Carrie. See you tomorrow afternoon. When's Melvin getting back?"

"I'm expecting him for supper."

"Then maybe you won't mind if I stay again? I'd like to talk the work over with him, and since I'll already be here…"

"*Ja*, fine."

"*Gut Nacht.*"

"*Hatge*, Joshua."

The door closed behind him and the sound of his boots thumped down the steps. Emma looked at her and raised a brow. "So much for a ride home. I hope you don't mind hitching Jimsy up for me."

"Of course not. But what on earth has gotten into him? I'm not sure what shocks me most—that he wouldn't stick around to give you a ride after dark, or his complete lack of concern about leaving you stranded on the other side of the settlement."

"Not stranded. If you couldn't take me, I'd just walk. Someone would be along to give me a ride."

"That's not the point." At last Carrie figured out what it was about Joshua that had been bothering her since he'd come to work on their place. "The point is that he didn't put you first, like a brother would a sister in the family of God. He put himself first."

She scrubbed the plates vigorously while Emma fetched the first bushel of apples and a knife. She sat at the table and began to peel. "I'm sad to say you're not the first person who has had that thought. I think it's the root of his troubles, even back when we were children."

"But did his parents not see it and take steps to check it?"

"I'm sure they did, but you remember how big their family was. He was the youngest of eleven, and his parents were older by the time he came along. Sometimes you can depend on the older siblings to take a hand in the bringing-up, but maybe it wasn't quite so successful in his case."

"That's right. He was the baby of the family," Carrie said. "That explains a lot."

"What do you mean?"

"He wasn't very kind when he got here this afternoon. He said some things that...well, that were meant to make me feel bad about having you girls here and forgetting that he was to come."

"Poor baby." Emma finished one long spiral of peel and picked up another apple. "Not getting your undivided attention. I hope you stood up to him. He needs that."

"So I saw. You really know how to handle him."

"It feels strange, standing up to a man like that, but it's the only way with Joshua. Jesus intended that we should be humble, walking beside our man, not ahead of him. But I don't think He meant we should lie down so he could walk on us, either."

Humility was a battle a woman chose to fight every day, obedience a decision she made every morning—and sometimes more often than that. But in most cases, your man would meet you halfway. It was a joy to be humble with a man who put you first, and no sacrifice to obey a man who included you in his decisions.

"Maybe that's Joshua's trouble," she mused aloud. "He's gone too long only making decisions for himself. It's an adjustment to take your partner into account every time you go to do something."

"Yes, well, he could take his sisters in the faith into account and get some practice at it," Emma said.

"We're fortunate in our men," Carrie said as she dried the last plate and put it away.

"God has been good to us," Emma agreed. "I thank Him every day on my knees, believe me. Now, look here. I'm already three apples ahead of you. Don't cut yourself catching up to me."

The drying boxes would be full tonight, and so would her soul, Carrie thought as the long peels curled away from her own knife. An evening of Emma's company was just the thing to heal up the scrapes and cuts from her hired man.

* * *

The running lights glowed on the buggy as Emma climbed in next to Carrie. "You really don't have to do this. I can walk."

Carrie shook the reins and Jimsy started forward. "Don't be silly. You're wearing dark colors, and with your coat and bonnet, even a car with headlights would have a hard time picking you out."

"I'm glad I wore a coat." Emma settled on the bench and wrapped her arms around her carry basket, which now contained several jars of freshly made applesauce. "Winter is definitely around the corner. And just three weeks from now..."

Carrie could practically feel the happiness and anticipation filling Emma's side of the buggy. "The time will flash by. Remember when we were planning my wedding? Even that morning there were things that hadn't gotten done, and I had nearly a year to prepare."

Emma was silent for a moment. "Would you have still made the choice you did, knowing what you know now?"

"You mean, about children?"

"That, and other things. Like Melvin's struggle to find work he's truly happy with."

Those things might have made another woman answer differently. But Carrie knew her answer even before Emma had finished speaking. "*Ja. Ja*, I would have married him still, even knowing how hard it would be. He has been the only man for me ever since we met, that night at the band hop."

"Love is a strange thing," Emma mused. "Or maybe I should say the will of God is sometimes beyond what our poor brains can imagine. Who would have thought it would be His will that I marry a man who married someone else first?"

"Maybe that time of waiting had its purpose," Carrie suggested. "Because I wouldn't want to think that poor Lavina's death was part of God's plan to bring you and Grant together."

"That's the part my brain can't comprehend," Emma said. "And I'm glad it doesn't have to. My part is to say yes, and I have. And will." A few minutes passed, the seconds clopped out by Jimsy's hooves on the asphalt. Then Emma said, "I can't regret these twelve years with Mamm, though. They've been very precious years, and I'll look back on them with gratitude."

"There you are, then." Carrie made the left turn off the county highway onto Edgeware Road.

They hadn't gone more than a hundred yards when the front lamps illuminated a figure wearing a white shirt. Tall, skinny, and coming from the Grohl place around the corner, maybe? That made it—

"Alvin Esch?" Emma called. "Is that you?"

The teenager turned and waited for them to draw up next to him. "Hallo, Emma. Hi, Carrie."

"This is awfully late for you to be walking," Carrie said. "I'm just going to drop Emma at the farm. I can give you a ride down to your folks' place if you like." It would take her back around to the county highway the long way, but it wasn't like she had anyone waiting for her at home, was it? Melvin wasn't coming back until tomorrow.

"*Denki.*" Emma jumped down and he folded himself into the back. Then she climbed in again. "I wanted to ask you something anyway, Emma." His voice sounded muffled, as though he were hiding his mouth with his hand. "Has any mail come to you lately?"

Carrie peered out into the dark ahead of them and kept her mouth firmly shut. It would not do for him to know that Emma had told her and Amelia all about his correspondence courses—and her part in it. She would let Emma herself break that to him if she chose.

"You don't need to be so vague, Alvin," Emma said matter-of-factly. "Carrie knows. She knows what you and I and Aaron King were up to last year, and she knows that your packets were coming to my house."

"Oh," he said faintly. "I thought we agreed…"

"We did. They found out another way. And anyhow, it's all water under the bridge, because I told you when the school year ended that I would not be getting the packets anymore."

"But I'm starting the first term of junior year this week. I don't know where else to have the people send them."

"General Delivery at the post office?"

"You know Janelle would blab."

"I thought the post office was supposed to keep people's mail confidential?" Carrie couldn't resist speaking up.

"We're talking about Janelle Baum," Emma reminded her, as if that explained everything. "She gave me a package for John once when I was in there. I could have been living in Strasburg for all she knew, and carried away his baler parts to sell at the flea market."

"Please, Emma," Alvin begged. "You've helped me this long."

"And I was wrong to do it," she said. "Besides, what good will it do you to have them sent to me for only a month? Come November, I'll be living over on the other side of Whinburg."

"You could get them there. I can send them a change of address."

Emma turned on the seat to look at him as though she could see in the dark. Maybe she could. "It's one thing to deceive Mamm for your sake, Alvin. But I will not deceive the man who will be my husband."

A long breath went out of him, and Carrie could almost feel sorry for the boy. Almost, but not quite. Because all three of them knew that he was disobeying the *Ordnung* and had been for two years. On top of that, it was just the run-up for something even worse. He could not go on with his education and join church at the same time. One precluded the other.

"Alvin, you have two choices," Emma said gently. "Either you stop here and be thankful for the two years you have more than everybody else, or you move to a district whose *Ordnung* allows its young men to finish high school."

"I want more than high school," he said stubbornly. "I want to be more than a farmer, or a harness maker, or a builder. I want to be a scientist, or an engineer."

Carrie supposed there were college graduates among other Amish groups, maybe, but she'd never heard of any. "Are you saying you will leave your family and friends, then, Alvin?" she asked softly. "Is it worth it? Besides counting the cost of such losses, how will you pay for it in actual money?"

"I'll work my way through, somehow," he said, ignoring the first part and going straight to the second. "I'll talk to a counselor at the correspondence school. They'll know."

"And what about Sarah Grohl?" Carrie persisted. "Does she know about your plans?"

"No." The word sounded as though it had been dragged out of him against his will.

"Then you have her to think of as well," Emma said. "Do you really want to deceive an innocent girl like that? Because you will have to give her up if you go ahead with this."

"Maybe she'll come with me."

"And maybe it isn't fair to ask that of her. While you're going to college and working your way through, what is she going to do with her eighth-grade education? Stay alone in your one-room apartment and mend your socks?"

Silence hung in the shadows of the back of the buggy, which rocked as Carrie turned into the lane of the Stolzfus farm. She drew Jimsy to a halt in front of the path under the trees that led to the *Daadi Haus.*

Emma climbed down. "*Gut Nacht*, Alvin. I pray God will help you with your choice. *Denki*, Carrie. Tell Melvin we're all anxious to hear about his trip to Philadelphia."

Carrie waited until the lamp in the sitting-room window dimmed and brightened to signify that Emma was safely inside, and then she turned the buggy. Alvin climbed into the front as she headed for the road.

"I'm not a fool," he muttered. "I'm just not cut out to be Amish."

"We all have to make our own decisions," Carrie said. "But it's when we involve other people in the actions we take that it gets dangerous."

"Correspondence courses never hurt anybody."

"No, probably not. But the attitude behind them, the deception, can hurt any number of people. Emma, your parents, Sarah. Think of them and how your unwillingness and disobedience can hurt them."

He propped his elbows on his knees and let his hands dangle between them, head down. Carrie knew when to plant a word in season, and when to let it rest in the soil. She made up her mind to enjoy the silence of the evening for the rest of the ride.

Alvin didn't speak again until she drew level with the lane to the Esch place. "Just drop me here," he said. "If they hear a buggy, everyone will come out to see who it is, and Mamm will have a hundred questions."

Giving a brother a ride didn't seem to Carrie worthy of a hundred questions, but she brought Jimsy to a halt anyway. "*Gut Nacht*, Alvin."

He mumbled something and jogged up the lane, keeping

to the grass on the wayside so his boots didn't crunch in the gravel. Carrie shook her head and started Jimsy for home.

Choices.

In the end, weren't they what created a happy life or a miserable one? And the problem with being sixteen was that sometimes you couldn't tell the difference.

CHAPTER 7

The next day, Joshua arrived after lunch, put away his horse, and got to work painting the equipment shed like the very model of a hired man. It was as though last night's brush-off of poor Emma had never happened...or since it had, he wasn't allowing it to bother him.

Carrie had often thought how lucky she was to be Melvin's wife. A man like Joshua just proved how right she was to feel that way. And now with Melvin coming home tonight, she wanted everything in the house to be perfect. She'd been up cleaning since six a.m. The house's inside sparkled, at least. There wasn't much she could do about its shabby exterior, but if Joshua pitched in to help them, maybe they'd get it painted before the rain started.

At five, she put a casserole in the oven, closed the chickens into their coop for the night, and hitched up Jimsy. She was leading him out of the barn door when Joshua came around the corner with a bucket of scraping tools and brushes.

"Where are you off to? I was hoping we could pick some apples."

"Melvin and your cousins will be getting into the bus station at quarter to six. I'm going to meet them."

"That's right. I forgot they were coming back today. You'll be glad to see him."

"Yes, I will." Carrie climbed into the buggy and gathered up the reins. "We should be back at quarter past, and the casserole will be ready to come out. Are you still planning to stay for dinner?"

"If you don't mind." He grinned at her as though her reaction to his presence ought to mean something.

Honestly. Melvin was an hour away and any man with a brain in his head would know Melvin's wife would be looking forward to seeing *him*, not Joshua. "Of course I don't. It's what we had planned."

"Do you want company for the ride?"

"*Nei.* You'd do better to spend the time cleaning those tools."

The mischief in his face seemed to increase at her tone. "You'd do better not to tell a man how to do his work. I'd like to come."

He was imposing on her, but to admit that out loud would be ungracious. "What if Brian and Boyd need a ride?"

"They have wives, who are probably just as anxious to see them as you are to see Melvin. What's the matter, Carrie? A man would almost think you were afraid to be alone with him."

Did he always refer to himself in the third person, like a king? "Don't be silly. Hop in, then. And try not to get dirt on my dress."

He swung in next to her. "I'm looking forward to telling Melvin all the things we got done while he was gone."

I would rather have spent the ride with him in private, and it's my place to tell him the news of our place, not yours. But she couldn't say that. If a sister could do something for a man when he asked her, then it was her place to make that sacrifice for him. Whether he was willing to make the same sacrifice in return didn't really matter. One didn't do things for people to get a return.

They had just passed the turn for Edgeware Road when the slight figure walking at the side of the road turned to see who was coming up behind her. Under her black cape and apron, she wore a dress of a fabric Carrie had seen some of the girls fingering in the fabric store. It was a coral so pretty that she had no doubt that being the first to wear it would kick off a fad among the girl's buddy bunch.

Not to mention attract the attention of the bishop's wife.

As they drew closer, Carrie got a glimpse of red hair curling under her white organdy *Kapp*. "*Guder Owed*, Lydia Zook," she called as she pulled out a little farther onto the highway to pass the girl.

"Hi, Carrie." Her shawl dangled from her fingers as though she were deliberately giving the whole world a look at her new dress, despite the rapidly falling temperature. She peered past Carrie to see who her passenger was, green eyes bright with interest. "Hallo, Joshua."

"Hallo, Lydia. That's quite the dress you have on."

"*Denki.*" She swished the skirt. "I was visiting north of Highway Three-forty, and lots of the *Youngie* wear colors like this. Yellow, pink, even cherry red. I decided it was time for a change down here in our district."

"Maybe it is," Carrie said, "if you can convince Mary Lapp that anything but green, burgundy, purple, and blue are appropriate."

Lydia made a rude noise. "Only old ladies wear those colors." Her gaze bounced off Carrie's green dress and lifted to take them both in. "Any chance of a lift to town?" she asked brightly.

"All the shops will be cl—"

"Sure, hop in." And before Carrie could finish her sentence, Joshua had squished her over to the right and Lydia was perching on the leftmost edge of the bench, with one foot outside.

"Lydia, get in the back." Carrie felt like she was about to fall out the door. "Joshua, we're not teenagers, for heaven's sake, with six people packed in here. Give me some room."

Lydia edged two inches to her left, and Joshua laughed. "Relax, Carrie. We're almost to town. It's not often this thorn gets to sit between two roses."

Two pressed roses, maybe.

Fuming, Carrie flapped the reins. The sooner they got to the bus station, the better. Being smashed up against a single man might be fine when you were a teenager like Lydia—thrilling, even, if it were someone less annoying than Joshua—but it was a different matter altogether when you were a married woman on your way to meet the husband you hadn't seen in a week.

Jimsy seemed to feel her tension, because he sped up to a very smart pace indeed. While Joshua and Lydia traded nonsense remarks—what a flirt she was! Did her father know she spoke to men like that?—Jimsy trotted through the last traffic light and they arrived at the bus station in about half the time it had taken the week before.

And just in time, too. Carrie had no sooner tied up to the rail than Melvin and the Steiner men came out the door. She threw propriety to the wind and hugged him right there in the parking lot.

"Guess I was too long away," he said to no one in particular, grinning down at her. "Are you well, *Liebschdi?*"

"I am now." The blue eyes she knew so well softened as he took in the smile she couldn't keep off her face, and it was a moment before he looked up at someone over her shoulder.

"*Guder Owed*, Joshua." He set Carrie on her feet, but pulled her against his side, where she was content to stay. "Have you come to meet your cousins?"

"*Nei*, I came with your wife to meet you."

"And Lydia," Carrie put in. "Where did she go?" For the girl had vanished, and a look along the two major streets that formed the intersection didn't offer even a glimpse of coral cotton. "We gave her a lift into town, but I can't think why. All the shops are closed."

"Maybe she was meeting someone." Joshua's hazel eyes twinkled. "Come on, Carrie, there's more to an evening than making supper."

"I'm surprised to hear that, considering I made supper for you, Joshua Steiner."

Melvin's arm tightened around her waist as he waved good-bye to the others, who were already climbing into their buggies. Then he pulled her in the direction of their own. "What's this about supper?"

"Carrie invited me for dinner." Joshua climbed into the back without an invitation, leaving Melvin standing by the driver's side with an eyebrow raised.

"She did?" As Carrie untied the reins and handed them to him through the tilted-up storm front, Melvin said, "I'd sort of hoped . . . well, never mind."

Well, what was she to say to that? *I'd hoped the same, but Joshua invited himself along.* That would have the dual effect of making Joshua feel unwelcome after all the work he'd put in for them, and calling him a liar to boot.

"Joshua was anxious to tell you about the progress he's made," she said quietly when she settled in next to him and they'd followed Boyd's buggy out of the parking lot.

"He could have done that tomorrow when he came over."

"I thought you'd be back at work," Joshua put in, "so I didn't make plans to come tomorrow. It's better this way. We can work out a plan for the rest of the week."

Carrie resisted the urge to tell her husband that the man had been over every afternoon, regular as a clock, and that there was no reason he couldn't come tomorrow. But she was no authority on Joshua Steiner's schedule—other than that if there were a way to gum up somebody's works or aggravate them into the bargain, it was guaranteed he would find it.

Maybe Hill Farms really did need him all day tomorrow. Maybe they didn't. But now that Melvin was home, he could deal with him and she could retreat into the background with relief.

Melvin put away the horse while Carrie hurried into the kitchen to check the casserole. It had browned nicely, so she turned off the gas oven and cut up a green salad, boiled some string beans with onion and bacon, and had everything ready by the time the men came in.

She wasn't expecting to enjoy dinner much. But to her surprise, Joshua seemed to relax, and between his funny stories of attempting to help with the apples, and Melvin's stories of the trade show—including one crazy *Englisch* man who wanted a full dining set for his store *by the following weekend*, custom made—two hours had passed before she looked up from dessert and realized what time it was.

Melvin finished his coffee and stretched in his chair so

hard Carrie could hear his spine crack. "That was a *gut* meal and *gut* company." He smiled at them both. "I'm bushed. Joshua, not to hurry you away, but maybe we can talk a little about what's left to do out in the barn, and I'll help you hitch up your horse."

Carrie had done the dishes, cleaned up the kitchen, and gone up for the night by the time she finally heard his boots drop on the kitchen floor, a piece of wood heavy enough to last all night being shoved into the stove, and his footsteps coming up the staircase. He never used a lantern to light his way. "I know my place by day or night," he'd told her once, and he seldom bumped into furniture or ran into doors the way she would. She had a lamp burning in the bedroom, though, and when he stepped through the door, she snapped an elastic around her long braid and went into his arms.

"I'm so glad you're back," she breathed.

"Was it so bad?"

"*Nei.*" It hadn't been as bad as other times, when the silence made her a little crazy, when she would rather sleep in the coop with the chickens just to be near another breathing soul. "Joshua was here, and I saw quite a bit of the girls, and I had dinner with Lena and Emma one night. But I still missed you."

"And I missed you." Gently, he set her away from him and sat on the bed to take off his socks. "How did it go with Joshua? You can tell me the truth, now that he's gone."

"He picked bushels of apples, so the drying boxes were full all week. And he scraped and painted the equipment shed, and got the chicken coop ready for its first coat."

"He told me all that. I meant, how did it go between the two of you? Believe me, I got an earful on that subject from Brian and Boyd, all the way to Philadelphia on the train.

It made me wonder if I'd have done better hiring one of the young boys to do the work. Alvin Esch, maybe, or your brother Orval."

"What did they say?"

"Nothing I'd want to upset you with."

"Dearest, you forget Emma is my best friend. She grew up with Joshua, and there isn't anything he's done that she hasn't told me about. Including the story of that girl up in Shipshewana."

Melvin's brows contracted briefly as he unbuttoned his shirt. "It's an ugly story. I don't want you to dwell on it."

"And an untrue one, as it turns out. The girl's baby had skin the color of a good walnut stain, and she married the father, according to Emma."

"Is that what he told her?"

She was silent for a moment, kneeling beside him next to the bed. "Is that not the truth?"

His shoulder touching hers, Melvin clasped her hand between both of his and began to pray. And when she had added her prayers to his and they were both in bed, Carrie snuggled up next to him with her arm across his chest.

She waited for some time, but the answer to her question never came.

* * *

Carrie had always been close to her sister Susan, probably because Naomi was several years older than the two of them. So even though Melvin had just come home Wednesday, on Thursday night they went to her birthday party at Carrie's parents' farm.

Susan loved the wreath she'd made from bright autumn

leaves, penny plants, red berries, and twists of wheat. "You're
the artist in the family," she whispered in her ear as they
hugged. "*Denki* for sharing your gift with me."

Drat her fair skin that showed every emotion with a
blush—especially in front of a room full of people. Carrie
squeezed her hand and hoped that Daed had not heard.
While their mother encouraged them to explore their gifts in
small ways that glorified God, Daed shared Bishop Daniel's
opinion that anything that brought attention to the self and
made it stand out was a thing to be tied on the altar of sacrifice. And the sooner the better, which was why Susan had
stopped singing when she had been nine and Carrie eight.
Oh, she sang in church, sure enough, but always under everyone else, blending in, instead of soaring above them like she
could have.

"Do you ever sing anymore?" she asked Susan under the
guise of hanging the wreath in the spot over the pantry doors
where Carrie had hoped it might go. "Do you ever want to?"

"Sometimes." Susan tapped a small nail into the paneling,
hung the wreath, and Carrie stepped back to admire the effect. "But I make sure the urge only comes when I'm alone
with the babies and the windows are closed."

"Does Thomas share Daed's views?"

"Daed's mellowed over the years, Carrie. He was never as
strict with Orval as he was with us."

"Maybe we taught him a thing or two."

"Maybe seeing you run off to those band hops and take
those trips to Hershey with that girl—what was her name?"

"Malinda King. And it was only the one trip. Once was
enough to take all the rebellion right out of me, and show
me my real friends were Amelia and Emma. Before that, I'm
ashamed to say I took them for granted."

"Oh, and speaking of rebellion, have you seen Lydia Zook lately?"

"Sure. I gave her a ride into town yesterday evening when I went to pick up Melvin."

"Did she look any different?"

Carrie chuckled. "She sure did. Have peach-colored dresses been blooming among the *Youngie* like roses in June?"

"Have they! Mary Lapp is going to have a conniption."

"I'm sure there are letters in the postman's bag even as we speak," Carrie said. "I've been on the receiving end of one of those. It's not something I'm proud of—or want to repeat."

"Mary is just giving a word in season," Susan said more gently. "She's doing it out of kindness and concern."

There were days when Carrie wished she had Susan's gentle, humorous spirit. It would make life so much easier. "I'm sure she is. But while she's giving that word in season, she might remember that a tiny pinch of compassion goes a long way to flavoring a pot of good intentions."

"I'll be sure to tell her you said so." Susan dimpled at her, and Carrie stuck out the tip of her tongue, crossing her eyes in an echo of the faces they used to make at each other when they were *Kinner*. "But getting back to Lydia Zook, it wasn't so much her appearance I was getting at. Or maybe it is. I don't know."

"What are you talking about?"

"Maybe it's my imagination, and definitely it's none of my business. But don't you think that she's...noticeable lately, in a way she wasn't before?"

Carrie eyed her. "She's sixteen. Of course she wants to be noticed. Reining her in is Abe Zook's business, though, not ours."

"There's a challenging job." Susan had been gazing at the

wreath far longer than its workmanship warranted. "How can you rein in a glow like that? Her *Kapp* so far back on that red hair that it's nearly falling off. And then there's that lift of the chin that dares you to comment about it."

This was hardly fair. "You're a mother." Something deep inside twinged at this gift Susan had been given that she had not. "But poor Lydia doesn't have one, and these are the most trying years of a young person's life."

Apropos of nothing, Susan said, "Carrie, all the young girls like you. At church you're always in the middle of a crowd of them, hearing their news and laughing with them. Sometimes the years fall away and it's like you're a teenager again."

It was true, she did get along well with the young girls. Maybe they saw her as someone standing in the middle. Someone who had achieved their goal—a husband—but who had not yet become that authority figure—a parent.

"What are you getting at?" Her sister was not just reminiscing. Gentle she might be, but she was also as inexorable as a snowfall. You hardly felt the effect until you were up to your knees in whatever she wanted you to do.

"I think you should have a word with her. Before Mary's letter gets there."

"What? Lydia Zook is none of my business, Susan. And what's she done wrong? Made a dress in a fancy color? That's nothing the girls north of the highway haven't done a hundred times."

"It's not that. Not only that. Please, Carrie. Something is going on with that girl, and as her sisters in Christ we must do what we can to help."

"She won't thank me for it."

"Maybe not. But if the medicine comes from you, it might go down a little better."

Carrie sighed. "If she gets offended, it will be on your head."

"I have more faith in you than that."

"Maybe Mary should talk to her father."

"Caution will come better from you, and you know it. Imagine if it were you. Much as we love Mamm, how much listening did we do when we were sixteen?"

She had a point. But that still didn't excuse Carrie making herself into a busybody. "I will pray about it, and if God opens a door and pushes me through it, I'll know it's the right thing to do."

Susan worried the edge of her apron, two little lines forming between her brows. "Lydia's mother, Rachel Zook, was one of my closest friends. In a strange way I feel I should look out for her daughter a little more—more than taking garden vegetables over there and helping to clean once in a while. If it's not too late."

"Have you talked about this with any of the other women?"

"Only Esther Grohl and Christina Yoder. Anyone else would think we're a bunch of worrywarts, and old ones at that."

"I think you are, too." Carrie nudged her with one hip toward her company in the front room.

"But you'll ask God for that push?"

"I'll ask Him." But hopefully He, in His infinite majesty, would have more important things to do than satisfy the vague uneasiness of an Amish woman who should have more faith.

CHAPTER 8

I f the Lord wanted her to stick in her oar and interfere in
someone's business, then He would make the way plain.

Carrie hopped down from the buggy of one of the many
Yoder cousins, and waved as he clopped off down Main
Street. It had been kind of him to give her a ride all the
way in to Whinburg. Once she was done at the fabric store,
she would walk over to Whinburg Pallet and Crate and ride
home with Melvin.

She actually had a real reason to go to Plain and Fancy
Fabrics besides sticking her nose into Lydia's life. Melvin had
come home from the trade show with a big tear in one of his
shirts that defied her attempts at patching, which relegated
it to the ragbag. It was time he had some new ones, anyway. With their purse strings as tight as they had been during
the last couple of years, opportunities for buying fabric had
been few and far between. And even then, she'd had to scrape
the bottom of the barrel, metaphorically speaking. She and
Melvin had their share of clothes made from the pieces nobody else wanted.

She browsed the short aisles in the shop, which was a
cheery meeting place for the women of the district. While
there was plenty of brightly patterned cotton up front for

the tourists who came looking for "authentic Amish quilt" fabric, the women from the church actually shopped in the back, where dress and shirt weights filled the racks with solids in colors from Lydia's peach to Sunday black. Downstairs you could get ready-made kitchen aprons, away bonnets, and *Kapp* strings, along with modest underclothing, shoes, and even sweaters and coats.

The place seemed to be empty except for a couple of women browsing quilt cottons at the front. From downstairs Carrie could hear the sound of the cash register. She was fingering a nice length of burgundy broadcloth that would look particularly fine on Melvin when a voice spoke up beside her. "Can I help you with that?"

And there she was. Lydia Zook smiled and indicated the material. "I can cut it for you if you like."

Well, so far God was on Susan's side. "*Denki*. Six yards, please, and I'll need some thread to match."

"It's a nice color," Lydia offered as she snapped the lengths out on the cutting table. "Are you making a dress?"

"Maybe, and some shirts for my husband. I like the warm colors on him, though he'd think I was crazy if I told him so."

"Men don't care about things like that," Lydia agreed. "I love color."

"So I see." On a cloudy October day, she was wearing a spring green that made her hair seem to burn in the light. "The one you have on is very...bright."

"Not as bright as some of the things we have in here." Lydia tilted her head toward the front. "There's a lime green up there that you could light a room with. Even I have my limits."

"I hope so," Carrie said, feeling her way into a conversational bramble. If she were going to run into a thorn, it would be now. "It wasn't so long ago that I was trying on bright colors, hoping to impress a certain someone."

Lydia ran the scissors up the cutting line, looking interested. "*Ja?* Melvin?"

"No, before I met him. It was a boy from the next district, and oh, didn't I think he was fine. But"—she shook her head with mock sadness—"he must have been color-blind, because he only had eyes for my sister Susan. I could have been decked out like a Christmas tree and he wouldn't have seen me."

"But then you met Melvin, who wasn't color-blind."

Carrie nodded, with a reminiscent smile. "God led him to me in the unlikeliest of places."

Lydia folded the length of fabric carefully, as though it might split. "Do you think God is in unlikely places?"

Careful, now. "I think He is in us. And sometimes, if we're lucky, we meet Him where we don't expect Him."

"So maybe it's not so bad to go to an unlikely place, then, if we find what God wants us to find?"

"Well, I wouldn't want to go into the Hitching Post to test that idea," Carrie said dryly, naming Whinburg's only bar. "He also gave us a conscience. Why, have you been looking into unlikely places?"

"Maybe." Lydia dimpled at her. "Or maybe just unlikely people."

"As long as you find God there. Do you?"

Lydia nodded, though her merry gaze had fallen and become a little pensive. But maybe that was just because she had finished folding the fabric. She held it out to Carrie. "Elizabeth will ring you up downstairs."

"*Denki*, Lydia. See you next Sunday."

And she went downstairs to find a couple of sets of *Kapp*

strings and pay for her purchases, feeling a little unsettled. For all her poking around in the bramble, what had she really learned?

Nothing much, except that maybe the girl was going places and seeing someone who might not entirely possess the presence of God. It wasn't so hard to believe that. She was sixteen and was clearly choosing a *Rumspringe* and the activities that went with it. So far, nothing seemed very harmful. What kind of real trouble could she get into in Whinburg, anyway, that Carrie and half the people Lydia's parents' age hadn't gotten into themselves?

Susan was worrying for nothing, and Carrie would tell her so the next time she saw her.

This was what came of poking your nose into someone else's window. You might not get the sash slammed down on your fingers, but you wouldn't get much of a welcome, either.

When she climbed the stairs again, Lydia was away in the back with a customer, and the two *Englisch* ladies had stacked a few bolts of cotton and worked their way over to the thread rack, where they were comparing colors.

Thread. That's what she had forgotten.

With the ladies and their bolts, there was no room in front of the rack, so she browsed idly over the interfacing shelves while she waited for them to move on.

"…can't believe he won't even consider it," the blond woman said.

"Since when has he ever listened to anyone but himself? I tell you, Tiff, that guy has severe empathy problems. He's probably a sociopath. I mean, how could you tell your wife 'No, you can't have a baby if we don't do it the old-fashioned way'?"

"It's an ego thing," the dark-haired woman—Tiff—said

with a sigh. "He doesn't want to admit his little swimmers are so weak they can't get up the river."

"But with IVF it's still his swimmers. That's what I don't get. It's not like she's asking to go visit the sperm bank and pick someone a lot better-looking than he is."

"Which I would totally do. I wouldn't be inflicting that nose on my kid, that's for sure."

"Seriously. Or that Neanderthal brain, either. I don't know why she stays with him."

"I've told her over and over there will always be another bus coming down the pike, but she won't believe me. She got on this one, and she's staying with it no matter what."

"I think you should go with that purple thread. The thread should be darker than the fabric, my mom says."

"Why?"

"I don't know. Some sewing rule. But you have a lot of purple here, so it would match the most."

"Fine. Come on. Let's go see if we can find someone to cut this. We should have gone to the place in Intercourse. This store is so quiet it makes me wonder if anybody actually works here."

As they passed, the blonde cut her eyes at Carrie, who focused on the interfacing as though it held the secret to eternal life. But in reality, she was hardly aware of it—or very much else.

Instead, she was trying with every ounce of willpower she had not to stop the two women and ask what they had been talking about. Another girl who wanted a baby and didn't have one, that was clear. But what was IVF? Something sketchy, it must be, if the girl's husband didn't want her to have it. And swimmers? Surely they hadn't meant... was that possible?

Carrie knew the basics of human reproduction—her mother had sat her down the night before she was married and struggled through the conversation, which had not turned out to resemble the beauty of reality very much. And over the years since, her *Englisch* doctor had broached the subject of her childlessness a time or two, shaming her so badly she could hardly get out of the clinic fast enough. But before Carrie had left the room, the doctor had said Carrie was healthy, if slightly undernourished, and there was no reason she could not have a baby.

Could this be their problem? Had she been blaming her thinness for her inability to conceive when it was really the "swimmers" that were weak and unable to travel far enough to do the job? And if it was so, what could she and Melvin do about it?

Oh, this was so frustrating. If she asked the women these questions, they would know she'd been eavesdropping, though in the quiet of the store their voices were impossible to avoid. But who else could she ask?

Well, she knew of one place to start. A place where you could be totally honest, no matter how shameful your question or confession. And that place was her own spare room, on Tuesday, with Amelia and Emma.

But until then, she had a few minutes to spare. Maybe she'd go over to the library and see if she couldn't find out a thing or two.

* * *

Oh, if only this week were a church Sunday! Carrie could have cornered Amelia and Emma and put her questions to them then. But maybe it was better this way. It would certainly be easier to talk in the privacy of her own home than it would be to find a quiet corner in all the crowd, with the distractions of family and friends visiting and greeting one another.

She was thankful that when Joshua came over to finish painting the chicken house, Melvin was there to manage him. Before she knew it, the two of them were walking the perimeter of the house itself, talking about getting the men together for a painting frolic before it got too cold.

That was good news. Carrie could never suppress a twinge of shame at her shabby house, but until now there had been no money to do the job. Now, even if they had only Joshua's help, they could do it in a couple of days—and with a whole crew, in one.

Carrie felt more hopeful than she had in many months. People saw autumn as a time of ending, of going to sleep, of pulling in and turning to inside activity. But the feeling in the air around her wasn't the slow easing of movement; no, if what she had read at the library thanks to a very helpful young lady librarian was true, it could be the season of beginnings for her.

Amelia and Emma had barely seated themselves and loaded up their needles with their first stitches when Carrie decided she couldn't keep it in any longer. "You'll never guess what I've been learning this week."

Emma smiled. "How to crochet afghans like the ones Susan makes?"

"I don't have the patience to make fabric for something. I'd rather just buy the fabric, make the blanket or quilt, and get to the point," Amelia said. "But Susan's afghans are beautiful. I've always liked the one you have downstairs on the sofa."

"No, it's not afghans. I've been learning about babies."

Amelia blinked at her. "What more do you need to learn? A woman marries, she has babies, she learns she needs a lot less sleep at night."

"Not every woman," Emma said softly. "Carrie, what do you mean?"

Carrie gave her a grateful look and told them about the women in the fabric store. "So I went to the county library and you would not believe the number of books about it. I spent the whole afternoon there…and *meine Freind*, I can't believe I never knew all this before."

"All what?" Amelia laid down her needle. But instead of looking as interested and excited as Carrie herself was, she looked calm. Too calm.

Never mind. Carrie hurried on. "I always thought I couldn't conceive because I was so thin. That if I just got to eating more, it would eventually happen. But our situation has been getting better and better, and still no sign. So then I wondered if it might be Melvin who is stopping it, not me."

"Melvin? But he wants children as much as you do," Emma said.

"*Ja*, I know. But what if there's something going on inside? The doctor said there was no reason I couldn't conceive. So it could be something in Melvin that isn't right."

"Have you told him this?" Amelia asked quietly.

"No, not yet. I wanted to talk it over with you first."

"That is what isn't right." Emma chewed on her bottom lip and concentrated on her needle until she completed the lily petal. "These are very private matters between husband and wife. You should be saying these things to Melvin."

"If he'll hear them," Amelia put in. "I'm not sure how any man would handle such an announcement from his wife."

"It's not like that," Carrie protested. "I just wondered if either of you had heard of IVF and the possibilities it could hold for us."

Emma shook her head. Amelia spoke slowly. "I have seen it mentioned in the papers. They used to call them 'test-tube babies,' didn't they?"

"I suppose so. But the egg is fertilized outside the body and then put inside the woman to grow. If Melvin's swimmers can't get to my eggs, then don't you see? This could solve it."

"I can't believe you're even thinking about this," Amelia muttered. "It's crazy."

"It's not crazy!" Carrie caught her breath and forced herself to speak calmly. "Millions of babies have been born to millions of mothers from such a beginning. Just think, Amelia, how wonderful *gut* it would be if I were one of them."

"It would be wonderful *gut* to see you a mother," she said. "But Carrie, these things can't happen in a lab. The gift of a child is from God alone. You can't just march into a hospital and have them go into your body and take an egg and put it in a test tube and expect a baby to come out of it, like putting a coin in the phone and getting a connection."

"Why not, if it's my egg and Melvin's sperm? If we can't conceive the natural way, why not use the hospital?"

"Because that would be man's way," Amelia said gently, "not God's. It would be saying that God's timing is too slow, that His will for you isn't good enough. That you know better than the God of all creation what is right."

"I'm not saying that at all." Carrie felt as though Amelia had put a hand on her chest and given her a good, hard push backward.

"Maybe not, but it's what Bishop Daniel will say."

"My problems are not Bishop Daniel's business." Carrie

was beginning to think she shouldn't have made them Amelia's business, either. "He doesn't need to know what goes on between Melvin and me."

"I'm sure he already does," Emma said to no one in particular.

"What I mean is, I don't tell the bishop when I go to see the doctor. Why would this be any different?"

Amelia gave her a long look. "Because it is different, and you know it. Before you eavesdropped on those women, you had never heard of IVF . . . and now you're ready to go to the doctor and have it done, just like that?"

"I wasn't eavesdropping. You could hear them all over the store."

Amelia let this go. "I'm just saying, *Liewi*, that you should think about it carefully—and pray about it, too."

"Do you think I haven't been?" Did she have any idea about the hours and hours she had spent on her knees, asking God for just one single moment of mercy—one tiny moment of conception?

"Of course you have." Emma's tone was soothing, and Carrie felt her hackles smoothing down in spite of herself. "But here is another thing to think of—something I had to think of when Grant got hurt this summer." She paused, loaded her needle again. "Money. It's one thing to go to the doctor and have the *Gmee* pay for it. We all do this and it's not a problem. But how much will this new procedure cost?"

Carrie bent her head over the quilt. She hadn't taken a single stitch yet. "A lot, I think."

"Even if you see a doctor about it in private, when it comes to paying for it, Bishop Daniel will have to know. He and the elders will have to approve." Amelia inclined her head so that Carrie was forced to look up to meet her eyes. "And if they would not approve a radical treatment when I thought I had MS, do you really think they would approve of a test-tube baby?"

Did she have to put it like that—so bluntly, so unkindly? Carrie's eyes filled with tears.

And Amelia saw it. "Oh *Schatzi*, I'm sorry. Carrie, please don't cry—you know I would never hurt you for the world."

"Well, you have," she blurted, and then wished she could grab the words and stuff them back where they'd come from. Amelia looked stricken, tears welling into her own eyes.

"My dear ones, don't do this to one another," Emma cried softly. "The whole subject is as spiny as a chestnut husk. Please, let's not say things to hurt when we come to each other for help."

Amelia pulled Carrie into a hug. "I'm sorry," she whispered. "I just don't want you to get your hopes up like I did, and suffer so much when they're disappointed."

"I'm no stranger to that," Carrie managed. But she couldn't say she was sorry in return. She hadn't done anything but speak the truth.

And God would not put this spirit of hope in her heart if He didn't mean to bring something good to her.

Would He?

CHAPTER 9

Amelia may not have meant to rain on Carrie's parade, but the cold drops still stung. Maybe that was why she'd got caught up on her quilting stitches so quickly afterward... she really didn't have much to say, which left her to stitch and Amelia and Emma to natter about Emma's wedding preparations. With only a couple of weeks left to go, the buzz of activity at the Stolzfus place was building like that of a hive of bees.

Carrie waved good-bye as the buggy rolled down the lane. As she turned, she scanned the lawn. Not a single hen pecked and scratched in the yard. A drop of rain hit her on the forehead. Aha. The hens could tell a raincloud from a hole in the ground. They had put themselves to bed early.

She put on her lumber jacket and went into the henhouse, where she found most of them already roosted up. As she filled the feed cans and topped up the waterers, she rehearsed with the hens what she would say to Melvin tonight after dinner.

Maybe it was just as well that Amelia had had her say. At least now Carrie was prepared if her husband didn't see things as she did.

When she sat, Dinah walked along the roost and settled

onto her shoulder. Carrie spent a few quiet moments enjoying her companionship...well, her body was quiet. Her mind was a jumble of arguments to marshal into order, of gabbled prayer, and snippets of conversation that might happen or might not.

This was no way to prepare herself. She should have brought home one of the books from the library. Why hadn't she thought of that before? Then she could have everything laid out sensibly, with all the information at her fingertips. As it was, she'd probably get things confused, or just like this afternoon, be unable to come up with an answer to what would probably be the same objections.

Gently, she set Dinah back in her place. Talk or no talk, Melvin still expected his dinner when he came in from work. That at least she could do. Then, when they were both full, but before he sat down with the paper, she would broach the subject.

So, when Melvin sat back in his chair with a sigh of satisfaction, Carrie was ready with a pan of apple crumble—his favorite dessert. She even had heavy cream to pour on top of it—a luxury she had cajoled out of Moses Yoder's wife the day before.

"I wonder what the rich folks are eating tonight?" Melvin said around the first big spoonful. "It can't be anything better than this meal."

"You always say that, even when it's only scrambled eggs." She ran her fingers up his arm and squeezed affectionately.

"I always say it because I always wonder. If the way to a man's heart is through his stomach, you've certainly captured mine, *Liebschdi*."

"Is that all that captured it?" she teased. His bowl was empty already, so she dished him another.

"I think you know. At this moment, I am a happy man." He waved his spoon to encompass the kitchen, the house, and the world outside. "I have everything I need."

Here was her opportunity, dropped into her lap like a present. God must really be in this. There was no other explanation.

"What about the things we want?" she asked softly.

He knew what she meant, of course he did. It was a subject that had come up so often there was no need to explain any further.

"What we want is in God's hands," he said gently. "I hope we are both willing for that."

"But what if God is encouraging us to find another way?" she asked softly. "I've been seeing signs lately that maybe He might be."

"What signs?"

She told him about the conversation in the fabric store, about the library books, about the possibilities that lay out there for them if only they would reach out and try. "At my last appointment, back in August, the doctor said there was no reason I couldn't conceive and carry a child. So Melvin, maybe, just maybe, we might visit the doctor and see if she says the same thing about you?"

Through her whole speech he had watched her gravely, not interrupting. That was one of the things she loved about him. She'd heard many a man interrupt to correct or contradict or simply cut off a woman in mid speech. Melvin never did that. He always listened, and when he was ready to speak, he did so.

Now his eyes looked shadowed. "I should go to the doctor?"

"In my reading in the library, I learned that one of the

things that can prevent conception is if the man's sperm aren't strong enough to swim all the way to the egg. In that case, there's something called IVF—in vitro fertile"— her tongue stumbled on the unfamiliar word—"fertilization. In the hospital they bring the sperm to the egg outside the body, and then put it back inside the womb to grow."

"That is impossible."

"*Nei*, truly," she said eagerly. "I can borrow the book that shows you the pictures of how it's—"

"I don't care what a book says. Carrie, how can you consider such an unnatural thing?"

Again she felt that sensation of being pushed away by a hand laid right over her heart. Carrie took a deep, steadying breath. "It's not really unnatural. These would be my eggs, your sperm, my body in which to grow. The procedure only shortens the distance between the first and the second, so that the third can happen."

"The only thing I see happening here is that you believe the fault lies with me."

"Melvin, *nei*, that's not so. That's why we should go to the doctor, to find out for sure."

"And then what? Walk into the lab and—and have relations with each other on a hospital bed?"

The heat of embarrassment scalded her cheeks, as no doubt he had intended. "Of course not. The egg is removed from me in surgery, and you provide sperm in a private room. They—" Oh, how could she say this? "They provide worldly men with magazines to make it easier, but you would not do that, of course."

"I will not do any of it!" He pushed the chair back, and before she knew it, she had jumped to her feet, too. "This is crazy. Unnatural. If I had known you were gadding about today, filling your head with this worldly nonsense, I would have locked you in!"

She reared back. "The door locks from the inside."

"You know what I mean. I forbid you to speak of this to me anymore."

"Melvin—"

"And I forbid you to go back to the library and read any more about this. It is obscene. Shameful."

"It's just a procedure."

"It's your own will, Carrie, going up against the will of God. And you know who will win that battle."

"I know who is winning this one, if loudness counts for anything."

He took a deep breath, and she could see him wrestle his temper under control. "I do not want to fight." The words almost sounded choked by that very control.

"I don't, either. But Melvin..." Her eyes were already swimming with tears, and one spilled over to track down her cheek. "You know what this means to me. To us. Will you not even talk with the doctor about it? Words will not harm anything."

"Words have done enough harm tonight. You have put images in my head that will take serious prayer to get rid of."

Why did he insist in making this about his service to God? "Millions of babies have been born this way, my dearest. It's not the unnatural thing you think it is."

He gazed at her for a long moment. "In all our years together, I have never once been afraid for your soul. Until now."

"My soul? Melvin, if we could have a child, no matter how, my soul would rejoice and flourish." As opposed to now, when her soul sometimes seemed as gray and wan as the cloudy skies of October.

"The wicked flourish like the green bay tree."

The tear had dried on her cheek, leaving a narrow track that felt stiff as her eyes widened. "Are you calling me wicked?"

"I'm just telling the truth. If you feel convicted by it, that should tell you something."

"I am not wicked. I just want a baby, like every other married woman in Whinburg. Why is that so impossible? And why is trying something new so sinful?"

"If you cannot or will not see why, then there is no use my talking about it anymore." He pushed his bowl away, the second helping only half gone. She had never seen him leave food uneaten, ever.

"But we must talk about it." Despair choked off the words.

"Not now. Not later." He paused in the kitchen doorway. "Put this out of your head, Carrie, and come and pray with me about it."

But she could not. If she knelt beside him, she would only pray for this thing she wanted so badly. He would pray that it would be cleansed from her soul, and all God would hear would be two conflicting appeals. What good would that do?

"I have to clean up the kitchen."

"After, then."

But he got no reply, only the clashing of pots and cutlery as she ran water into the sink as hard and hot as it would go.

* * *

Carrie could count on the fingers of one hand the number of times she and Melvin had quarreled. The few times they had fought were over silly things—the way he drove on the county highway (far faster than necessary, in her opinion), or the time she'd miscalculated while cutting his hair and neither of them had noticed until they were on their way to church. Little spats over little things were easily made up, and the words her father had said to her on the morning of her wedding had remained like the pretty lace tablecloth in her hope chest, there for when it might be needed, but until now, unused.

Let not the sun go down upon your wrath. Do not go to bed angry with one another, or you will wake in the morning with cold ash.

She cleaned the kitchen within an inch of its life until finally Melvin decided he couldn't outwait her, and went upstairs first. She had broached the sore subject and offended him; it was her place to tell him she was sorry and ask forgiveness.

But it was the same as with Amelia this afternoon—she had not really done anything wrong, so how could she apologize? Wanting something good and right and offering a plan to achieve it wasn't wicked.

But the fact remained that he was offended—or at least, gravely disappointed in her. They had almost never allowed each other to go to sleep angry, and if they did, all was forgiven with a kiss in the morning. But tonight…

Carrie hung up the washcloth when there was nothing left to clean, and took the lamp upstairs with her.

Melvin was already in bed, lying on his side facing the window. Away from her.

All right. She had expected that. She took off her apron and dress and hung them up, then slipped into her warm flannel nightgown—the one with the tiny eyelet frill around the yoke. The *Ordnung* in many districts stipulated that plain dressing extended even to nightwear, but she had always been glad that Bishop Daniel, while he was vocal about externals like house colors and the number of reflectors on buggies, kept diffidently quiet about things that were extremely private. Maybe Mary Lapp went to bed in a silk nightie with satin ribbons. No one would ever know, and Bishop Daniel wasn't about to tell—or go looking in other people's houses to make sure the standards were kept.

Carrie shook her wandering thoughts into order, and sat gingerly on the edge of the bed, in the crook of Melvin's body where his knees bent.

"*Liebschdi*," she said softly. "Please don't be angry with me. I can't bear it."

Silence, except for his breathing. He was not asleep; she knew the cadence of his every breath, and these were not the long, relaxed breaths of sleep.

"Melvin? We have not prayed together."

"I have said my prayers."

She bit her lip as a spurt of pain arrowed through her. "You did not wait for me? We always pray together when you're home."

"I prayed for you."

"I like it better when you pray *with* me."

For answer, he moved away from her, closer to the middle of the bed.

Fine. He was determined to be angry. Very well, then, she would say her prayers on her own side, and they would make it up in the morning. Silently, she got up, but when she settled onto her knees on her side, the floor seemed so hard she could hardly concentrate.

Dear Lord, thank You for opening up another way to me and for giving me the eyes to see it. Please help Melvin see it, too, so that we can stand together in this matter. It's clear we must do it together. Help him to see this is the only way if we hope ever to be parents. Help him see this is Your will, no matter what he thinks or the bishop thinks.

And Lord, I pray he would forgive me for upsetting him and see beyond it to what You want for both of us—to be a family and have little souls to care for and bring up in Your love.

Amen.

* * *

Carrie woke to the sound of rain hard on the roof, and snuggled deeper under the quilts. On mornings like this the woodstove downstairs was nothing short of a blessing. It would be a good day to cook down the last of the apples and get them into the canner. The house would smell wonderful when Melvin got home from work.

Poor man, having to hitch up and go into town on a day like today. She reached over to his side of the bed.

And found it empty.

Shoving the covers off her face, she gaped at the tousled sheets, then looked wildly around the room. He never left their bed without a kiss. Never.

She tossed on her dressing gown and knotted it as she padded barefoot down the stairs. "Melvin?"

"In here." He stood at the counter, pouring a cup of coffee. The clock over the door said 5:45 a.m.

"You're up early. Is there a big project at work?"

"No. I just couldn't sleep."

Her rest hadn't been the best, either. She slipped her arms

around his waist and laid her head on his back, the clean cotton of his green shirt crisp under her cheek. "It was my fault." Her poor attitude of last night seemed foolish in the light of those cold sheets. "Forgive me."

And to her enormous relief, he turned and wrapped her in a hug. "I already have, *Liebschdi*. I had to, last night, before I could pray."

You might have told me so, and I would have known the sun hadn't set on your anger. But she kept the words back—words that might upset this moment of hard-won peace.

She released her hold and went to the refrigerator. "We have cream for your coffee this morning."

"What about you, Carrie?"

"Oh *ja*, I'll have some, too. What a treat."

"I didn't mean cream, I meant prayer. Were you able to approach God last night?"

She nodded as she poured a dollop into the mug he held out to her. The silence stretched out as she poured her own, and when she sat in her place at his right hand to take her first, satisfying sip, his gaze had not left her. "What?"

Something changed in his eyes, and his lashes dipped. "Nothing. It's just as well I have an early start today. We're expecting a load of lumber early at Brian's, for that dining suite. The buyer decided it wasn't such a rush after all, but he still wants us to make it."

Sensitive to his moods, she was always glad to see his satisfaction in the word "us." It was *gut* he had work he liked, and a good business to be part of. The solitary work of a farmer was just not what he was cut out for.

"You'll be home at the usual time?"

He looked down at the tabletop. "*Ja.*"

Was he waiting for something? She had asked forgiveness and received it. What more could there be?

"I'll start breakfast, then." She began to get up, but he covered her hand with his.

"Carrie, how can this be true?"

She settled into her chair. He had lost her again. "How can what be true?"

"That you could pray, believing as you do that this medical scheme is acceptable in the eyes of God."

What answer did he want from her? She did believe that, no matter what everyone thought. "It's as you say."

"But how can you think so?"

"I think the blessing of the child is worth the inconvenience of the way it's conceived."

"Inconvenience?" he whispered. "Is that all this blasphemy is to you? An inconvenience?"

She pressed her molars together and breathed a prayer for a soft answer, even though her head was uncovered and her *Kapp* upstairs. "If you forgave me for these thoughts last night, why are you bringing them up again?"

"Because I thought that when you knelt before God, He would have changed your heart. Or maybe I should say your mind, because clearly it's man's thinking at work here, not God's."

"And you know how God thinks?"

"Of course not. The Bible says His thinking is far above ours."

"Then where in the Bible does it say that IVF is wrong?"

His jaw firmed and his lips thinned in the way they did when he was coming to the limits of his patience. "It does not, of course, as you know very well. But the *Ordnung*—"

"There is nothing in the *Ordnung* about it, either, and if

you didn't know that before, when we go into the *Abstellung* at Council Meeting in three weeks and Bishop Daniel goes over it, you'll know then."

"And of course he'll say nothing about it. Because such a thing is not covered. Because no one has ever wanted to do it. No one has ever been bold and proud enough to put herself above God on this matter!"

Carrie glared at him, so angry she dared not speak.

"And when he asks you if you are ready for Communion, *Fraa*, what will you tell him?"

"I will tell him I am." Carrie lifted her chin. "I will have done no wrong, even if I do go to the doctor and ask her questions about it."

"Then you will not be in unity with the *Gmee*," he said slowly. "You cannot take Communion if you have a quarrel with even one person."

"And are you that one person? Are you going to bring this up in public?"

"Of course not. We must resolve it well beforehand so we can take the bread and the cup with peace in our hearts. We must be right with God."

"Or must we just be right?"

"I don't know what you mean." He pushed back from the table as though he meant to leave without his breakfast.

"Where are you going? You haven't eaten yet."

"I'm not hungry. I must go. Someone has to meet the truck."

At six in the morning?

She tried to kiss him good-bye. And he let her. But she may as well have kissed a fence post for all the joy it gave either of them.

CHAPTER 10

By two o'clock, Carrie had finished two dozen quarts of applesauce, gently flavored with cinnamon, and lined them up in rosy rows on the counter. The kitchen smelled just as she'd imagined...which was about the only lovely thing about the day.

With a sigh, she settled at the table with a cup of tea, a piece of apple crumble drowned in cream, and pencil and paper. If she was to make Emma's wedding cake, she would need to take a trip to town to buy the ingredients she didn't have on hand, and to refresh her supply of food coloring for the bird cutouts.

So when a buggy rattled into the yard and footsteps came up the porch stairs, she laid her pencil down on the paper with a snap. Who was this, now? And how fast could she send them on their way so she could catch the bus?

"*Ischt mir,*" Joshua said cheerfully, opening the kitchen door and leaning in. "Hey, that looks good. Any chance of a helping before I get started on the barn?"

"You're working today?" she said, a little blankly. She'd forgotten all about him, as thoroughly as if he'd never been born.

"Melvin asked me to help him replace the loft floor before

someone falls through it. By the time I'm done, the *Youngie* will be able to hold a hoedown up there."

So much for the bus. Mentally, she waved good-bye to it and moved her list off the table.

"That's not very likely," she said dryly. She beckoned him in and dished up a good helping of crumble. No cream. That was for Melvin's dessert tonight, and Joshua could comment if he wanted to, he wasn't getting any.

But he didn't say a word, just dug into the bowl with enthusiasm. "I hope you're well?" he asked when he came up for air.

How to answer that? Carrie couldn't very well tell him the truth—*I'm quarreling with my husband over a new cure for an old problem*—so she settled for nodding her head. "And you?"

"*Gut*. But I think you're just being polite. The light's gone out of your face."

Goodness. How could such a harum-scarum man who made a career out of being irritating say something so perceptive...and so kind? And once again, there was no reply she could make that wasn't disloyal...or any of his business.

"Now I've made you blush. Come on, Carrie. What's the matter? You can tell old Joshua."

"I can't say."

"Can't or won't?" He polished off his bowl and pushed it aside, then leaned on both elbows on the table.

"There are things a woman doesn't talk about with a man who isn't her husband," she told him, swiping the bowl and taking it to the sink.

"Oh." His tone said he knew exactly what she was talking about, though that was impossible. "I wouldn't be so sure about that. We men can surprise you with what we know."

"I'm sure you can. But that doesn't mean we women are going to talk about it with you."

"Guess I'd do better with an *Englisch* woman. They don't seem to have any problems talking about personal things right out in public."

Carrie froze. He was just babbling, talking to fill the silence. He couldn't know about what those two women had been talking about in the fabric store. "Maybe."

Now he'd caught her gaze and wasn't letting her look away. "I think I know what's bothering you—and believe me, plenty of other people will be bothered about it, too."

"I don't know what you're talking about," Carrie said through stiff lips. "If you're going out to the barn, you'd better go, or Melvin will find you still here and not a single board laid."

"Have it your way," he said. "Maybe you're wise to keep it to yourself. There's sure to be a to-do once it gets out that you've even let that thought enter your head."

That tied it. "Joshua Steiner, either speak plain or stop talking. Or maybe you just like the sound of your own voice, whether it makes any sense or not." There, if that didn't sound like Emma, she didn't know what did.

To her surprise, he laughed. "If you said that to anyone but me, they'd feel sorry for Melvin, having such a bossy wife on his hands."

"No one flaps his lips the way you do, so I don't have to speak so to anyone else. Now, tell me what you're talking about."

"I heard a rumor, is all."

"What rumor?"

"That there's a newfangled medical practice that could result in the pitter-patter of little feet at the Miller house. And I don't mean those chickens of yours."

A sudden, awful thought struck her. She had only confided in three people—Melvin, Emma, and Amelia. And not one of them would ever break such a confidence. Or so she thought. But with all his faults, Emma still harbored a soft spot for Joshua, believed in him when many others did not.

Oh, surely Emma hadn't...

"I'm not saying a word," Joshua said. "But I know a lady in Shipshewana who went through the procedure. And she's now the mother of a two-year-old boy."

"An Amish woman?"

"Well, no. But she'd been married a long time and come to find out her husband couldn't father a child. So they did the test-tube procedure using someone else's, er..." Finally, he looked a little embarrassed, as though it had taken this long for him to figure out how inappropriate this conversation was.

"Swimmers?" Carrie supplied, not without an edge to her tone.

Please say Emma didn't betray my confidence. Not Emma.

"A good *Englisch* word for an *Englisch* idea. Yes. And now she's a happy mother."

"But she's *Englisch*. She doesn't have the *Ordnung* to contend with."

"Such a thing is in the *Ordnung* here?" She'd never have believed she could surprise Joshua. But then, there were a lot of things she wouldn't have believed last week that she was forced to look in the eye this week.

"No, of course not. But both Amelia and Melvin have given me their opinions in no uncertain terms, so it might as well be."

"But Amelia and Melvin don't go over the *Amstellung* every year, do they?"

"*Nei*, Bishop Daniel does, as you know very well." Goodness, what silly things he said.

"So Bishop Daniel is the one who can say if this is right or wrong, not Amelia or Melvin."

Silence settled in the kitchen. Finally Carrie said, "I will not speak of these things with you. It's not right."

He only shrugged and got up. But she couldn't let him leave before he answered one question. "Who told you about these things? Who said I was thinking of it?"

"There are certain things I can't speak of with you, either." And he smiled, the most innocent, maddening smile—the kind that would get him shaken by the shoulders if she were only tall enough and brave enough.

And instead of laughing and telling her, he moseyed out the door as though he had all the time in the world and a clear conscience to enjoy it with.

Carrie had never stamped her foot in all her life.

Next time, she would remember to wear shoes. It hurt.

* * *

At dinner, Melvin enjoyed his crumble and cream, and neither of them brought up the subject. All the next day, Carrie made meals and spoke gently, and saw him visibly relax. But by Friday morning, she had made up her mind.

They were expecting Brian and Erica for supper, so she made up a salmon casserole in the morning and put it in the cooling porch for the day. Dessert would be fresh apple-and-cranberry pie, and there were any number of vegetables in the garden to pick yet for side dishes.

Doing everything early meant she was free to take the shortcut along the creek to Edgeware Road and the Lapp farm, which lay on the other side of the road and about half a mile from the Stolzfus place.

God must have been with her, because there were no visiting buggies in the yard, and from what she could tell, the buggy horses were out in the pasture, grazing. Chances were good that Mary Lapp was home.

Mary Lapp's eyebrows practically disappeared under her hairline. "Why, Carrie Miller. Whatever are you doing all the way over here? You didn't walk, did you, on such a blustery day? Come on in."

"I did walk, but not in faith that the rain would hold off. I brought an umbrella in my bag."

"Daniel has to go and see Moses Yoder on church business later this afternoon. He can give you a ride back."

Mary Lapp had a terrible reputation for talking—in conversation, you could hardly get a word in edgewise, and chances were good that whatever you said would wind up on the grapevine sooner or later. But Carrie pulled her courage together. All she could do was ask the bishop's wife for advice and beg her not to say anything about it. After that, it was up to God—and Mary's conscience.

"So what brings you here today?" Mary's black eyes sparkled with interest…and kindness, too, if the truth must be told. More than one or two of the casseroles that had appeared now and again during the lean times had come from Mary's kitchen, with never a word said about it. But a woman's cooking was as distinctive as her handwriting, and Mary had a talented hand with the herbs she grew in her garden.

"I came to ask your advice about something," she said slowly.

Mary looked pleased, then puzzled. "But why come to me and not Miriam? Surely a mother knows more about her daughter and is in a better position to give good counsel?"

"Not about certain things," Carrie said. "Things that might fall under the *Ordnung*."

"Then you would want the bishop," Mary said.

"Female things," she said, a little awkwardly. "I wouldn't know how to put this matter to Daniel in a way that wouldn't embarrass him."

"Goodness." Mary got up and put the kettle on. "Sounds like we might be here for a few minutes. Let me cut some pumpkin pie and we'll have a nice cup of Ruth Lehman's new tea blend with it."

Once she'd seen Carrie settled with a cup of steaming tea and nearly a quarter slice of pie with cream—no holding on to that for special occasions here; they had a pasture full of dairy cows—Mary sat down opposite her. "Now. Suppose you tell me what's on your mind. Daniel's out in the barn and he won't interrupt."

Where to start? Mary already knew how it was with her—how every month was a disappointment and every year a cause for grief. So she began with what had put her on this path: the ladies in the store.

"So then I went to the library and read some books about it, and it seemed that if it were possible to do this thing, then maybe there was hope for me becoming a mother after all."

Mary gazed at her, then took a sip of tea and a forkful of pie. And still the silence lengthened. At last she swallowed and said, "What does Melvin have to say about it?"

"He... well, it was something new for him."

"And for me, too, I must say."

"He didn't seem in favor of it right off the bat," Carrie said carefully. "But I think that if he thought about it a little, he might see it from my point of view."

"What did he say, exactly, Carrie?"

"He said it was an abomination and I was flying in the face of God," she said miserably. "That I was putting myself above the will of God to use worldly medicine to get what I wanted."

"Our human wills tend to grasp at anything to get what they want," Mary said tactfully. "But I have to say that Melvin is probably right."

A man's feelings were one thing. Men wrote the laws, after all. But there had to be a way to convince another woman that this idea had its merits, even if no one around here had given them any thought before.

"I know this is a new idea," she said. "But I don't think it's wrong. Thousands of babies have been born this way."

"What way, exactly?"

Carrie told her, as gently as accuracy would allow. Mary's eyes widened. "Well. I see why Melvin thinks the way he does."

"But the question is, will the bishop think the same way? Council Meeting is coming up soon, and Mary, if Daniel were to say some little thing about it—leave me some way where I could have this procedure done and Melvin would be satisfied that it did not go against the *Ordnung*...do you think that would be possible?"

Just a few words. That was all she asked for. Just a hint that such a thing would not be a sin, and Melvin could say nothing against it. Whether he would actually go to the hospital and submit to the tests was a whole other matter, but that was something she could handle. His spiritual objections were a much higher fence to jump.

"What would you have him say?" Mary asked gently.

Send me the words, Lord. "Maybe something about the blessings of welcoming little ones into the world, no matter how they are conceived, or a word or two about the medical procedures the church will fund...." She looked up from her pie and saw the pity in Mary's face, and the words trailed away.

"You know my husband," Mary said quietly. "He is a conservative man, a traditional man. Maybe another bishop could stand up in front of the congregation he is responsible for and say those things, but I do not think that Daniel could."

The little green shoot of hope that Carrie had been nurturing in her heart shuddered under a blast of cold reality. "Could you just talk to him about it? Maybe on this one subject that is so important he might be willing to consider being a little less traditional?"

"More important than the needs of those who are under medical treatment now? More important than Sarah Yoder's hip replacement? Or Grant Weaver's hospital stay, which the *Gmee* is still paying for?"

"Not *more* important," Carrie whispered. "Everyone's needs must be cared for. Daniel makes sure they are." Except Amelia's, when she wanted that treatment in Mexico. She had not had the elders' approval for that, and Daniel had been the one to tell her so.

"These situations are real, physical problems, Carrie. Sarah cannot walk without her motorized chair. This new hip would allow her to come and go to church with freedom again. And Grant's ability to work and provide for his children was at stake. Childlessness is not an injury, or a disease. It is simply God's will."

"It isn't an injury, or a disease, as you say. But it is a condition, a medical condition that has a medical cure that has worked in thousands of cases."

"Amish cases?"

"I don't know."

"I don't know either, and I suspect it's because there have been none."

Carrie grasped at another straw. "But what if there have been some? What if we wrote to the other bishops and asked if they had allowed it?"

"What good would that do, Carrie? Other bishops allow lots of things that Daniel will not. Radios in buggies—red trim on houses—yellow dresses on the young girls—the approval of one of these men will hold no water with Daniel, I'll guarantee you that."

Another long silence fell while Carrie stared at her slice of pie and tried to imagine swallowing some. She would not cry. She had drained herself of tears on this subject so many times that all she was capable of now was a tired sense of surprise that they still kept coming.

"Thank you for talking with me about it," she said at last, when for once Mary showed no signs of taking the conversation elsewhere. "I'm sure you have other things to do."

"I do, but they'll be there when I'm ready to turn my hand to them," Mary said comfortably. "I was ready for a little rest, anyway. I've been putting up squash all day. Maybe you'd like to take some with you."

"I would. Melvin loves squash."

Mary gazed at her, compassion soft in her eyes. "I will talk this matter over with Daniel. I just can't promise that he'll do or say differently than I told you."

Carrie nodded. "*Denki.*"

"I'll write to you with his answer. Now, finish up that pie. I hate to waste it by giving it to the hens."

"I don't give mine anything with sugar in it. They'd still eat it, but I don't think it's good for them."

"As long as it fattens them up before we butcher them, that's all I care."

Oh dear. She should have taken her leave before this. She shoveled down the pie and escaped before Mary could really get going on the subject, a couple of jars of golden mashed butternut squash in her bag to keep the umbrella company.

It was a long walk home, but she couldn't bring herself to stay and talk about the poor hens until Daniel was ready to hitch up the buggy. She didn't mind. The rain was holding off, and there were even rents in the clouds with blue sky showing.

Even so, the little shoot of hope inside her did not survive the walk.

CHAPTER 11

Carrie was an old hand at covering up her feelings and getting on with life. Company was coming for dinner, which was something to be thankful for. She could tidy and cook and even spend a few minutes outside picking the last of the autumn chrysanthemums for the table, keeping her hands busy and sometimes even her mind.

At least the Steiners were good company. Brian and Melvin had a lot to talk about, and Erica was a gentle soul, shy and prone to sitting in the corners of couches, where holding the baby gave her a good excuse not to talk. But she was a little more forthcoming when there weren't so many people.

When dinner was over and she and Erica were doing the dishes, the baby in her basket on the floor, Melvin shrugged on a jacket. "I'm going to take Brian out to the barn so he can see what his cousin has been up to lately."

"I still can't believe Joshua is working for you." Brian tugged on his own jacket and held the door. "I mean, actually working."

"He's doing a good job on that loft. You'll see."

The door closed behind them, and Erica hung up her dish towel while Carrie wiped down the counters. "It still surprises Brian that any good can come out of Nazareth."

"He shouldn't be surprised. Joshua picked bushels and bushels of apples, painted our sheds, and has started inside the barn. After the loft, I think Melvin is looking at having him wall off the lower section of it for a shop, with shelving and benches and things."

"So he'll be around here for a while, then."

"Until Thanksgiving, I think. Maybe longer."

"And it doesn't bother you, being alone with him?"

Carrie shook her head. "He's just an overgrown teenager. Sometimes he's sensible, and sometimes he has his 'me first' blinders on. Emma told me how to handle him, and it seems to work."

Erica laughed and picked up the baby. They went into the sitting room and she handed her to Carrie with no ceremony and no comment. When the bathroom door closed behind her, Carrie settled the baby in her arms as naturally as though she were one of her own siblings.

And waited for the pain.

Little Elsie reached up and patted her cheek, and Carrie touched her perfect hand, chubby and warm. Tiny fingers wrapped around hers with a grip that was surprisingly strong. Elsie gurgled happily, her eyes crescents above plump cheeks, with lashes that were going to play havoc with the little boys when she went to their local one-room schoolhouse for the first time.

When Erica came back, Carrie realized with a kind of dazed relief that holding the baby had been like a gift, not the tearing in her soul that she'd felt in the past.

Was this resignation, then? Or had her heart simply given up?

Erica tucked herself into the corner of the sofa, her feet up under her like the girl she still was. "She likes you."

"And I like her." She smiled down at Elsie and was rewarded by a big-eyed gaze that made it impossible not to make silly noises and a goofy face.

Elsie giggled, and the two of them laughed in response. "You're so good with the young ones," Erica said. "I see you at church with a crowd of the girls around you, and it always makes me smile."

"It makes me smile, too. I don't know what it is, or why they include me in their little news about flowers and birds' nests and boys, but I love it."

"That's probably your secret." Erica watched Elsie's eyes close and made no move to take her, so Carrie settled in to enjoy the moment while she had it. "You said a minute ago that Joshua was like an overgrown teenager. Do you suppose that's why he's still in no hurry to find himself a wife?"

"I think it's the opposite—why none of the girls of marrying age are looking at him for a husband."

Erica raised her brows briefly in acknowledgment. "A woman wants to look to her man for safety and sound judgment. I'm not sure Joshua is a judge of much but a good time."

"There's nothing wrong with a good time, but sensible girls eventually settle down and look for a good man instead."

Erica didn't respond for a moment, and Carrie got the impression that she was working up to telling her something. Silence was the most fertile ground for confidences to grow in, so Carrie let it deepen.

"I think Lydia Zook might not be one of those sensible girls," she said at last, in such a low tone that if the house hadn't been utterly quiet, a person would have missed it.

"If she isn't, she's probably being pretty discreet." How

discreet, though, if people other than Carrie's immediate circle were concerned about it already?

"Most girls would tell their parents if they were seeing someone, but Abe Zook doesn't seem the kind who would welcome a girl's confidences."

That was an understatement.

"My youngest sister, Mariah, is in her buddy bunch with Sarah Grohl, and she says she's been leaving the group volleyball games and outings and going for long walks and finding unnecessary errands in town and dressing in clothes you can see from a mile off. Goodness knows it's hard to keep a secret in this district. I just get the feeling it's because the boy isn't suitable."

Bright hair and reckless eyes, squashed into a buggy in a way that would embarrass most girls. Too much familiarity. It had been staring them in the face all this time. They hadn't met Lydia on the road by accident. It had been carefully planned.

"It's Joshua."

Erica looked up with an expression that told Carrie this was what she'd deduced, too—and it wasn't what she'd wanted to hear. She pulled one of the sofa pillows into her lap and hugged it as though, without the baby, she needed something to cuddle. "He's twelve years older than she is— and about two centuries older in experience. The kind of experience that good husband material shouldn't have."

"He's been baptized, though. Is she thinking of it?"

"I don't know. I suppose we'll see on Sunday. But she's only begun *Rumspringe*. She doesn't seem like the type to cut it short and join church so young. And there are other things. If I were Abe Zook, I'd be worried."

"What things? What's worrying you?" The echo of Susan's

voice sounded in her mind, asking her to talk to Lydia. Had Erica tried and failed, too?

"There are only six years between us, you know. It used to be that the young girls in Mariah's group could come to me and talk about anything. But lately…" She sighed, put the pillow aside, and held her arms out. Gently, Carrie put Elsie into them.

"Lately?"

"I've seen Lydia walking on the county highway in the direction of Hill's. The hired man has his own rooms in the barn there, did you know that? Joshua stays with his folks so the room doesn't come out of his pay, but he still has the use of it. There's a kitchen to make a cup of coffee, a bathroom to wash up in, and a furnished bedroom. So he told me once, when he first got the job."

"You think they might be…?"

"I think that a sensible girl would not put herself in the way of temptation."

And they'd already concluded that Lydia was not a sensible girl. "Erica, if you've tried to talk to her, and maybe if Mariah has tried, we've done all we can short of locking her in her room."

"But no one has tried to talk to Joshua."

That was true. "I could ask Melvin. They seem to get on fairly well."

"I don't think he would take correction from a man. That teenage-boy tendency would get in the way, *nix*?"

"Then who? Maybe Emma?"

"He is here in your yard during the day," Erica said softly.

Carrie swayed back, her shoulders flat on the rear cushions of the couch. "Oh no. I'm done with meddling in people's business. Lydia has probably already told him about my attempts to talk with her. He'll think I'm a busybody—and he'll be right."

Erica subsided and began to coo at the baby, but Carrie could tell that her thoughts on the matter hadn't changed one bit. And she was using the same tactic that had worked on her—a little silence went a long way.

* * *

By New Birth Sunday, when the congregation was streaming into Old Joe Yoder's huge barn for the service that included the baptism, Carrie's feelings hadn't changed. She had no business talking to Lydia, or to Joshua Steiner either, about whom they courted or how.

But there was Lydia, whose reckless ways seemed to have triggered a "project" among the women of the community. Susan, Miriam, herself, Erica…well, that was how it was done, *nix*? When there was a problem to be solved—whether it was a quilt that needed to be stitched or a young woman who needed guidance—the community pitched in.

Carrie watched with interest as the folks who were taking the step of baptism filed into the front row. A number of young people had been taking instruction from the bishop for the past eighteen weeks—among them, she noticed, Sarah Grohl, who was in Lydia's buddy bunch.

But not Lydia. So did that mean she was not thinking of marrying Joshua? Not that a girl so young had to marry the boy she was dating. That would be unwise, especially if he had no means of supporting a wife yet. It would have been quite the surprise to see, anyway. A young woman joined church when she had matured enough to make the most important decision of her life—more important even than the man she would marry. Because earthly marriage ended at death, but the choice of Jesus as her eternal bridegroom lasted for all eternity.

There were one or two others in the front row as well...a man who had left the church at least a decade ago and gone out into the *Englisch* world had come back during the summer. His mother wept silent tears of joy on her bench near the front when she saw him walk in, head bowed and hands covering his face as a sign of his unworthiness.

The baptism always left Carrie feeling clean and joyful— as though the bishop were pouring the cup of water over her bare head, washing away her sins. But today, though her body sat quietly in her place toward the back of the barn—ahead of the *Youngie*, but behind the older women and the women with families—she felt her mind to be one step removed.

Or maybe it was her heart that stood at a distance, looking on instead of being involved. She was standing on a path that no one else had walked, and no one *would* walk if Melvin and Amelia and Mary Lapp all had their way. Everyone else in the *Gmee* trod the familiar paths, said the familiar things, sang these hymns and murmured prayers that generations of their families had before them. And here she was, all alone on her narrow road, pulling her courage around her and hoping it would keep her warm.

After the noon meal, she found Emma walking toward the pasture with one of Grant's girls on either hand. "We're going to see if the pond froze over last night," Emma called gaily. "Come with us."

"Are you planning to skate?" Carrie fell in beside seven-year-old Katie. "If it did freeze, you'll be able to break it with your finger."

"*Nei,*" Katie said, respectfully enough, but Carrie got the impression her intelligence had been found wanting. Nobody skated until Christmas, when a good three or four inches of ice on the ponds had been tested by someone's *Daed* and his approval given. "We're learning in school about animals hibernating. I want to see if the fish have gone into the mud, like Miss Hannah says."

"You wouldn't be able to see them," Carrie said.

"I don't think that's the point," Emma said as both girls let go of her hands and ran down the slope to the pond. The dried brown stalks of the cattails clattered in the wind being pushed toward them by the big clouds overhead. Even the blackbirds had deserted the pond, and gone where cheery summer birds went when the winds blew down from Canada. "Grant says the girls were a handful this morning, and I think they're avoiding him."

"A little too much wedding excitement?"

"*Ja*, I think so." She turned to Carrie, her eyes sparkling from much more than the wind. "Only think, Carrie. By the time we meet for church again, I'll be married."

To which the only reply was a hug.

After a few moments, Carrie saw that the girls were beginning to tire of not finding sleepy fish in the crunchy mud at the edges of the pond. She would miss her opportunity if she didn't take it now.

"Emma, can I ask you something?"

Emma raised a brow. "That is the most unnecessary question I've ever heard. This is me you're talking to, remember?"

"And I'm glad of it." She took her arm and hugged it close, the fringes of their shawls blowing together. "Have you heard anything of Joshua Steiner and Lydia Zook courting?"

She felt Emma's body stiffen and knew the answer before Emma even spoke. "I haven't. But you have, evidently."

"I've seen them together, and I was talking to Erica, and to my sister Susan, and everyone seems to agree that there might be cause for worry there."

"If there is, it's Abe who must deal with it."

"I don't think he can. Not alone. I think it might just turn into a 'project.'"

"Ah." Emma watched the girls, who had discovered that if you tore the fluff out of the tops of the cattails, it would catch the wind and sail away by the handful.

"I just wondered if Joshua had spoken with you." *And if he has, if you told him about my private worries.*

"I don't talk much with Joshua anymore—nothing more than hello at church and when I see him on the road."

Well, that seemed to answer one question. Relief trickled through Carrie. She should have known better than to doubt her friend. But there was still the other question.

"But could you talk with him about it? A man his age has no business courting a girl of sixteen, especially with his reputation. I'm surprised Abe hasn't put a stop to it, if he knows."

"Carrie." Emma turned to face her, concern etched into her smooth skin. "I decided that Grant was the man for me when I was only a little older than Lydia. I would have thanked God on my knees if he had given me more than that one ride home from Singing."

"But Grant is steady. Dependable. And he doesn't have—"

"—a reputation. So you said. The truth is, *Liewi*, I don't have time to go chasing after Joshua to give him a talking-to. With all the work there is to do in the next ten days, I'll be lucky if I *have* a wedding. Do you know I haven't even made my cape and apron yet?" Emma scraped an errant wisp of hair out of her eyes. "I'm so grateful that the cake, at least, is in your hands. That's one thing I don't have to think about."

She needed to make it up to Emma for doubting her—
even if Emma never knew it. "Let me make those for you as
well, then. Bring them to quilting on Tuesday and I'll have
them back by Sunday."

Emma wavered. "But I wanted to make my wedding
clothes myself."

"Who's making Grant's things?"

"Christina. They're close, and she offered before I had a
chance to."

Carrie nudged her. "You'll be making his shirts and pants
for the rest of your life, dear one. Let Christina make these
and it will be the last thing any Yoder woman will do for
him."

"There is that," Emma admitted.

"In the meantime, while the cake is baking, I can have
your cape and apron done. Please."

"All right." Emma hugged her. "I'm so thankful for friends
I can count on."

Carrie hugged her back. And wondered whether, if the
women of the community did not do something, poor, reckless Lydia would be able to say the same.

CHAPTER 12

Trailing cattail fluff, the little girls joined them and they began to climb the gentle slope back to the house. But before they walked out of the trees, Will and Kathryn Esch waved and walked toward them in a way that said, "We need to speak to you."

"Run and find your *Daed*, now, girls, while I visit." Emma squeezed their hands and they ran off, *Kapp* strings flying behind them. Carrie glanced curiously at Emma. Had that really been necessary?

"Emma," Will said, settling his black broad-brimmed hat more firmly on his head. "It's a blustery day for a walk."

"It was also a long time for two little girls to sit," Emma responded with a smile. "If I wear them out now, they'll be willing to color in their books this afternoon without jumping around like a pair of grasshoppers."

"Thinking like a mother already," Kathryn said, but she did not smile. Instead, she gave Carrie an apologetic look. "We would like to speak to Emma privately, Carrie. I think I saw your man getting ready to go."

Whether this was true or not, Carrie never found out, because Emma put a hand on her arm. "Carrie knows everything that goes on with me. She is free to stay if she wishes."

Oh my. Oh my goodness. There was only one topic in the whole world about which this couple would want to speak to Emma.

They had found out about the correspondence-school packets. And now the fat was in the fire.

"Does she?" Will's face was grave. "Then I wonder that she did not do one of two things when she learned that you have secretly been letting our son study high school subjects in your home. It is very strange to me that she would not have come to us, or at the very least, counseled you against this behavior."

Carrie's cheeks felt cold, her fingers nearly numb. *Amelia and I did counsel her*. But to say so would be disloyal. What could be said had already been said months ago. All she could do now was stand beside Emma and hope that they could both hold each other up.

"How did it come to light?" Emma asked. Carrie knew her well enough to know that that calm tone had not come easily.

Kathryn's distress showed in her eyes, though her voice was steady. "Janelle Baum at the post office stopped Will when he was getting stamps, and asked him if a certain parcel had been misdirected. It was addressed to our Alvin, but care of the Grohl postal box. She found it very odd."

That Janelle, getting people into trouble under the guise of being helpful.

Then again, if folks didn't practice to deceive, they wouldn't get into trouble, would they? There was no hope for Emma now. She had sown her tares with open hands; now it was time to reap them.

"When we opened it, we found his correspondence-school papers," Will went on. "And when we asked him about it, the whole story came out. How you and he have been deceiving us for nearly two years."

"I am very sorry you found out in this way," Emma said.

"But not sorry enough to say no when he asked you to be part of this plan?" Will asked.

"Is that where he's been going all this time when we thought he was courting Sarah Grohl?" Kathryn asked. "He has been studying at your place?" She rubbed her hands over and over, as if they were cold, too. "I cannot imagine Lena being a party to such a deception. *Es wunnert mich.*"

"Mamm knew nothing about it." Emma leaped to her mother's defense. "Alvin would come and use our kitchen table late at night, after she was asleep. I alone am responsible. Not her."

"What will happen to Alvin?" Carrie ventured, her voice hardly above a whisper.

"He has not joined church, but he is still living under my roof," Will said. "I have told him that this will stop, or he will not be welcome anymore. There will be no more packets, and he will turn his hand to being a better apprentice at the buggy maker instead of filling his head with nonsensical *Englisch* ideas."

"And he has agreed?" Emma asked.

Both parents looked at each other. Will's jaw set. "He will see sense."

He had not agreed. Carrie resisted the temptation to look at Emma, but she could imagine what she was thinking. Alvin was slender and studious. The kind who wore glasses and pored over books by lantern light, not the kind who could control a six-mule team or wrestle buggy parts together.

"I noticed that you were sorry we found out," Will said, "but not so sorry you took part in this deception."

"I can't say that I am sorry."

Carrie drew in a surprised breath. How could she not be?

"Alvin is a smart boy—far smarter than I was at his age. He wants to be more than a farmer or a buggy maker, Will. He wants to be an engineer or a scientist."

"I know what my son wants better than anyone," Will retorted. "Better than you. And if he does not understand the will of God for his life, at least I expect you would, even after your gallivanting around the country and taking up with people from New York."

Emma began to speak, then bit back the words.

"Kathryn and I—we would like to hear that you repent of what you have done, and promise never to help him in this way again."

After a moment, Emma said carefully, "Let us put this behind us. What's done is done, and now it's up to Alvin to choose his path with God's help."

"That sounds to me like no answer," Kathryn said. "My husband has asked you to say that you are sorry for your actions." She touched the shawl wrapping Emma's arm. "You don't want to live with this on your conscience, Emma, I'm sure."

Emma covered the other woman's fingers and squeezed. "I don't, Kathryn, truly. *Ja*, it was wrong not to tell you. But it was Alvin's secret to tell or not tell. He asked for help and I gave it. I cannot be sorry for that, when it made him so happy."

"Of course getting his own way made him happy," Will snapped. "Cars and electricity in our homes and cell phones in our pockets—these things would all make the *Youngie* happy if we were foolish enough to give in to them. But do they make God happy? And do they help our brothers and sisters to walk in His will?"

There was only one answer to this, and Emma would not give it. Why wouldn't she just say "I'm sorry" and be done with it?

"It's finished," Emma said at last. "He has already asked me to get the packets at our place for the new school year, and I told him no. And I told him I would not be getting them on Old Orchard Road, either. That's why the packet was sent to Sarah's, I expect. He couldn't think of anywhere else to have them send it."

Kathryn's chest rose and fell with what Carrie could only imagine was relief. She looked up at her husband.

"But you are not sorry for this sin," Will repeated.

"I am sorry that my actions have distressed you," Emma said. "Very sorry. But I cannot be sorry that a young man whose mind can challenge any boy his age in the county should get on with his education. If he lived in the Beachy church over in Douglas County, he would go to high school and no one would think a thing of it."

"He is not in the Beachy church, nor will he be if I have anything to say about it," Will said heavily. "Emma, I must know that you repent."

She was silent.

"How are you going to go to Council Meeting in two weeks and say you are at peace?"

"Because I am."

"How is that possible? I can't stand up and say so. This trouble has put me miles away from peace. We must resolve this. We must both be in harmony on this matter."

"Will—" Kathryn began softly.

"And what about Grant Weaver? How can he marry a woman who cannot tell the bishop she is in unity with the congregation?"

All the color drained from Emma's face. "This has nothing to do with Grant, or with our wedding."

"I say it does. I say a man who would marry a woman who is proud and stiff-necked, and not afraid to defy the *Ordnung* if she feels like it, needs to think twice about his choice."

"Will—"

"Silence." Will shook off his wife's restraining hand. "I will have words with the bishop about this. If you will not repent, then it is his place to step in."

Emma's jaw flexed, and when Carrie slipped a hand into her elbow, her arm felt as hard and unyielding as bone.

Will made a sound very like the snort of an angry bull, and turned on his heel. "Come, Kathryn."

"I will pray for you," Kathryn said over her shoulder as she was marched away, but the wind snatched at her words and Carrie could hardly hear them.

"Emma, what are you thinking?" Carrie demanded in the softest tone she was capable of.

"I'm thinking of Alvin," Emma said softly, watching the Esches' retreating backs. "And the look on his face when he got his grades. They were good grades, Carrie. I wasn't tutoring him—he was far beyond my little bit of knowledge. He's a smart boy."

"His brains better be able to find a roof over his head, if Will goes through with what he said."

"He will. He's not a man to say something and not live by it."

"But that wasn't what I meant, you know. I meant, what are you thinking, to put yourself forward now of all times?"

Emma dragged her gaze away from the Esches, who had found Bishop Daniel and were talking to him urgently, bowed toward him as though to keep the sound of their words to themselves. "I couldn't lie. I'm very sorry Alvin was foolish enough to send a package anywhere near Janelle Baum. I'm sorry that I've distressed them. But I'm not sorry I gave the boy a place to study. Not one bit."

"That's the part they want. They want the whole sacrifice."

"I know. Look, here comes Amelia."

They waited for Amelia to join them, and Carrie could see from the look in her eyes that she already knew. "Emma, *Liewi*, what trouble have you got yourself into now?"

"That didn't take long."

"I was coming up to say good-bye—Eli has taken the boys to hitch up the buggy—and I heard Will Esch telling Bishop Daniel. I don't think it's gone much farther. Everyone else has gone into the house to get out of this wind."

"She won't tell him she's sorry," Carrie blurted. "Amelia, please talk to her. She isn't listening to me."

"I listened," Emma said.

"Yes, but you didn't *do*. What if he makes a fuss and the bishop is forced to come and talk to you?"

"Then I'll offer him some coffee and a slice of pie, the same as I always do."

"And what if he says he will not marry you and Grant next Thursday? Marriage is a holy covenant, Emma. You can't make your vows when you're out of kilter with your brother in the faith."

"You're getting that mixed up with Communion, Carrie," Emma said in a tone that was maddeningly calm. "I can face Grant with this on my heart, though facing God is a little more serious."

"I would say the whole thing is serious," Amelia put in.

"No, it isn't. It's just a tempest in a teapot," Emma retorted. "Will Esch has never cared about what Alvin has done or not done. He's the youngest boy, and if that man even re-membered he was alive half the time, I'd be surprised. He's just mad because someone put something over on him. His pride is smarting, and I'm not going to pander to it."

Carrie looked at Amelia helplessly. "Maybe Grant can talk some sense into her."

Amelia's gray eyes were as troubled as the cloudy sky around them. "You know I think you were wrong to do it," she said. "But here's a chance to put it right. Even if you don't believe you were wrong—even if you think Will's dan-der is up and he's like a rooster looking for a fight—Emma, you must humble yourself and say the words."

"Even if I don't mean them?"

"Sometimes we have to do what we don't want to so that we can make peace."

Emma eyed her. "The words would be a lie. Is that what you want me to do?"

"I want you to do what is right."

"By lying."

"By putting our own thoughts aside and thinking of the other person. You're not exercised by this. Will is. It's up to you to think of him and not yourself."

Emma kicked at the brown grass and started down the hill. For one horrified moment, Carrie thought she was turning her back on both of them, but when Emma looked over her shoulder and gave them a quizzical look, she took Amelia's arm with a sigh of relief and joined her for the walk to the house.

Will and Daniel were still there, though Kathryn had gone in. Daniel lifted a hand when Emma changed direction to go around them. "Emma, a moment."

Oh dear. Surely he wouldn't speak to her right out here in

the yard, where it was freezing and anyone could hear? Carrie glanced around wildly. Where was Grant? She should go find him. She should—

"Our brother Will tells me you have wronged him and Kathryn in the matter of their son Alvin," the bishop said slowly.

"I let him study in my kitchen," Emma said. "And the packets from the correspondence school came to our mailbox."

"Did Lena know of this?"

"No. She would have stopped it if she had."

Carrie's stomach sank as Daniel Lapp noticed her and Amelia, standing a little to the side and clinging together as much for warmth as for moral support. "I think there are others who should have stopped it if they had known about it." His gaze settled on Carrie. "There are all kinds of worldly thinking going on in this district that must be stopped."

Carrie's breath seized up in her lungs.

She didn't need that letter from Mary Lapp now. She had her answer.

Amelia gripped her arm. "Are you all right?" she whispered. "What is he talking about?"

She nodded—a lie without words. She was not all right. But she couldn't have spoken if her life depended on it.

The bishop turned his attention back to Emma. "Emma, we must have harmony in the *Gmee* if we are all to take part in Communion four weeks from now. You saw those who were baptized today. They have been washed clean. This is how we must be if we are to take the body and blood of Christ." He paused, and gazed at her. He really was a kind man, Carrie thought. It wasn't his fault that he had no tact and that he found dealing with the problems people brought to him painful. He would much rather be out in his barn with his horses, where speech and action had direct results, and the animals didn't need counseling on the consequences of their behavior.

"Will you not apologize to your brother and sister, and be in good fellowship with them again?"

Come on, Emma. This can all be smoothed over if you'll just say two little words. Whether you mean them or not is between you and God.

CHAPTER 13

The silence crept in, behind the wind and the sound of the leaves being tweaked from the trees.

Bishop Daniel's gaze did not leave Emma's face. "Emma, when you came to us asking for our approval to sell your book to these *Englisch* people, you remember that you made us a promise."

Emma chewed on her bottom lip. "Yes."

"Can you tell us all what it was?"

"I promised that I would not let worldly ideas take root in my mind, and that I would remember that my place is here and only I can fill it."

Carrie risked a glance at Will Esch. She expected him to look triumphant. Instead, he only looked troubled.

"Would you not say that this business with Alvin was prompted by worldly ideas? Ideas about schooling and a man's place in the world?"

"I suppose," Emma said, so quietly that if Carrie had been standing a foot farther away, she would not have heard her.

"God does not want a service that has to be extracted from people by threats. But I will offer that reminder."

"She sold a book? To *Englisch* people?" Will said as though

his mind had got hung up on that and hadn't moved any farther. "And you gave your approval for this?"

"I did, and it is not your concern," the bishop told him.
"Your boy's education is what we're discussing here."

"But it's all of a piece," Will said. "This New York business. Planting crazy ideas in my son's head. Next we'll hear
that she's planning to send Grant Weaver's children to the
public school in Whinburg."

Amelia reached out and gripped Emma's wrist—and just
in time, too. Emma's mouth was already open on an angry
breath.

She closed it with a click of her teeth.

Bishop Daniel seemed to think it was better to let the wind
carry such talk away, too. "I remind you of your promise,
Emma, and remind you that what the elders approved, they
can also disapprove."

"The book was sold some time ago," Emma said, her voice
scratchy with the need to keep her composure. Carrie and
Amelia both swung to gawk at her.

And when had she been planning to share this with them?
They should have been laughing and crying around the quilting frame, hugging each other in joy, instead of standing here
frozen, hearing the words dragged out of Emma in front of
such an unsympathetic audience.

"That is beside the point," Bishop Daniel said. "I don't
want this to go so far as Council Meeting when all our
brother desires of you is repentance. Wouldn't you rather
give that gift to him here and receive his forgiveness than
have to go down on your knees in front of the entire *Gmee*
and confess to what you have done?"

Carrie's cheeks prickled as the blood drained from them.
Surely not. Surely this little tiff between neighbors would not

escalate to a public confession? How would Grant feel to see his wife of only a few days on her knees on the floor of Moses Yoder's barn? How would that affect the girls, knowing their new mother had had to undergo such a trial?

Emma lifted her head and met Will Esch's gaze. "I am sorry for helping Alvin, Will," she said in a monotone, almost exactly like the dial tone on the phone in the shanty out on the highway. "Please forgive me."

He took a deep breath and released it. "I do." Then he said, "It is a whole sacrifice. You have already said that Alvin will not receive help from you in the future."

"*Nei.*"

"Then I am satisfied." He held out his hand, and after a moment, Emma shook it.

She stared blindly into the distance while the bishop exchanged a few words with Will and Kathryn, and Amelia gently took her arm and moved a few steps away. Then another few steps. Carrie took her other arm, and between them, got Emma away from the house and out into the yard, where Eli had just loaded Elam and Matthew into the buggy.

"You came so close to losing everything you worked and prayed so hard for in the summer," Amelia told her urgently. "Don't throw away your harvest now."

"I lied," Emma whispered. "I lied so that Will Esch would be satisfied."

"You said the words that would give him peace," Carrie told her.

"But who will give me my peace?" Emma turned away, pulling her shawl around her shoulders. "I'm going home."

When Grant came out with his children to fetch the horse and hitch up the buggy, Amelia and Eli had gone, and it fell to Carrie to tell him where his fiancée was.

"Walking home? In this cold?" Grant handed his little son, Zachary, to Carrie while he backed the horse between the rails. "I hope I can catch up with her, then."

"Be gentle with her," Carrie said quietly, thankful the two little girls were busy climbing into the buggy and arguing over who was going to sit next to Daed in the front. "I don't know which was worse—having the bishop threaten to take away his permission about her book, or having Will get her back up so bad she'd have to make a public confession before Communion. There was even some talk about this affecting your wedding."

"Nothing can affect our wedding except for Bishop Daniel refusing to perform it. And I don't think it would come to that."

"I wouldn't have put it past Will Esch to insist that it be delayed until Emma was brought to her senses."

"He does not have that power."

Carrie wondered about that. "He sure seems to have an influence on Daniel."

"Any strong personality does. I often wish…" Grant's voice trailed away. "Never mind. Daniel was chosen by lot to be bishop, and it's not for us to question God's will."

Carrie smiled. "Melvin says that if he's ever tempted to, it would be an open invitation for the lot to fall on him."

Grant climbed into the buggy next to his eldest daughter, who had evidently won the fight. "If anyone is suited to be a preacher, it's Melvin." He raised a hand, and Carrie looked over her shoulder to see her husband coming across the yard to get their own horse. "There is a work frolic on Saturday at the Stolzfus place. We will see you there."

The Stolzfus place already sparkled like a new pin thanks to Karen, but the benches had to be set up in the barn, and the upper floor given a final cleaning before the girls hung decorations.

Carrie stepped back as Grant clicked his tongue and the buggy started forward. Melvin came up behind her and put his hands on her shoulders.

"Emma's not going with him? And the wedding only a few days away?"

She leaned into him so that his beard brushed the organdy of her *Kapp*. "He'll catch up to her." And then she surprised them both by turning and giving him a kiss, quick as the touch of a butterfly's wing. "*Denki* for not being a proud man."

He looked astonished, as well he might. "What brought this on?"

"I'll tell you at home. *Kumm mit*, let's go find our horse before it rains."

* * *

Amelia glanced at the clock over the stove and then at Carrie. "Where do you suppose she is? Emma's never late on Tuesdays."

"With her wedding next week, do you need to ask? Or have you forgotten those days so soon?" Carrie teased.

"I haven't forgotten. In fact, we still have wedding visits to pay to some of Eli's family in Maryland. But that wasn't what I was thinking of." She walked through to the sitting room, where the windows overlooked the yard and the lane.

"You were thinking of Sunday." Carrie followed her, pausing to gaze out at the familiar view.

"You don't think she's angry with me, do you?" Amelia crossed her arms and rubbed them as though she were cold, but the woodstove was going and it was toasty in the house despite the rain spattering on the windows.

"Nobody could be angry with you," Carrie reassured her.

"But what if she was offended? She thinks I told her to lie in order to make peace. What if she thinks I sided with Will Esch instead of standing by her like a friend should?"

"A good friend gives the counsel we *need* to hear, not what we *want* to hear."

"She may not appreciate that." Amelia's shoulders drooped while she gazed down the empty lane. Then she shook herself. "We should get started or we won't accomplish anything today. I'll walk over tomorrow and make sure she's all right."

They had barely sat down at the quilting frame when the sound of footsteps thudded on the stairs. "There she is." Amelia ran down, Carrie right behind her. "How did she come? Surely she didn't walk in this rain?"

The door opened, and Carrie practically skidded to a halt on polished floorboards that were still a little damp from Amelia's arrival. "Joshua!"

"And me." Emma came in behind him, rain dripping off the brim of her away bonnet. "Carrie, we're going to need a towel. I feel like I've been swimming."

"Hello, Joshua," Amelia said. "*Denki* for bringing her safely."

"I was on my way to town and saw her climb out of the creek bed next to the highway."

"You make me sound like a fox or a weasel living in the culvert." Emma shook water from her coat out on the porch and then hung it on the tree next to the door. "But thank you for the ride." She took the rag Carrie offered and mopped up the puddles.

"Would you like a hot drink to warm up with?" The

girls could get started on the quilting while she attended to Joshua. After his carelessness from the other week, Carrie couldn't let a good deed go unrewarded.

"Not me. I'm having dinner in Strasburg."

Which was in the other direction. From under her lashes, Carrie saw Emma and Amelia school their features to smiling acceptance without so much as the lift of a brow.

"You'll have a wet ride."

"So will everyone on the roads today. *Guder Owed*."

"*Guder Owed*," they chorused softly, and Carrie closed the door behind him.

"Dinner in Strasburg, but he's going to Whinburg first?" Emma asked no one in particular.

"He'd be picking up his date," Amelia said.

"Who is probably Lydia Zook," Carrie added. "Who has likely never been to a restaurant in Strasburg in her life."

"So it's true," Amelia said quietly. "They make a very odd couple."

"They could have picked another afternoon for a date. A Tuesday? In a downpour?" Emma shook her head. "It was nice of him to give me a ride, though. I wouldn't have made it yet. That'll teach me to start a job I can't finish before it's time to go. Come on. Let's get to work."

The relief on Amelia's face at Emma's natural tone told its own story. If Emma chose to bring up what had happened, then she would. Until then, Carrie decided, she wouldn't say a word to upset the balance.

They settled into the rhythm of the stitching, loading needles and progressing around the whorls and curves of the flower patterns an inch at a time. It was soothing work, keeping the hands busy while ruffled spirits soaked in the quiet and the sound of the rain.

"You did the right thing, *Liewi*," Emma said quietly.

Carrie sifted through all the "right things" she could mean, but Amelia got there first.

"I was afraid I had offended you. Put Will Esch before you."

"Grant came over yesterday and we talked it out. He made me see that I was setting my opinions higher than the feelings of others. I may think that I was doing right for Alvin last year, and Alvin may think so, but if his family and the church don't think so, then that's that."

"We're a conservative district," Carrie ventured. "It would not be wrong somewhere else, maybe, but it is here."

"It's wrong plenty of places," Emma said. "But what's even more wrong is me putting myself above the boy's father. He was right to ask for my repentance."

"Let's put it behind us." Amelia reached across the quilt to touch her hand. "Now, what's this about your book? I nearly fell over when you blurted out that you had sold it."

"Technically, Tyler West sold it." Emma smiled at them, and Carrie rejoiced to see that it reached her eyes and brimmed over. "And just in time, too. The bank had already sent Grant a second 'payment due' letter in glaring red type. He was able to take the book contract down to the bank and tell them that the check was on its way."

"And you will have a home to move into next week." Carrie clasped her hands against her chest, as if to keep the joy inside. But it still came out in her voice. "I'm so glad. I've been trying not to think of what we would do if you had to move to Paradise or . . . or somewhere even farther away."

"I couldn't think of it," Emma said bluntly. "Somehow I felt that if God even heard a whisper of it in my mind, He might take it as a prayer and answer it."

"Well, now your prayers will be full of thanks," Amelia said. "Ours, too."

Silence fell again, filled with the warmth of happiness and a feeling of safety. *We will not be separated.* Carrie's heart lifted. *No matter what happens in this life, we will be together to help one another. Each of us experiences life's trials in a different way, but somehow it all pools together so that each of us has help to offer when we need it.*

"Amelia," she said slowly, "when you were going through such a hard time last winter, how did you get through it?"

"Prayer," she answered. "Lots and lots of it. If I couldn't have brought that burden to God, I don't know what I would have done. It was like trying to walk through the orchard at night—every time I tried to take a step, I ran into something hard and it hurt."

"That's exactly how I feel," Carrie said eagerly. "Every time I try to get anywhere with this IVF possibility, I run into a tree."

Emma and Amelia exchanged a silent glance. Carrie would have missed it if she had been stitching the way she was supposed to.

But she did not miss it.

"I know what you're thinking," she said. "That you've given me the counsel I need, not what I want. But I still think you're wrong." She paused a moment. They may as well know it all. "Bishop Daniel is, too. Having children is a woman's matter, and shouldn't fall under an *Ordnung* made by men."

"Men who have been prompted by God," Emma said quietly. "Carrie, please don't pursue this. I put myself above Will Esch...but you're putting yourself above Bishop Daniel— and God."

"Is that what the *Englisch* women are doing? The ones who all have babies to love?" Carrie demanded.

"The *Englisch* women and their babies have not made vows before God to submit to the *Ordnung* and His will."

There was a point you couldn't argue with.

"I heard him," Amelia said. "I was there on Sunday, too, remember? When he said there was too much worldly thinking going on and he looked right at you."

"But he hasn't taken me aside and told me the *Ordnung* won't allow it. And no letter has come from Mary, either." Carrie stabbed her green square with the needle instead of working it gently up and down. "So I'm going to make an appointment with the doctor this week."

"And what will you find out there," Amelia said, "that she hasn't already told you many times over the last ten years?"

"A different doctor. I'll get a reference to a fertility doctor to talk about my options."

Another silent glance. Really, why didn't they just come out and say what they thought?

"What does Melvin say?" Amelia asked, her eyes on her stitching.

"After the first time, we haven't spoken about it again. But I have hope that his mind will change if the bishop says a little word about it at Council Meeting."

"It didn't sound to me as though he will," Amelia said. "I'd prepare myself for the opposite if I were you."

"Even so, I'm still going to the fertility doctor. I wish I'd found out about this years ago. I could have had a baby by now."

"Is that why you're so set and determined?" Emma wanted to know. "Because you're going to be thirty soon? There's still time to wait on God."

"Are you planning to have children with Grant?" Carrie fired back as though she were spiking a volleyball made of words.

"If that is God's will—and I hope it is—then yes. I'm a little old to start, but look at Old Joe's Sarah. She had her last when she was forty-two, and he was perfectly healthy."

"Then you should understand, Emma," Carrie said. "I've spent so many years waiting that I feel I'm running out of them."

"I do understand. At least you had a husband while you were waiting. And trying."

"But if it's not God's will for you, you still have Katie and Sarah and Zachary. I don't have anything."

"Except a husband who adores you," Amelia reminded her. "And a home. These are blessings many women don't have."

"Like Esther Grohl." Emma's needle dipped and rose like a narrow boat on waves of green. "I feel very blessed, children of my own or not."

They said they understood, but they didn't. Not really. Much as she loved her friends, neither of them had this burning urgency under the breastbone, this wild hope that saw the light shining in the darkness and was running toward it at breakneck speed, despite the trees standing in the way.

She would go to that fertility doctor. She would find a way.

Even if her friends and her husband and her church were not willing to help her.

CHAPTER 14

Dr. Neuhaus was a woman in her fifties who struck Carrie as being as comfortable in her own skin as she was in her white coat. Her own doctor had been happy to refer her to New Hope Fertility Center, which was not in New Hope, but a mile on the far side of Intercourse.

New Hope on the far side of Intercourse. Carrie resisted the urge to giggle.

The doctor who might just have the power to change her life settled into a chair in the consulting room and leafed through a folder. "Well, Mrs. Miller, your personal physician seems pretty convinced that you're healthy, and the fact that you're here tells me you're committed."

"Please," Carrie said, "call me Carrie. We don't use honorifics."

"Carrie, then." The doctor gazed at her. "I can't say I've ever treated a member of the Amish church. I have two Amish neighbors, and I always got the impression that fertility treatment wasn't..." She searched for the word, and Carrie supplied it.

"Approved?"

"Yes. Can you educate me a little on that?"

"Our folk believe that having children is a blessing from

God." She hesitated. This nice doctor was not going to judge her. She was here to get help, and Dr. Neuhaus was the one who could provide it. "And not having children is also the will of God."

"But you don't believe this?"

"I wouldn't say that...I mean, I have believed it. But I think that if the *gut Gott* reveals something to you, it's your duty to act on it. And I believe this is what has happened to me. I heard these ladies in a shop talking about IVF and it was like a whole new world opened up to me."

"'World' being the operative word," Dr. Neuhaus said. "I can guess that, along with electricity and cars, scientific technology of this nature is probably frowned upon."

"Our *Ordnung* says nothing about it," Carrie said cautiously. Surely this woman wouldn't turn her away because she thought Carrie ought to be obedient?

"I imagine it probably doesn't come up very much. Ah well. That's none of my business. My business is babies, so let me stick to that. It says here that you're married. What does your husband do?"

"He works at the pallet shop in Whinburg."

"So he's not farming, then. We'd want to ensure the best possible environment for you, Carrie, which includes following the protocols precisely, being available to come in at a moment's notice, and having both of you engaged and committed to the process. Your husband must be as involved as you are—his support and willingness for the testing and labs is just as important as your ability to carry the child."

She must choose her words carefully. "My husband is a faithful man. At the moment we are waiting for word from the bishop about whether we can do this."

"And if you don't get that word? Will your husband—"

"Melvin."

"—will Melvin be coming in? He'll need to be tested for sperm production and motility, and after that, we'll need multiple samples from him for the actual IVF process."

Oh dear. This was going to get awkward.

Dr. Neuhaus was silent, watching Carrie's face. She turned a page in the folder and Carrie jumped at the snap of the paper.

"Carrie, does your husband even know that you're here?"

She wanted to say yes, but she had never been able to lie. Her skin flushed hot, a flag of guilt that anyone could see from across the room. "N-no."

"You realize that we must have his complete cooperation, don't you? That it's impossible to conceive using these methods unless your husband is willing and able to supply viable samples, preferably here under controlled conditions?"

"Yes."

Dr. Neuhaus closed the folder. "Then I suggest that you go home and have a long talk with him. Then make another appointment, and I'll go through the process with you." She stood as though their appointment was at an end.

But it couldn't be. She'd only just got here. "Please—wait."

"Certainly." The doctor settled back into the chair.

"What is the process after that? Please tell me."

So the doctor told her. About the drugs she'd start on, and the ones that would need to be injected by needles in the stomach, and about egg maturation and ultrasounds and "extraction," which was nothing more than sucking eggs out of tubes with more needles; and fertilizing them with yet more needles; and "implantation," which was putting them back in....

She showed pictures, too. Carrie felt a little sick. The books in the library must have been out of date. Or incomplete. Or something. How had she missed so many steps that had to do with needles? She couldn't even watch when the vet had to give the horses a shot. She stayed in the house.

Don't be a coward. You can do this. You want this. You've come this far. You can't stop now.

"So you see, your husband is a vital part of this process. He's your coach, your cheerleader, the person who drops everything to get you into the clinic every day when we're monitoring the oocyte growth. Or in your case, the person who makes sure the car and driver are ready at a moment's notice."

"I can do that myself. There's a phone shanty only a quarter mile away."

The doctor took a breath, obviously changing her mind about her next words. "That's not the point. The point is, this is something you do together. And there's another thing," the doctor said gently. "The church would have to approve the funding, wouldn't they?"

She should never have come. This was what you got when you didn't listen to your friends. You got to sit here and have facts flung at you—facts you hadn't considered or wanted to consider. Facts that hurt just as badly as running face-first into an apple tree.

"We're talking anywhere between fifteen and thirty thousand dollars, Carrie. Is the church prepared to give you that? And if not, do you have that amount or can you get it through a loan with a bank?"

"I didn't know it would be that expensive," she said faintly. It was all they could do to pay the mortgage and eat. With Melvin's job at the pallet shop, she had just begun to feel safe in handing over money for a beef brisket or a pork shoulder once in a while. Even if the church did give them money, it would be a loan. One that would send them under.

"It's certainly cheaper to do it the old-fashioned way," the doctor said with the hint of a smile. "But for some, the old-fashioned way doesn't work so well." She gazed at her for a moment. "Go home and think about it. Talk to Melvin. And then we'll talk some more."

Carrie nodded and collected her purse, shawl, and away bonnet. She made sure she took everything she had come in with.

Because she would not be coming back again.

* * *

On the off Sunday before Emma's wedding, Carrie wondered how Emma was dealing with the temptation to do just one tiny little wedding-related task on her day of rest. She hoped her friend could spend this quiet time with Lena—it would be her last before her new life began.

On off Sundays, she and Melvin usually spent the morning quietly, singing a hymn or two as they did the dishes, and then spending a little time with Scripture. Some people took their day of rest so seriously that a woman wouldn't even turn her stove on, which meant she'd have to work twice as hard on Saturday to have three cold meals ready for the next day. However, the elders in Whinburg were sensible— and appreciated a good meal as much as anyone. If a person's own convictions led them to keep the stove off, then that was their business, but such a thing had not been added to the *Ordnung.*

Neither had anything about having babies, from what she

could tell. Next week, during the *Abstellung*, she would know for sure, but no letter from Mary Lapp was going to appear now. That meant either that the bishop was going to make a point of it as he went over the standards the people were to keep, or that what he'd said to her in front of Emma and the Esches was his final word on the subject.

Melvin sat at the kitchen table and opened the Bible. "Come and read to me, *Liebschdi*. Your voice turns these old words into poetry."

She might be in the depths of despair, but who could help but smile at something like that? She settled opposite him and turned the book so she could read it. "I think the Psalms were written that way. Old Joe Yoder could read it and it would still sound the same."

"Old Joe doesn't read English. At least, not if it doesn't have to do with crop prices and the weights of bags of grain."

She looked down. "Oh, is this the English one?" They had two—one in *hoch Deutsch* and one in English.

He pointed to Psalm 113. "Here."

> *Who is like unto the LORD our God, who dwelleth*
> *   on high,*
> *Who humbleth himself to behold the things that are*
> *   in heaven, and in the earth!*
> *He raiseth up the poor out of the dust, and lifteth the*
> *   needy out of the dunghill;*
> *That he may set him with princes, even with the*
> *   princes of his people.*
> *He maketh the barren woman to keep house, and*
> *   to be a joyful mother of children. Praise ye the*
> *   LORD.*

Her voice only broke once, on the last line. She looked up. Was he trying to punish her? Had he found out somehow about her journey in the market wagon on Friday and this was his way of telling her?

"Carrie, don't look at me like that."

She closed the book. "How did you find out?"

His callused hands, which were reaching across the table, hitched. Then he took hers in both of his. "Find out what?"

"That I went to the fertility clinic on Friday."

For a moment, the kitchen was so quiet she could hear the clock ticking over the door. "You did? And what did you learn there?"

So she told him. It was pointless, but she did it anyway, more to punish herself for having such hopes and being so foolish, than to give him information. The samples, the drugs, the needles, the cost—she told him everything.

"Thirty thousand dollars to have a baby?" He sat back, and her hands slid out of his. She folded them on top of the Bible.

"That's just to conceive it. I think it might cost nine or ten to go to the hospital and have it."

"I think our way is easier," he said with a feeble attempt at humor. "As you say, the old-fashioned way."

"I want you to know," she said steadily, "that I've given up. Even if the bishop were to say the treatment is the next best thing to a Honda generator and everyone should have one, I wouldn't do it. We have no way of coming up with that money short of selling the farm."

"Which would not be wise. I suppose we could bring up our family in a buggy, but it would be cramped."

His face was so gentle, his eyes so kind, that her own filled with tears. "I'm sorry I've put you through this. I know I've

made you think that I think less of you somehow—that because we can't have children that you're less of a man and
I'm a defective woman. But it's not so. You're far too good
for me."

"God does not create defective people," he told her. "Every
one can serve Him in their own way. Ours will just have to be
as friends and neighbors, not as parents. Until God decides
otherwise."

"He won't."

"Don't be so sure." He reached under her hands and
opened the Bible again, where a slip of ribbon lay between
the pages to mark Psalm 113. "He has kept all these promises
to us so far, Carrie. Look. We were poor and needy, and he
raised us up with better work that I can do with joy and confidence. We live among princes—His chosen people. You are
certainly keeping a home of our own instead of living in that
buggy or in someone's empty *Daadi Haus*. The only promise that He has left in this Psalm is to make you the joyful
mother of children. Not a child, my dear one. Children. An
abundance of them."

She could point out that the Psalmist was probably not
writing directly to her. But maybe that was not so. Maybe
these words had been preserved in this book so that this
morning, the last Sunday in October, she would read them
to her husband and be reminded of how good God had been
to them.

"I've been so selfish," she whispered. "All these gifts.
Emma is always telling me about the little gifts she sees everywhere, and I've taken even that for granted." Her throat
swelled. "I'm sorry, Melvin. I will put this away in God's
hands, where it belongs, and leave it there."

"I will not stop praying," he said, covering her hands on

the fragile onionskin pages with his warm ones. "And neither will you."

"But I will stop plaguing everyone with my wild ideas."

"Don't give up hope. God will provide. You'll see."

She nodded. This morning, in her kitchen, sitting across from the man she really would live in a buggy with, if it came down to that, it was almost possible to believe.

Almost.

CHAPTER 15

Three things would make Emma's wedding something Carrie would never forget. The first was the look in Grant Weaver's eyes as he took his bride's hand and led her to the front of the congregation packed into John and Karen's house. He stood for just a moment, holding her hands and gazing at her as though he couldn't quite believe she was there, dressed in a new blue dress and the crisp white organdy cape and apron Carrie had made, all for him.

"*. . . und glaust daß es vom Herren ist und durch dein glauben und gebet so weid gekommen bist?*"

"*Ja,*" Grant said to the bishop, but his voice was pitched just for Emma.

With the simple vows that followed their declarations of belief that they were obeying God's will, she became Grant's Emma . . . and Carrie knew down to her bones that for her friend, life could hold no greater gift until she met her Savior in heaven.

The second thing was that the cake Carrie had made was mistaken by just about everyone as having come from an expensive bakery in Lancaster, where a wedding cake could cost as much as five hundred dollars. Carrie pressed her lips together to keep from smiling as she sat in the *Eck* at the bridal table and heard someone murmur about it just loud enough for them to hear.

"Do you want me to tell them?" Emma leaned over to whisper. "After all the work you put into that cake?"

Carrie shook her head and tried to keep a giggle under control. "You can give me the five hundred dollars later."

That set them off, and somehow Amelia, who was serving, caught the joke, and pretty soon all three of them were wiping tears from their eyes and trying to fend off their husbands' questioning looks.

She didn't care about who got credit for the cake. Her little weaverbirds were for Emma's eyes alone, and if other people liked them, well, that was just... icing on the cake.

The third thing might have overwhelmed her and spoiled the day entirely if it hadn't been for the gift of the first two. The arrival of Melvin's mother, Aleta, for the wedding was preceded by a letter, giving them just enough warning to make sure the second bedroom—not the one she usually stayed in, because that one held the quilt frame—was in fit shape for company. Aleta was Mary Lapp's sister, and had been in Miriam's buddy bunch decades ago—both very good reasons to come for a visit and see "that poor Stolzfus girl" safely married to a widower who had a family in need of her care.

Carrie pushed the third thing out of her mind. Beside her at the wedding meal, Emma glowed with happiness as she talked with her agent, Tyler West, who had come to her wedding from New York City in a navy suit with a lime-green tie. Even Grant's face, usually so solemn with care, had lightened with the ability to tease his wife and be teased in return.

And the weaverbirds had not been lost on him, either, much to Carrie's satisfaction.

The one thing about being *Neuwesitzern* was that neither she nor Kathryn, the sister closest to Emma in age, who was also standing up with her, had cleanup or serving duties. As members of the wedding party, their job was to make sure the bridal couple had whatever they needed, from another glass of punch to an extra pin for *Kapp* or apron. Likewise, as the mother of the bride, Lena Stolzfus allowed others to work, and simply enjoyed her family and Grant's parents at their table close by.

Meanwhile, in the big house, Karen directed the delivery of all the food to no fewer than three sittings with clockwork precision. Carrie had no idea how many were there, but as Emma had estimated, it had to be over two hundred. But by two o'clock, everyone had eaten, and Emma had a few minutes to visit with her guests before the singing began at three.

"I've always liked wedding roast," Emma said to Carrie and Amelia, "but I don't think I've ever enjoyed it as much as I did today."

Carrie adored the chicken-and-stuffing concoction that went by the prosaic name of "roast," even though none of her own chickens would ever contribute to it under any circumstances. "There was a lot of love and answered prayers in that roast. I bet that's why it tasted so good."

"I'm so full I'm going to burst." Out of the corner of her eye, Amelia watched Eli take the boys to the outhouses in back. Even though the farm had indoor plumbing, it wasn't capable of handling the influx of people who came on church Sunday, or for weddings and funerals. The outhouses had to be kept in good repair as backup. "But you can guarantee the *Youngie* will be ready to eat again tonight."

"You will be, too," Emma said. "Even if it's only another piece of Carrie's cake."

"How many cakes have they cut so far?"

"Six," Emma told her. "Christina Yoder made two really pretty chocolate ones. They were the first to go. I'm trying to save your sheet cakes for last, Carrie, because they're the nicest thing this old barn has ever seen. They won't get past the *Youngie* after tonight's Singing, though."

"I like how you say that word," Carrie teased. "You *relish* it—because you'll never be one of them again."

"Will you last until after the Singing?" Amelia asked affectionately.

Emma raised a brow in acknowledgment. "Usually I'm the first one to run away from a crowd. But"—she surveyed the happy congregation, the roar of conversation like that of a huge waterfall of words—"this is *my* crowd. I've been waiting for it my whole life. So I'm going to enjoy every single minute."

They soon lost her in a throng of well-wishers, many of them from their buddy bunch and quilters' groups who had traveled a long distance on trains, buses, and buggies to join her on her wedding day. Grant took Tyler West away to join the men, including Melvin, as though he were one of them, despite the fact that none of them could look at his tie and keep a straight face. Carrie had some time while the waiters and waitresses who had looked after them at the *Eck* had a chance to eat their own meal there, so she made her way outside.

The day couldn't have been nicer if they had ordered it from a catalog. The midafternoon sky was a deep autumn blue, tinged with frost and garlanded with hawthorn berries and the last of the chestnuts. She wandered toward the cornfields, bare now, behind the house, wondering how many couples would be made public tonight at supper, when the bride traditionally paired off the *Youngie*.

"That's quite a crowd in there," a voice said behind her, and she turned to see Joshua Steiner coming over the grass, his long stride eating up the yards between them. "Are you looking for your man?"

"*Nei*. He and Grant took Emma's agent away somewhere, since the barn is wedding territory today instead of men's territory."

"Fortunately for us all, John Stolzfus has more than one barn. You'll likely find them with my cousins in the dairy, where John is planning to make some changes."

"He wants cabinetry in the dairy?" Carrie couldn't keep the disbelief out of her tone, and Joshua laughed.

"*Nei*. But he does want some good opinions. Mine isn't worth much, but Brian's is."

"But you work at the Hills' big dairy. If you have an opinion, wouldn't you offer it?"

"With John, I'm afraid, you wait until you're asked." Joshua's smile changed as he looked over her shoulder. "I think someone is looking for you."

Carrie turned, expecting Melvin, or at the very least Amelia or one of her own sisters. But instead, steaming up the hill like a very determined train, was her mother-in-law.

What had she done now?

There had been a time when Carrie had humbled herself literally to the dust and done what was right—washing Aleta's feet—one of the most difficult experiences she'd ever passed through. She had put Aleta before herself, and found a measure of peace, even if it had gone down hard. Not that she expected some kind of return—that wasn't how *Uffgeva* worked.

Uffgeva—that giving up of oneself to God, to one's brothers and sisters, to one's community, was the principle that enabled disparate personalities like theirs to rub along together.

But usually the other person practiced it, too, with peace as a result. Maybe Aleta's attention drifted during that part of the *Abstellung*.

"Carrie," she called when she was about ten yards away, "you'll be wanted down there. The *Youngie* are getting ready to sing."

One look at the barn was enough to tell her that the young men hadn't gone in yet. Since they were the last to be seated and no one looked to be in a hurry to stop talking, she still had a few minutes.

"Mamm Miller, you remember Joshua Steiner? He's helping us on the farm this fall."

Her mother-in-law drew level with them, her chest heaving under her neatly pinned cape. "I do. In fact, I wanted a word with him, now that I have the two of you."

The two of them? Carrie didn't like being paired, even in thought, with anyone but Melvin. You'd think Melvin's mother would feel the same way.

"It's nice to see you again, Aleta." Joshua sounded as sincere as though he really did pay attention to the occasions when one meddlesome widow was in town. "I hope you're well?"

"I'd be better if you weren't up here with my daughter-in-law in front of the whole *Gmee*."

Carrie's mouth dropped open while she tried to decide which would be worse—laughing or saying something that would betray what she really thought.

"Better in front of the whole *Gmee* than hiding, wouldn't you say?"

Aleta huffed and blew and finally corralled some words. "So what I'm hearing is right, then? You're hiding your sinful attentions to my son's wife, and she's going along with it?"

Carrie turned to run. She didn't know where. Out to the other barn, maybe, where she could grab Melvin and get him to take his mother home. She was clearly out of her head.

But before she could take a single step, Joshua laughed. "Is that what they're saying? Seems to me the grapevine must be hurting for material if it's reduced to making things up."

"My sister does not make things up."

"Ah, our good bishop's wife. She certainly is blessed with the gift of husbandry."

Goodness. What a thing to say! As though Mary Lapp cultivated the grapevine as assiduously as she did her own garden. Which she sometimes did—even if half the time it was accidental.

Aleta shot him a narrow look. "She's also blessed with the gift of discernment, and if Carrie is so blind she can't see it, then I'll speak up myself. You stay away from her, Joshua Steiner."

"Aleta, he works for us," Carrie managed to get in.

"Is that all he's doing? He's eating meals alone with you and helping you in the kitchen and who knows what-all?"

"Last I looked, eating a good meal wasn't a sin," Joshua said easily. Carrie wondered how he could be so calm and speak with such good humor. Did nothing bother him—even being accused of—of—

Of what?

"Yes, that's all he's doing," she finally managed to get out. "If anyone is saying different, then shame on them."

"A man's work should take him outside," Aleta pressed,

"not inside in a woman's world. Helping to peel apples. Hmph!"

Where was she getting her information? But no. She couldn't ask that. It would look as though it were true. Except it was. "He isn't very good at it," Carrie said. If Joshua could look like he found it funny, then so could she. "The peeling only lasted one evening and then he went back to picking, which he's much better at."

"So it's true?"

"That I'm a terrible peeler? *Ja*, sad to say."

Aleta's lips thinned. Carrie wondered how often she was teased. Clearly she wasn't used to it, and had mistaken it for mockery.

"I meant, it's true you're in my son's house, flirting with his wife and getting up to who knows what kind of tricks."

This time Joshua laughed out loud, and by the time he got control of himself, Aleta's face could have made a thundercloud look like a harmless puff of quilt batting. "Aleta Miller, if I were a vain man, you would put the polish on me. But I have the least reason in the world to be vain, so let me tell you the truth. Your daughter-in-law and your son have been nothing but kind to me. And I mean that in its simplest sense. Kind."

Aleta folded her arms and glared at him, as if being told that her son was indeed the man she'd brought him up to be was as bad as a single man talking back to her.

"Melvin gave me a job, when he could have chosen any of the other young men around here, despite what my cousins might have told him about me. Carrie fed me and put up with me and made me work whether I had any liking for the task or not. I may not have learned anything useful in the kitchen, but I learned how good she is. You can be thankful to the *gut Gott* that you have such a family, Aleta. I know I would be."

By this time, the folded arms only made her look as though she were cold. Carrie took off her jacket and settled it around her shoulders.

"You don't need to tell me what I already know, Joshua Steiner," Aleta said, but the anger had gone out of her tone.

"Even the best of us need a reminder of our blessings once in a while," he said cheerfully.

"I'm far from that."

"You care about your family and you're willing to stand up for them," he said.

Carrie would not have put it that way, but she was just a bystander to this conversation. If she had taken lessons from Emma on how to handle Joshua, then she'd better take a few from Joshua on how to handle Aleta.

The two of them had never understood each other. Carrie had always felt that Melvin's mother would rather have seen him married to anyone on the planet but her. No matter how well Joshua was smoothing this over, she would just have to overlook the fact that Aleta had had no problem believing Carrie would step out on her son.

The first notes of the ninety-seventh *Lied*, "*Wohlauf, Wohlauf, bu Gottes G'mein,*" where the church is exhorted to put on its bridal ornaments for Christ, drifted up the hill. All the young men and boys had gone in and been paired off with the single girls already, and her place was empty.

"Looks like I missed out on getting a singing partner," Joshua said. "I'll be at the farm tomorrow afternoon as usual, Carrie."

"It's the singles table for you. I'm going to be here tomorrow, helping with the cleanup. I guess I'd better go and take my place, too, before Emma thinks I've deserted her."

Joshua loped off, and Carrie would have followed him except that Aleta laid a hand on her arm. "Just a minute." She swung Carrie's jacket off her shoulders and handed it back to her. "*Denki* for this. The wind is cold." She paused and pursed her lips. "I was a bit hard on you."

Was this an apology? Carrie couldn't very well agree with her, and to deny it would be a lie, so she kept silent.

"I came up here to talk to you, and when I saw that man, I suppose everything Mary told me rose up and got the best of me."

"Does Mary believe all that?"

"I don't think so. She doesn't believe hardly any of what people tell her. She winnows through it all, looking for bits of truth, but it's like trying to find a grain of wheat in a measure of rice sometimes."

Is that what she did? Pass on the winnowings as though they were truth? Carrie shook her head. Really, the ideal bishop's wife should be deaf to gossip, blind to faults, and dumb when it came to the first two.

"Well, now you know the truth," she said at last. "Melvin likes Joshua, and he trusts me, and between the two there's no room for...winnowings."

Aleta nodded, watching Abe Zook head across the field to find his horse. "Now, there's a man who's been winnowed so many times there's nothing left. And to think we courted once."

If Carrie hadn't been standing firmly on two feet, she would have fallen over. "You? And *Abe Zook*?"

"Oh yes. Years ago, before I left Whinburg. I went to take a job as a school teacher in Douglas County, and I met

Melvin's father and stayed. But Abe Zook and I..." Her voice trailed away while Carrie tried to wrap her imagination around this stormy woman and sticklike Abe Zook, living together in that awful house and riding roughshod over their daughter and any other children the union might have produced.

"Lydia works at the fabric store in town now," Carrie said.

"Does she? Well, it gets her out of the house, I suppose, though goodness knows it must need looking after. Does no one come?"

"We do what we can. What he allows us to do."

"That girl. I would never believe she was his daughter. That coloring must come from Rachel's side of the family, though I can't recall any redheads there, either."

Rachel was Lydia's mother. Or had been. "Didn't Rachel have a sister?"

"A twin. An older sister died when they were real young. That branch of the family's had its share of misfortune, and now here's another bushel of it on the way."

Carrie eyed her, very much afraid that they were gossiping now, themselves. "What do you mean?"

"Well, it's as plain as the nose on your face—or will be, soon. Believe me, when you've had as many *Bobblin* as I have, you know the signs."

"What?" Something was squeezing Carrie's chest, as if a pair of massive hands had her heart and lungs between them and she couldn't get a breath.

As though she'd heard them talking about her, Lydia Zook emerged from the barn and trailed reluctantly across the yard to the pasture gate. She moved so slowly it looked like some magnetic force was pulling her back in the door. She gripped the post and gazed back toward the barn, looking for a face or a silhouette in the lamplight that glowed in its sashed lower windows.

"The girl's breeding," Aleta said. "She's not very far along yet, but far enough to know it. Abe is going to have his hands full, and that's a fact."

Carrie watched the slender figure push open the gate and stand next to it as her father drove the buggy through. At a word from him, she closed it and climbed in beside him, stiffly, the way a teenager would if she were doing it under orders and not because she wanted to.

Pregnant.

Pregnant.

For unto every one that hath shall be given, and he shall have abundance: but from him that hath not shall be taken away even that which he hath.

CHAPTER 16

Emma and Grant left at eleven o'clock to spend their first night as husband and wife at the Stolzfus *Daadi Haus*. Lena had gone home with Katherine and her family hours before, and when Christina Yoder asked if the children were going with relatives, Emma shook her head.

"We're a family now," she said, taking little Katie's hand and hefting a sleeping Zachary higher on her shoulder. "We're going to start off as a family." Smiling, Christina had taken her own children home.

Carrie glanced around the barn to make sure there weren't any stray dishes left on the tables. Melvin found her with a drinking glass in one hand and a small stack of empty candy dishes that had somehow found its way on top of a crossbeam. "This will all be here tomorrow, *Liebschdi*. I have the buggy outside."

Feverishly, Carrie clutched the dishes and hustled them out the door. "Are the dishwashers still here? We should get these—"

"*Nei.*" He took them and set them on the end of one of the tables, where someone would see them first thing tomorrow. "Carrie, you've been working like a plow horse ever since the

Singing. Now that Emma and Grant are gone, aren't your duties done?"

She wished there were more. Thank heaven for work. Work was a blessing, keeping the hands and the mind busy so that she didn't have to think about teenage girls barely out of the schoolroom who were facing motherhood without neither husband nor home.

Carrie spent a sleepless night, which meant that getting up at four the next morning was a relief—an end to the torture of her own thoughts. She made a big breakfast for Melvin, let the hens out of their coop and fed them, too, and they were back at the Stolzfus place by six to break down the tables, scrub the barn floors, and pack the silverware and dishes into their chests, ready for the next wedding.

Early as she was, Emma and Grant still beat her there. But then, they had only been a few steps away, which was the very reason the newlywed couple usually spent the night at the bride's home. Besides, if the couple were young, they often didn't have a house built yet, so there was no time to waste on cleanup, because a farm's other jobs still waited.

By noon, the work was mostly done, and after Carrie helped cook the lunch for the cleanup crew, Emma practically had to force her to sit and eat a plate of it herself.

Carrie finally came out of the inferno of her own mind to gaze at her friend across the plate of ham, macaroni and cheese, buttered beans, and biscuits. "Emma. Look at you." Emma blushed and looked down at her own plate. "Happiness is beaming out of you."

The flush on her cheeks made her look softer, and her eyes glowed in a way Carrie hadn't seen before, even if the corners of them drooped just the tiniest bit from lack of sleep. Marriage definitely suited her.

"I have every reason to be happy," Emma said quietly, her gaze finding Grant at the men's table. As though he could feel it, he looked up and smiled at her, and Emma blushed again. "Even if between us Zachary and I managed to spill his milk down his shirt this morning. I wonder how on earth Amelia managed with *two* boys under two. Zachary is a good little guy, but my goodness, he takes a lot of watching."

"You should ask her," Carrie said. "Do you still mean to have our quilting time on Tuesday?"

"I do. Nothing can keep me away." She tucked into her macaroni and the words that trembled on Carrie's lips fluttered into silence.

She would save the news about Lydia until then. It would do no good to bring it up now, at a table with twenty other people clattering their dishes, and brothers and sisters close enough to hear what she said. And what if she started to cry? No, no. Tuesday, in the quiet of her own spare room, was soon enough.

Maybe by then she'd have found out a thing or two. Like whether it was actually true, or if Aleta was just imagining things.

She hoped Aleta didn't plan to stay for the Peachey and Kurtz weddings next week. At best, she could encourage her to do some visiting on Tuesday afternoon, so that the three of them could have privacy to talk.

Melvin decided to join Eli Fischer for the remainder of that day at the pallet shop, which meant he took the horse and buggy into Whinburg. After all the busyness of the past week, a quiet walk home along the creek bed would be good for her. The old-man's-beard—the seedpods of the wild clematis—was finished now, and there were hardly any left, but there might be something she could make into a wreath.

She had no idea if Joshua was at the house or not, but worrying about it wouldn't get her there any faster. She was just about to head out across the field when Emma leaned out of the Weaver buggy.

"Can we give you a ride?"

Carrie shook her head. "I know you want to start setting up your house right this minute, so I won't keep you from it."

"Nonsense." Grant backed the horse, and Carrie walked over to Emma's side of the buggy. The two girls were in school, so only Zachary rode on Emma's lap. "She's had her kitchen set up the way she likes it for weeks. And after all you've done for us, the least we can do is give you a ride. Hop in."

Emma slid over and he put his arm around her and the baby both, still holding the reins. "Eyes on the road, you," she teased.

"I can see this old road any day. Seeing my bride is a different matter."

"You won't be saying that in ten years." But Emma couldn't keep the impish smile off her lips.

"Watch me."

The three miles over to her house had never seemed so short as they laughed and talked over the wedding. How often was a woman's heart's desire granted to her? And yet Emma had both—her book was to be published, and she was married to the man she'd loved since she was eighteen.

Thank you, Father, for little gifts like a steady hand with cake frosting, and for big gifts like a lifetime's happiness for someone I love. Father, You know my heart's desire. You also know I've given it into Your hands. I know I've done that a hundred times over the last ten years, but this time I won't be taking it back. It's

*staying with You, to do with as You will. Give me the strength
to leave it there, Lord. Amen.*

"Looks like Joshua Steiner is here," Grant said as he pulled
the horse to a halt in the yard. Joshua's horse cropped grass
placidly in the pasture closest to the barn, while the buggy
had been pulled neatly to the side of the lane to allow others
to pass.

"The weather is supposed to be clear today and tomorrow," Carrie said. "I hope he plans to paint my chicken
house." She gave Emma a quick hug and jumped down. "Enjoy your day at home. Are you beginning your wedding visits
right away?"

Emma nodded. "We're going down to Katherine's first,
but we'll be back Monday night. I told you I wasn't missing
our quilting time, and I meant it."

"I look forward to it. I want to talk something over with
you." With a wave, she stepped back and Grant turned the
horse, shook the reins over his back, and they rolled down
the lane.

"You mean women are scheduling their gossip now?"
Joshua came around the corner of the barn wiping his hands
on a rag. "That doesn't sound godly to me."

Carrie climbed the steps. "What goes on at our quilting
frolics is not for men's ears. And we don't say anything we
wouldn't want the Lord to hear, anyway."

"The Lord hears it whether we want Him to or not."

"If He is fine with it, then you should be, too."

Joshua laughed as though he'd gotten the rise out of her
that he'd wanted. "Do you ever talk about me?"

Carrie rolled her eyes. "Such pride, imagining that of all
the subjects in the world, we would choose that one." Which,
of course, they had.

"I've probably given you reason to."

Something in his tone told her that they were no longer being frivolous. She put her big bag—now full of pieces of the cake's architecture, washed and dried—on the porch, pulled her jacket around her against the chill, and walked with him over to the chicken house.

It was freshly painted. All that was left to do was the green trim, and she could do that herself. "You've done a good job," she said. "This place looks nearly new."

"I had to let the chickens out. They were getting a little panicky."

"That's all right. They usually wander all over the yard anyway, keeping the bugs down."

"Carrie—"

"Is there something you want to talk with me about?"

"*Ja*," he said on a long breath that could have been relief, or maybe trepidation. "There is."

She busied herself filling the feed cans. Sometimes it was easier to talk when your whole concentration wasn't on the other person, making them uncomfortable. "I'm listening."

"I wasn't just being *batzich*, you know, about being the subject of people's talk. I know I am."

"In what way?"

"In a 'who is he seeing now' kind of way."

"Are you courting Lydia Zook?"

"Is that what they say?"

"I don't know who *they* is, but I've noticed you in her company, so it looks to me like you might be courting."

"And if I am?"

"Honestly, Joshua, you don't need my permission. But if you did, I might say you ought to look at someone who isn't two years out of the schoolroom."

She took the basket down from the wall and began to collect the eggs. Dark brown, light brown, green, and blue, their colors delighted her. When she put them in the egg cartons to sell in the summer, she would put them in an order that made pretty designs that probably only she could see, twelve at a time.

But it was November, and there were only three eggs in all six nesting boxes. The birds had begun to molt last month, so that was to be expected. A bird could use her body's protein for eggs or for feathers, but not for both, so most hens stopped laying in the winter.

Joshua watched her. "What would you say if I told you it wasn't true?"

"What wasn't?" She shouldn't have let her mind wander. She didn't want him to think she didn't care about his confidences.

"Me courting Lydia Zook. Because it isn't."

She nearly dropped the last egg, which would have meant no chocolate-zucchini loaf for Melvin's breakfast.

"Then if it isn't you, who's the—" She clamped her mouth shut and put the egg carefully in the nearly empty basket. Blurting out something like that—well, that really would be gossip. People were going to talk quite enough. She didn't need to add to it.

"What have you heard, Carrie?"

"Nothing."

"What were you going to say?"

He wasn't going to let her get out of this. "I was going to say, 'Who's the father?' but that would be cruel and unkind if—if people are wrong."

"You know?" He sounded astonished. "She just told me yesterday, at the wedding. Who told you? Lydia herself?"

"No. My mother-in-law. Right after you left us."

It took him a moment to absorb this. "Mamm Miller was having a busy afternoon."

Carrie wasn't going to touch that. All she needed was for it to get back to Aleta that she was talking about her behind her back, and things would become even more prickly than they were now. Bad enough she'd be coming home at any time from visiting Mary Lapp, and Joshua would still be here.

"She's had five boys and four girls. I guess she knows the signs," she said. "Nobody told her that I know of."

He took a sharp breath and let it out just as sharply. "But the baby isn't mine, I'll guarantee you that. Lydia and I— well, it hasn't progressed to that."

Hasn't progressed? But to progress, you had to start somewhere. People didn't practice bed courtship anymore in Whinburg Township, but that didn't mean things still didn't get out of hand.

"I know everyone thinks I'm courting her," Joshua went on, "and as soon as she starts to show, everyone will say I'm the father, but I'm not. I can't be."

He'd said that twice now. It sounded almost desperate. "Then who is?"

"She won't tell me," he said miserably. For once in his life, he wasn't the joker, the careless scapegrace who turned every word to produce a laugh. "I'm practically the only person she has to talk to around here, and she won't tell me."

If she thought they were an odd couple before, it was nothing compared to this. "Doesn't she have friends? She needs to talk to a woman about these things, not you. Isn't there an aunt in Strasburg?"

"And how is she going to get there? Abe won't let her out of the house, so she has to wait until he goes to sleep or gets busy with something and doesn't notice she's gone. Taking the buggy to Strasburg would be next to impossible."

"She must have girlfriends with mothers."

"Who is going to let their daughter get close to her?"

Carrie thought of the peach-colored fabric. "Sarah Grohl used to be her friend. And the girls certainly follow her lead." Or maybe it was more a case of watching to see if she was spoken to, and if not, then assuming it was safe to do the same.

"That may be true, but it doesn't mean she has the kind of friends she could confide in." He finally met her gaze. "Otherwise, why would she say these things to me?"

Because you dance along the edges of God's will, too, just like her. "You know, my mother and some of the women who have been looking out for her—making her a project—they could—"

"Carrie, she needs someone like you," he interrupted. "Even if she tells you to mind your own business, it's all a show. She needs someone desperately who knows about—about—"

"Pregnancy?" Carrie's stomach turned over and she tasted something sour in the back of her throat. "I am the last person who could talk about that."

Joshua didn't seem to hear the bitterness in her tone. "But you have friends who have. You have sisters—and a mother who can advise you. Lydia doesn't have any of those things. Maybe she can—I don't know—use your family instead. Through you."

"Do you know what you're asking me?" she said hoarsely. "What I've been longing for and praying for these ten years past? Are you mocking me?"

"Of course not. I'm begging you."

For probably the first time in his life, Joshua was putting

someone else ahead of himself—someone whose loneliness and need were probably even greater than his own. Even if people would think he himself had been the cause of the latter.

Be that as it may, God was clearly working in him, and a sister could rejoice at it. But a sister also had her limits beyond which she could not go. Especially when she'd been rebuffed once already.

"Joshua, I can't do it. I don't have the experience, so she'll never take me seriously. But I will talk to the other women and get them to help. She needs to see a doctor and get advice on the right things to eat and vitamins to take."

"I don't think she'll take kindly to the other women. She'll see it as meddling or being bossed."

"Then she'll have to open her eyes and see that they only want to help."

"She knows that about you."

"No, she doesn't. I tried to butt in once before and got exactly what I deserved—nothing. I can't do it, Joshua. Please don't ask me."

Blindly, she turned away and walked back to the house, out of his sight. When she climbed the porch steps, she realized every single hen in her flock had followed her and stood on the steps and planks of the porch, their necks craned up to look into her face.

She set down the nearly empty pail, sat on the step, and let their warm, feathery bodies crowd around her. But somehow, even their unselfish companionship did not offer her the comfort she craved.

CHAPTER 17

When Aleta came home, she was driving the Miller buggy. Joshua had been about to leave, but he tied up his horse and led Jimsy into the barn to remove his harness and brush and feed him.

"That was a neighborly thing to do," Aleta said, removing her away bonnet and hanging up her winter coat. "Not what I would have expected of him."

"He's here to help," Carrie said for what felt like the dozenth time. "A cup of coffee?"

"*Ja*, that would be *gut*. I suppose you're wondering why your buggy is home and your husband isn't."

"I imagine he's working late?"

"Yes. Mary and I went into town and we stopped at the pallet shop to visit. Apparently they got some good news in connection with that trade show they went to last month— good news that means Melvin won't be home for dinner. He put me in the buggy with that message for you, and told me to say that Brian would drop him off later."

"Good news means more work for the shop. I'm glad to hear it."

Aleta settled into a chair at the table with a cup of coffee while Carrie dished up creamed corn, biscuits, baked apples, and pork chops for the two of them. She made up a plate for Melvin, too, and put it in the oven in case he was hungry when he got home...whenever that might be.

They gave a silent thanks and began to eat. Carrie never knew what to say to her mother-in-law. She was touchy on some subjects, opinionated on others, and wouldn't speak about the rest. That didn't leave much conversational ground to cover. Some folks believed the table was for eating at, not talking at, and Carrie was willing to live by that philosophy tonight.

"My sister agrees with me," Aleta said when her plate was nearly empty. "That Zook girl is breeding, and your hired man is the father."

"No, he isn't."

Aleta nearly dropped her fork and knife, probably as surprised that Carrie had contradicted her as Carrie was to have done it. "What?"

"No one knows who the father is except Lydia, and she's not telling."

"Says who?"

"Says Joshua himself."

"Then he's lying, and shame on him." Aleta reached for the corn and took another helping.

"I don't think he is." Something perverse made her defend him, when privately she thought Aleta was probably right. "There were tears in his eyes when he told me, because it upsets him that she won't ask for help."

"She'll get none from Abe, from all accounts. He never used to be such a hard-hearted man."

"Surely he'll see that she goes to the doctor." Even as she spoke, Carrie wondered. Abe's own wife had died of an infection that could have been cured by simply hitching up the buggy and taking her to the emergency room in Whinburg. There had even been talk that the police might file charges against him, but nothing had ever come of it.

"If ever there was a candidate for a project, that girl is it."

"I'm going to speak to some of the women. Among all of us, we'll see she's looked after."

"Why you?" Aleta gazed at her across the table, eyes black as sloes and missing nothing. "You're not a mother."

If she hadn't already been through this with Joshua, the words might have slashed at her composure and left her trying to draw the rags of it around her. But she realized that Aleta was simply speaking the truth without the trappings of consideration or tact. As was her habit.

"In these matters I don't have any experience. But someone has to do something, and Joshua feels—" She stopped.

"Joshua? If he's not the father, what does he have to do with any of this? Not that I believe he isn't, of course."

"He's been a friend to her, the way he's been a friend to me." A mocking, annoying friend, but still...she had apples in the pantry and three newly painted sheds, didn't she?

Aleta snorted. "Sounds like he's preying on needy women. I've half a mind to tell Melvin to pay him his money and send him away."

"He isn't preying, and he isn't taking money from us." She would never have believed she would be defending Joshua to Melvin's mother, of all people. "He just asked me to help, to talk to Lydia and act as a kind of mother in Rachel's place, but I can't. The whole subject of children is so hard..." Her throat closed up, and the lump felt so big even the glass of water in front of her wouldn't help.

And now Aleta was staring at her, the silence in the kitchen drawing out to the point where something must break it or Carrie would run from the room.

She gripped the seat of her chair, intending to push it back.

"Sarai was a mother in Israel long before she ever had children," Aleta said.

"Sarah who?" Carrie sat back, feeling a little winded by the abrupt turn in the conversation.

"Sarai, Abram's wife. Before she became Sarah, she led that congregation. Don't you think she was called in at plenty of births, because she was the woman they looked to as their leader's wife?"

"I see what you mean, but I don't know how that applies here," Carrie said. She needed to go to bed. Her mind just couldn't keep up, what with the lack of sleep from last night and all the revelations of today.

"You can be a mother in Israel, Carrie. Much as I used to think of Abe Zook, he's not the man any of us once knew. He's turned to vinegar, that's what, and gone sour in his place instead of ripening like the Lord intended. You know he's not going to put out a single finger to help that girl. It's got to be the women of the *Gmee* who band together, and if folk are already looking at you, then there's a reason for it."

"Not a very sensible reason."

"God's ways are not our ways," Aleta said firmly. "And besides, can you see any girl bringing a newborn *Bobbel* into that house? For one thing, it needs repair so bad the wind probably blows through it without stopping."

Frankly, Carrie couldn't. Even a desperately wanted baby would find no warmth from this grandfather—and who knew how desperately Lydia wanted her child?

"A blessing it might be if she were properly married," Aleta said, "but a sixteen-year-old girl who was foolish and careless and didn't take seriously what upbringing she had? I don't know."

Carrie thought of that glowing, alive girl who had swirled her dress by the side of the road, and contrasted it with the haunted, hunched silhouette that had held the gate and climbed, oh so slowly, into the buggy.

"What can I offer?" she whispered, half to herself.

"You can be a friend to her," Aleta said. "And who knows? Maybe she will not be able to keep that baby. Heaven knows Abe Zook isn't going to welcome it, and he's been estranged from what's left of his and Rachel's family so long it's not likely they would, either. And here are you and Melvin with a room ready and hearts long prepared to be parents."

Carrie heard a rushing in her ears, as if a flock of birds had taken wing right behind her chair or a fire had leaped up into a blaze. "What are you saying?"

"I'm usually pretty clear when I speak. You'll see that I'm right. That baby will have no home unless someone reaches out a hand to give it one. And your hand will already be extended to Lydia, won't it?" Aleta narrowed her gaze. "You're as white as a flour sack, girl. Don't tell me you're about to faint."

She was not. Carrie gripped the edge of the table. She would not faint. She had to think.

A mother in Israel? Is that what you want of me, Lord?

The sound of wings, of fire, faded into silence.

And after the fire, a still, small voice.

* * *

She could not do this.

Carrie curled up next to Melvin's sleeping form and wished she could sleep, but for the second night in a row, that blessing eluded her.

How was she to help, except by rallying the other women? Why, she had about as much experience in pregnancy or childbirth as Lydia herself.

No, that wasn't quite right. There was that deliriously happy few months six years ago, before the endless, dreadful night she'd blocked out of her memory. Could she share that somehow? Bring it out of the depths of grief, where she'd stuffed it and refused to look at it, if it meant she could help Lydia?

Carrie gritted her teeth and rolled over, pressing her back against Melvin's warm side.

All things work together for good for them that love God and are called according to His purpose.

Oh, not that thing. Surely not. That couldn't work for anybody's good, and she would just put it out of her mind right now. What she needed to do was gather the women together to give Lydia support and information, not frighten her with what might happen.

Somewhere between two and three o'clock, her eyes finally slid shut, and she found the place of peace.

In the morning, after she'd made breakfast and they'd said their prayers and Melvin had gone out to work in the barn, Aleta went back into her room to do her morning reading. Carrie's path seemed clear. If a mother in Israel was a leader, then she would lead the women. She wasn't the kind of social leader that Ruth Lehman and Karen Stolzfus were, but she'd organized her fair share of quilting frolics and work parties. A project was no different—it was just a lot more subtle.

To begin with, she would have to include Mary Lapp. She supposed it was a blessing that Aleta had already filled her in on the situation. She was probably already expecting the pretty note card Carrie had open on the kitchen table. She'd painted and stamped it herself, using a kit she'd found at the secondhand store.

Dear Mary,

If you are free to come for coffee at our place on Wednesday after baking, we might get together with a few others who could help Lydia Zook in her time of need. Say two o'clock?

Your sister in Christ,
Carrie Miller

She sent similar letters to Amelia, Emma, her sister Susan, and Christina Yoder. Then she got out the district directory and addressed an envelope with care.

Dear Priscilla Bontrager,

You don't know me, but I believe you know Mary Lapp, the bishop's wife in our district in Whinburg Township. My mother-in-law is her sister, if that helps to place me.

I'm writing to give you news of your niece, Lydia Zook, who is in a family way and expecting in early summer. She does not have a mother or sisters to help her, so some of us are gathering to stand in that place for her.

If you would like to come to my house on Wednesday at two o'clock, you would be very welcome. I am going to speak to Lydia today and make sure she is there, too. Among us all we will do our best to keep her and the *Bobbel* safe and healthy.

Your sister in Christ,
Carrie Miller

The postman didn't come until three, but she pulled her shawl around her and walked down the lane to put the letters in the mailbox as soon as she'd stamped them. Once they were in the box, she couldn't change her mind.

Now all she had to do was to make sure Lydia came on Wednesday. And that meant going over to Abe Zook's and seeing if she was there.

"Would you like to come with me?" She poked her head into the spare room.

Aleta looked up from *The Martyr's Mirror.* "*Nei.* The last thing I want is for Abe Zook to think I was looking to warm up cold soup with him."

"I don't think a visit to his daughter is going to make him think that. He's probably not even in the house. The weather's holding—most of the men are probably out plowing the silage under."

"I'll keep out of it," Aleta said. "She needs a friend and a word in season."

Meaning that was not what Aleta herself might bring? Carrie decided not to ask.

When she hitched up the buggy, Carrie saw that Aleta had the right idea. The November wind cut bitterly, sawing right through her skirts and black stockings. At least she'd worn boots, so her feet were warm, and the buggy blanket was thick over her lap.

At the Zook place, even Jimsy wondered what they were doing there. "I won't be long," she told him as she tied him to the rail. "If Abe Zook throws me out, I could be back in five minutes. And then we'll go home and I'll give you an apple for your trouble."

Jimsy swiveled an ear toward her, his brown eyes skeptical.

She had to knock twice before she heard movement inside and the door swung open. Abe Zook towered over her, seeming even taller because he wore his work boots in the house. "*Ja?* You're Melvin's Carrie, ain't you?"

She nodded. "I came to bring you this"—she pulled a jar of applesauce out of her carry basket—"and to have a visit with Lydia. Is she home?"

He took the applesauce with an expression even more skeptical than Jimsy's had been. "This is a first."

It wasn't, but she would not argue. "I don't often get the opportunity to share, but our trees were loaded this fall."

He hefted the jar, the way a man might who suspected he was being shorted. "Melvin's working at the pallet shop these days, I hear. Not much of a farmer."

If she disagreed, she'd be lying, and if she agreed, she'd be disloyal. What kind of man would say such a thing to another man's wife? "He enjoys his work at the shop."

"Man's got to find what he's good at, I suppose. Me, I was never much for farming, but it was that or go hungry."

She was not going to debate life choices with Abe Zook. "Is Lydia home?"

"Nope. Said she was going for a walk, but she was probably meeting that no-account Joshua Steiner. Now, there's a man who needs to find his work, and soon. Among other things."

"I don't think she'd be meeting Joshua," she said cautiously. "He's due over at our place anytime."

Abe snorted. "Don't know, then. Maybe she was telling the truth."

Carrie smiled vaguely and wished him good morning, then got into the buggy and beat a hasty retreat. No wonder Lydia took so many long walks. The state of the sitting room! Why, there were probably fourth-generation spiders spinning mansions in the ceiling corners, not to mention the furniture. If someone were to sit in one of those chairs, they would wind up flat on their behind on the floor. Either Lydia had no housekeeping skills at all, or she absented herself so much that Abe just shrugged and went outside.

But she was not here to teach her how to manage a household. She was here to help her be a mother.

God's ways certainly were far above her ways. Like Moses, she was the last person who should have been chosen for such a task. But the letters had gone out, and her course was set. Now all she had to do was find Lydia.

In the end, it was Jimsy who found her. Carrie was doing more thinking and fretting than driving, and he turned onto the hard-packed dirt track the harvest machinery used between the back forty of the Stolzfus place and Moses Yoder's field, which ran along the creek. It was a short cut she'd taken before, and clearly Jimsy was anxious to get back to his warm barn. Among the leafless trees it was easy to see Lydia's bright hair and her white *Kapp* moving slowly along the path.

In less than a minute, Carrie had tied Jimsy to a bare branch and was making her way down to the creek.

"Are you finding anything good?" she called cheerfully.

Lydia jumped—as though she hadn't heard Carrie slapping away branches and sliding the last three feet down the bank. "I'm not looking for anything. What are you doing here?"

"I'm the lucky one, then. I was looking for you. And a few clematis or wild-grape vines to make a Thanksgiving wreath with." She pointed to an overgrown thicket that partially blocked the creek bank. "Like that. Give me a hand, will you?"

Lydia bit back what was probably a comment on the state of Carrie's mental health, and reached up to pull on a likely-looking bit of vine, drying now and losing its pliability as winter breathed closer.

"That's it. *Denki.*" Carrie wound the vine into a circle, the way she might a garden hose, tucked the loose ends in, and slipped it over her arm. "I suppose you're wondering why I'm looking for you."

"I can guess."

"Guess, then." Carrie stopped to admire a cache of chestnuts that had rolled down the slope, and chose a few of the nicest ones. "I should have brought my basket. There's more down here than I was expecting. God is good that way, isn't He?"

"If you say so. I suppose Joshua told you after I told him not to."

"He's concerned about you, Lydia. As any good friend would be."

"Is that why you're here, getting your feet muddy? Because you're concerned?"

"*Ja.* I am."

"Well, that's nice, but I don't need anything."

"Have you seen a doctor?"

"*Nei.*"

"Are you taking your vitamins? Do you even know what ones to take?"

"*Nei.*"

"Then you do need something. In fact, I'd like you to come over on Wednesday afternoon. I've invited some of the women to sit down with us so you'll know who to turn to for the things you'll need."

"What women?" Lydia stopped picking through the bramble and straightened.

"Amelia, Mary Lapp, my sister Susan. A few others. Among them they've had nearly a dozen children. There won't be too much they don't know, and they want to share it with you."

"Thanks, but I'm okay."

"Lydia—"

"Carrie, look. I appreciate what you're trying to do, but I don't need it. In six months this baby will be born and everything will go back to normal."

The depth of her ignorance surprised a laugh out of Carrie. "My dear, you've got it backward. Nothing will ever be normal again. It will be so much better."

"For whoever adopts the baby, maybe. But for me, I'll be leaving and never coming back."

Again, that squeezing sensation around her heart. Carrie sucked in a big breath of cold air and tried to stay calm. "You're putting the child up for adoption? What about your family? What do they say?"

"What family? Daed? Are you kidding?"

She didn't dare say what was really in her mind, so instead she said mildly, "I was thinking of your aunt. I've asked her to come on Wednesday, too, because I didn't know any of your other female relatives."

"Thanks to my father, I don't either. But even if I had aunts coming out my ears, it wouldn't matter. This kid isn't growing up Amish."

Breathe. You have to breathe or you'll fall in the water. "Not Amish?"

"Nope. If they won't take it in the hospital, I'm going to leave it at the fire station on the way home. If I can't do anything else for it, at least I can make sure it doesn't grow up the way I did."

The daughter of Abe Zook.

"Lydia, not everyone is—has been hardened by life like your father. Some of us—I—would fall on my knees rejoicing to have a baby to care for."

For the first time, the hard lines of the girl's mouth softened. "I know you would. And I'm sorry. I hope you have a baby someday. But my mind is made up."

Carrie had a moment's vision of a tiny newborn on the cold steps of the fire hall, where men in great big boots clomped in and out and the sirens shrieked and it would be all too easy to lose the sound of a cry. All too easy to miss a tiny body until the cold stilled it. Even in early summer it could be cold.

Who could throw away her child?

Her stomach turned over. *Breathe. Don't be sick. O Lord, please give me the words.*

"Do you think an *Englisch* family would love it more than an Amish family?"

"I get along just fine without love." Before Carrie could think of a word to say to that, Lydia went o:. "I'm thinking of how she'll grow up. She'll be free of the *Ordnung*. Free of always being judged all the time. Free of having to do stupid things like drive a buggy. She'll grow up and get a driver's license like it's normal. Bake a cake in an electric oven. Wear high heels if she feels like it, or work boots if she doesn't." She chucked a chestnut across the creek, where it hit a tree with a *clack*. "I'm going to do all those things, too. Just as soon as I can get away from here."

"What about the baby's father? Wouldn't his family—"

"*Nei.*"

"Does…does he know?"

"Of course."

"Is he Amish?" She couldn't imagine any family allowing the baby to be left on the firehouse steps. Grandparents, aunts, and uncles would absorb the child into the family and make sure she grew up healthy and loved.

"*Nei.*"

It took a moment for this to sink in. "The father is *Englisch*?"

"If he's not Amish, he'd have to be, wouldn't he?"

Carrie made an effort not to react. This was an emotional time for a woman. Hormones were going crazy. A little rudeness could be forgiven. "And he thinks it's okay for his son or daughter to be adopted by strangers?"

"What's he going to do with a baby?"

"I don't know, Lydia. I don't know who it is, unless you're going to tell me."

"I'm not. I don't even know why I'm telling you what I have, except that everybody seems to tell you everything."

"I wouldn't say that."

"The girls say it. They know you don't pass things on." She chucked another chestnut and missed the tree this time. "Except for now. Your little get-together of women will have lots to chew over when you tell them, won't they?"

"I'd rather you came and told them yourself."

"No, thanks. They'd only preach at me and try to stop me. Especially Mary Lapp. Why did you invite her?"

"She already knew."

"What?" Lydia spun, her jade-green skirts swirling to catch up. "How? Did Joshua blab to her, too?"

"It's not a secret you can keep forever," Carrie told her a little dryly. "The older women have eyes, you know. They know the signs when they see them."

"They need something else to keep their minds occupied, then."

"They are occupied...with helping you. Please let us."

"*Nei*. There's no point."

"Are you afraid they'll talk you out of this?"

Lydia crossed her arms, her black quilted jacket making a soughing sound, like the rush of the creek behind them. "I'm not afraid of anything. Not anymore." She turned and took a few steps downstream, away from the buggy and the prospect of a ride home. "Thanks for the visit, Carrie. And for being concerned. But you should just go back to your *gut Mann* and your nice house and let it go."

Carrie watched her pick her way along the creek bank, then duck under a tree, where she was lost to sight around a bend.

The rush of the water filled her ears. Her lungs pulled in cold air and couldn't seem to warm it into breath.

She wondered if you could actually suffocate from grief.

CHAPTER 18

Groggy and out of sorts from a third night without sleep, Carrie made breakfast for herself and Melvin and wondered how she would get through the Sunday preaching and Council Meeting. At least they didn't have far to go; in fact, Melvin suggested they leave Jimsy in the barn and just walk across the frost-hardened fields to Abner Yoder's place, which bordered theirs on the east side.

He took her hand as they walked. "Are you all right, *Liebschdi*? I don't think you've been sleeping very well."

It was barely light enough to see, but dark enough to hide your face if that was what you wanted.

Carrie squeezed his hand. "Too much thinking and not enough sleeping."

"Thinking about what?" Caution crept into his voice.

"Not about that. I've put my IVF notions into God's hands. If it's His will, then Bishop Daniel will say something about it today during the *Abstellung*. If not, then I guess that will be my answer."

"But that was days and days ago that we talked about it and I told you how I felt. What is bothering you now?"

She couldn't tell him. If she did, and he said, oh, something crazy like, "Of course Abe would take the child in," or that he knew an *Englisch* family who would be glad to adopt, she didn't know what she would do. Fall to pieces and never come back together, maybe.

"I don't know. Winter. Weddings. Maybe I've overdone it lately."

"Maybe you have." They were almost to the yard, and the light was strong enough now that the buggies rolling in no longer needed their lamps on. "Tell you what. I have a surprise—one I was going to save until tomorrow so we could keep our minds on the Lord's Day. But maybe now would be a good time."

"A surprise?" Melvin cooked up lovely surprises. One time he'd kidnapped her in the buggy and taken her swimming at a lake some twelve miles away, abandoning his stubborn fields and her laundry. They'd played like children, and she'd done the washing on Tuesday instead. She'd been the only woman in the settlement with a row of dresses and shirts on the clothesline, but she didn't care.

"*Ja.* Turns out Brian wants me to go up to Rigby to the big RV factory, and talk them into buying our cabinetry for their high-end vehicles. I want you to come and we'll turn it into a little vacation."

"A vacation? In November?" She couldn't imagine what there would be to do in a big place like Rigby, which was all the way up by Pittsburgh.

"*Ja.* In a nice hotel, with a swimming pool. Brian said he would pay for two nights if I paid for the train ticket."

They were in the yard now, and this was a highly inappropriate conversation to be having on the way in to one of the holiest days of the year. "We'll talk about it at home."

Melvin nodded comfortably and stopped to talk with some of the men. Carrie went into the machine shed, which was huge and filled now with benches, and took her place among the married women. Though strictly speaking, she was supposed to sit between Christina Yoder and Erica Steiner, she fudged a little and slipped in next to Amelia.

"I've missed you," she whispered. "I can't wait for our time together on Tuesday."

"Neither can I," Amelia whispered back, "after that tempting little hint you gave out the other day."

After the preaching and the hymns, it was time for the *Abstellung*, whose purpose was to go over the *Ordnung*—the standards of behavior and the expectations to which the community held its members. Carrie had heard these same things since she was old enough to be carried into church in her mother's arms. Some of them were obvious—how a buggy was to be fitted out modestly, without a lot of reflectors or those looping strings of dangly things the boys were enamored with. How a home was to have no wiring, even if it was an English one that an Amish family had purchased. Some of them were not so obvious but were equally familiar—the number of pleats in a woman's dress, the width of a man's hat brim depending on whether he was married or not, or a church member or not. These things did not change from one year to another, especially with Bishop Daniel standing in the place of responsibility. He was a traditional man, and no modern changes such as generators in the back room of a house or rubber tires on buggy wheels would find their way into the community on his watch.

But at the end, after all the *Ordnung* had been spoken in order to remind the church of its example, the bishop would deal with the new and the troublesome. This was for Carrie the most interesting part—doubly interesting today, when he might bring up what had been lying so heavily on her heart.

The bishop fell silent and then lifted his head, as if beginning a new chapter. "I am placed in front of this room as the least among you," he said, "but I am given authority by God's grace and keeping. There are things I wish to talk of now that have been troubling to me. I hope they are troubling to the church, too. I have been in prayer a long time about them, and so have the ministers and preachers who serve at God's command and stand in the breach for the *Gmee.*"

In their places, Moses Yoder, Young Joe Yoder, and Abram Steiner nodded gravely.

"We have heard of some who have been considering going to worldly doctors to have procedures done that are contrary to the will of God. I will not go into details, but I will say that this seeking after *Englisch* technology to achieve a blessing that only God can give—the blessing of children—is a sin, and must not be considered by a man or woman who is a member of God's family."

Amelia's arm, which pressed softly against Carrie's because of the number of women on their bench, went rigid. Carrie bowed her head as her face flamed scarlet. She turned slightly toward her friend, who leaned against her in the most comforting of silent support.

Here was her answer. Sin.

She had expected it, known it would be this way, but some wild, fluttering hope in her heart had wondered if the result might be different—if God would speak to these men and help them see the question from a woman's point of view.

Yes, she'd put it in God's hands. But He could put it in the bishop's hands, couldn't He?

No, it seemed He could not. Had not.

The bishop's voice faded in and out. She caught snippets

of things like "colors becoming to modesty" and "tractor tires" and even "single curtains in the windows—two is over-doing it."

Then Amelia elbowed her sharply in the ribs and Carrie sat up. Bishop Daniel was giving the final blessing, and then he said, "Would all those who are not baptized into the family of God please leave us. We will have a members' meeting today."

This was unusual. Members' meetings happened several times a year, when the *Gmee* decided as a whole on matters brought before the church, following Jesus's words about two or three being gathered together in His name. But during Council Meeting, which had already gone nearly four hours with the *Abstellung*? What matters could be so urgent that they couldn't wait until after Christmas?

"—must wipe out sin from among ourselves and present each one a pure and living sacrifice to God. There is one among us who has committed sin. In order to keep her place among us, she must cleanse her conscience and present the truth to her brethren by means of public confession."

Not for worlds would Carrie look behind her for the one he was referring to. It just wasn't done. The congregation kept their heads bowed, as if to avoid looking upon the sinner—and the sin. Carrie heard the rustle of dresses and the tap of shoes as the *Youngie* and the unbaptized filed out.

"Lydia Zook, please do not leave. Please come forward and confess this sin on your knees before God and your brethren."

Carrie grabbed the bench on either side of her skirts, feeling as dizzy as if she were about to be thrown off it into a tossing sea. She needed to focus on something. The back of Selma Byler's apron would do.

Footsteps came slowly up the center aisle. A skirt swished. The soles of a woman's shoes scraped once, twice. She was kneeling.

"What sin do you come before your brethren to confess?" Bishop Daniel asked gently.

"Fornication," Lydia said in a voice so low and shaky Carrie hardly recognized it. The room was so quiet that her voice sounded clearly.

"And do you confess?"

Lydia's breath scraped in her throat. "I confess that I have sinned. I b-beg God and the *Gmee* for patience with me. F-from now on I will be more concerned and be more careful, with God's help."

"We hear your confession," the bishop said. "This sin…I understand it will bear fruit?"

"I will have a baby in June," she said, the words hitching on a sob. "I think. Thereabouts."

"And whose baby is this?"

Silence. Carrie held her breath.

"Lydia Zook, you kneel before God, Who knows what is in your heart. Whose baby is this?"

"No one you know. A—a summer boy. A tourist. He's gone."

Skirts rustled as people shifted on the hard benches. Carrie exhaled. An *Englisch* boy, she had said, who knew he was to be a father and had chosen not to acknowledge it, leaving Lydia alone.

"Lydia Zook, please step outside while God's people take counsel together."

The girl practically fled down the aisle. The shed door closed behind her with a bang.

Bishop Daniel regarded his flock. "The elders and I have

consulted on this matter. Lydia Zook has not yet been baptized, but all the same, the Bible is firm on the subject of fornication. With prayer and fasting, we have come to the conclusion that she should be shut out of the body of Christ for the space of six months, until after her baby is born. Do you agree with this remedy?"

One by one, the members responded. "*Ja*, I agree," Carrie said when it was her turn, echoing the voices around her.

When everyone had agreed, the bishop glanced at Abe Zook, who went to the door and called his wayward daughter. His thin cheeks were as pale as granite.

"Lydia Zook," Bishop Daniel said to her, "know that you are not under *die Meinding*, but are excluded from fellowship and communion with your brothers and sisters until after your baby is born. You will take admonition from the ministers humbly and with grace, and you will attend church and sit here in the front row, where all may see you. Do you accept these consequences?"

She nodded, and returned to her seat in silence. The bishop announced the final hymn, and while Carrie's mouth moved with the familiar words, her mind was churning.

The rebellious teenager by the creek yesterday had not been in the frame of mind for confession. Had old Abe Zook forced her to do this? And why so fast? On the very rare occasions that someone had to undergo a public confession, there was at least a couple of weeks between the announcement of it and the performing of it, so that the person could repent privately before the elders and not have to make a spectacle of herself.

Were they making an example of Lydia, to keep the *Youngie* in line? Though, Carrie had to say, there weren't a lot of rebels in Whinburg—not like in some districts, where fast living and cars and all-night parties presented temptations the young people couldn't resist.

Carrie shook her head and filed out with the others when the service was over. What was done was done, and it was none of her business anyway. What was her business had been dealt with during the *Abstellung*.

And that was enough for anyone to handle for one day.

* * *

Aleta Miller whipped a kitchen apron off its hook on the back of the pantry door. She tied it behind her with movements so jerky that the fabric practically snapped.

"That man." The frying pan barely missed the fruit basket as she banged it onto the stove. "Of all the performances I ever saw in my life...that poor girl."

"It's not the first time one of the *Youngie* has had to make a confession," Carrie ventured, staying well clear of the pan and concentrating on slicing the potatoes to go in it.

"Maybe not, but there aren't too many who have had to do it practically the day the bishop found out." The fat sizzled briskly, and Carrie put the potatoes in, unsure which would hurt worse—her mother-in-law's uncertain temper or the bacon grease. She stepped away from both.

"Abe Zook is behind this, I'm sure of it."

"What makes you say that?" It wasn't like he was one of the elders, or ran the biggest farm in the district, or was even related to the Lapps. Abe Zook probably had less influence in the community than Carrie herself. Meaning, next to none.

"I don't know, but I'm this close to marching over there and giving him a piece of my mind."

"Bishop Daniel?"

"No. Abe."

"Maybe he didn't want to be shut out from communion along with her." Sometimes that happened—with an offense as serious as fornication, the parents were held responsible for the behavior of their wayward offspring who had not yet joined church, and underwent the same discipline. It was surprising how quickly the child shaped up when the consequences of his wrongdoing spread to his family.

"Maybe," Aleta conceded. "But I didn't like the look on his face. It was almost as though ... he was glad."

Aleta had been looking around during the whole episode? Other than one quick glance when he'd gone out, Carrie had not had that much nerve.

"He couldn't have been. That's a terrible thing to say."

"I saw what I saw." Aleta pounded egg and oatmeal into the meat loaf as though she had Abe's head under her hands. "And I don't like it one bit. Something is going on there that shouldn't be, I know it."

Melvin came in from the barn looking for his supper then, and the subject dropped.

But Carrie turned it over in her mind, looking at it from all angles the way she looked at the apples to see if they were ripe yet, and by Tuesday, the sight of Amelia and Emma was a relief.

They had progressed to quilting the feathers on the borders of the quilt, which twined around their central column so gracefully they looked like the furled wings of angels. "By the time Emma gets back from *die Flitterwoch*, we'll be finished," Amelia said with satisfaction. "This has to be the longest quilt project Whinburg has ever seen."

"Or not seen, as the case may be." Emma stitched with

serene concentration. "I have no problem with my wedding quilt being for Grant's and my eyes only."

"It makes me happy to think you'll be sleeping under something that has part of all three of us in it."

"Though I do wish we'd got it done by your wedding day." Amelia stitched carefully into one of the corners. "I suppose we could have if we'd been stitching more than talking."

"At the time, the talking was more important," Emma said. "I don't know what I would have done without Tuesday afternoons. When we finish this one, we'll have to start a new one."

"A baby quilt for Lydia Zook." The words popped out of Carrie's mouth before the idea was much more than a bud. "Goodness knows that girl hasn't much else."

"She'll have all she needs after we get together tomorrow," Amelia said. "I'm sure it will comfort her to know she's not alone in this, even if it might have felt that way on Sunday."

What happened in the members' meeting was supposed to stay in the members' meeting, but Amelia filled Emma in on the details anyway. Carrie reflected that nobody seemed to be paying much attention to that rule lately.

"I don't think she's coming," she said.

"Not coming?" Emma's stitches halted. "How can she not come? Does she have to work?"

"Maybe. I don't know. I went to see her on Saturday and she told me to mind my own business."

"She'll be sorry she said that when her back aches and she has to let out all her dresses," Amelia said. "What foolishness—to turn down help when it's offered freely? What is she thinking?"

"I don't believe she is thinking," Carrie said. "It sounds

like she's going to ignore the unpleasant fact that she's getting fatter, not bother with a doctor until it's time to have the baby, and leave it there in the hospital."

"For what?" Amelia looked honestly perplexed. "Is there something wrong with it? How would she know if she won't go to the doctor?"

"For adoption," Carrie said quietly. "By *Englisch* people."

Amelia's face lost its color. Even her hands, flat and motionless on the quilt top, looked as though the blood had drained from them. "She's giving up the baby to the *Englisch*?"

Carrie told them what she'd learned there in the creek bed, and the facts lost none of their sting in the retelling. She felt emotionally bruised once the last word had fallen into the quiet room.

"How could she?" Amelia whispered at last. "And you right there practically offering to give her child a loving home. How *could* she?"

"She's desperate," Emma said. "Desperately unhappy, emotional, and not thinking straight. She'll change her mind. Surely when the little baby is put into her arms, she'll decide to do what's right."

"What's right for Lydia, or what's right for the baby?" Carrie couldn't keep the bitterness out of her tone. "I have to say that taking it home to Abe Zook's tender mercies doesn't seem like the right thing for anyone."

"What a mess." Emma watched Amelia from under her lashes. "Amelia, are you all right?"

"I'm sorry." Amelia picked up her needle. "I'm shocked, that's all. I didn't think one of our—I mean, it seems so heartless, just to leave the child there as though it were one of those paper gowns you leave behind on the table when you're finished with your examination." Tears welled in her eyes. "We have to change her mind. We can't let this happen."

"It's her baby," Carrie said.

"It's a soul born into God's family," Amelia retorted. "We can't give up on her for the baby's sake. *You* can't give up."

"Me?"

"*Ja*, you. If she's determined to put it up for adoption, then you should be the one to adopt it."

"But I'm not *Englisch*," Carrie said, "and not likely to be by June."

"That's crazy talk. Of course the child should grow up Amish. It's his or her birthright. All we have to do is convince her."

"You're welcome to try. I practically got down on my hands and knees to beg her, and it didn't do any good."

"We'll work on it from all sides." Color was coming back into Amelia's face the more the idea took hold. "The men can work on Abe Zook, and the women on Lydia."

"What do you mean, 'work on'?" What was wrong with her? Carrie asked herself. She should be diving headfirst into plans to bring Lydia around to their way of thinking, not finding reasons to stay out of the metaphorical orchard—and all those painful tree trunks.

"A continual dropping on a rainy day," Amelia said. "We just won't let up until she agrees to either keep the baby or allow you and Melvin to adopt it."

"Wait a minute." Emma held up the hand with the needle in it. "Does Melvin want to adopt Lydia's baby?"

"I haven't talked about it with him. I mean, he knows she's pregnant, of course, after Sunday, but he doesn't know anything other than that the news upset me." She paused, uncertain about whether to tell them the next part. But these were her friends. They had bared their souls to her more than once, and had held her while she wept over her own short-comings as many times. "His mother is all in favor, though. In fact, she was the first one to bring up the idea of an adoption."

"Aleta?" Amelia sat back in astonishment. "She is the last person I would have—"

"—seen downstairs," Emma put in smoothly. "I heard her come in a few minutes ago."

As though she'd been waiting for her name to come up, Aleta climbed the stairs and stood in the doorway watching them load their needles as industriously as though they'd been working all along.

"It's a nice quilt," she said at last. "Is it for the auction?"

"It's my wedding quilt," Emma told her. "We've been working on it for a year."

Aleta's eyebrows rose. "Seems you would have had half a dozen made in that time." She raised a hand when Carrie took a breath to explain. "But I know how it is. It's what we talk about while we quilt, sometimes, that's as important as the patches and stitches."

"That's how I feel, too," Emma said. "So I hear you're in favor of Carrie and Melvin giving a needy child a home?"

"I just got back from seeing Abe Zook."

Carrie could swear she felt the floor heave, her surprise was so great. "But I thought you didn't want him to think—"

"This is not about me," Aleta said briskly. "It's about what's best for that child." She didn't specify whether she meant the baby or Lydia.

Amelia pulled over a chair, reached into her sewing box, and handed Aleta a needle. "Come. Join us."

Any other week but this, Carrie would have jumped up

with an excuse to get her mother-in-law out of the room. To not sully the stitches in their quilt with those of a stranger— or someone who wasn't a kindred soul. But somehow, Aleta seemed to have changed. Or perhaps Carrie herself had.

Carrie couldn't put her finger on it, but she seemed less critical, less vigilant about Carrie's faults, and more inclined to lend a hand or a piece of advice. Even though her tactics hadn't changed—she was still as sharp as vinegar. But the vinegar tasted more mellow somehow.

With one glance, Aleta took in the direction of Amelia's stitching and began on the other end of the panel. Her stitches were close and even—ten to the inch, for sure.

"I was lucky enough to find him in the barn," Aleta said, picking up where she'd left off. "Trapped between his horses and the buggy, where he couldn't weasel past me."

"Was he inclined to weasel?" Emma asked.

"I'd say so. He couldn't do it physically, so he laid into me verbally." Aleta snorted. "As though he was ever any competition in that department. 'You just listen to me, Abe Zook,' I said. 'What do you mean by looking so happy when your girl had to humble herself before the whole *Gmee?*' And you know what he said? That even the Lord rejoiced when one of His own humbled herself before Him. The nerve! As though he had personal insight into the infinite mind of the *gut Gott.*"

"He was happy?" Amelia echoed. "Not ashamed?"

"Not happy," Aleta told her. "To my mind, he was gloating, and there's just no cause for that, no matter what your child has done."

"So then what did you say?" Emma asked.

"I learned a long time ago that Abe Zook holds a short fuse and a long grudge," Aleta replied. "I counted the cost, and then I decided I'd rather get to the bottom of this and risk offending him than play nice. So I set out to rile him." A smile touched lips that were usually pressed together, whether from annoyance at the world or a desire not to voice that annoyance—Carrie could never decide.

"You riled Abe Zook on purpose?" Amelia shook her head. "You're a braver woman than I."

"I just know him better. 'Abe,' I said, 'Rachel would have been ashamed of you. She never meant for Lydia to grow up this way—running around and looking for attention from who knows who because you never had time for her.' Well, that was all it took. I thought he was going to strike me."

Carrie gave up all pretense of stitching, and even Amelia poked her needle into the quilt and left it, eyes wide.

"But instead, that fuse got itself lit well and proper. 'You know nothing about it, woman!' he roared at me like I was standing half a mile away instead of right there in his barn. Which was as neat as though he was about to have church in it. Have you seen the house? My stars. I went there first, and a hasty retreat I made down those steps. Anyway. Where was I?"

"Being shouted at," Emma prompted.

"So I was. 'I know a thing or two,' I told him. 'I know that girl is starved for love, and she wouldn't have been chasing after it from any summer tourist if you'd brought her up with a shake of it now and again.' So then you won't believe what he said." She didn't wait for anyone to answer. "'If that girl was my own, I'd have loved her the way a child is supposed to be loved. But if she's chasing everything in pants, then she comes by it honest. Her mother was no better.'"

Carrie gasped. "How could he say that? His own wife!"

"He married Rachel," Aleta allowed. "But according to

him, she was expecting when he asked her. Expecting another man's baby."

A long breath eased from Carrie's lungs. There it was. An old mistake, an old deception...and a lifetime of retaliation and misery. *The sins of the fathers shall be visited on the children.*

"A man with red hair?" Emma asked after a long moment.

"Many a woman has had a baby come early," Aleta said. "But it's hard to explain away hair like that when there are no redheads within three or four generations, and your husband is no slouch between the ears."

"How cruel," Carrie breathed. "None of that is Lydia's fault. How could he blame her for her mother's sins?"

"You don't think he—" Amelia stopped. "No. I'm sorry. That is wicked, to even say such a thing aloud. Please forgive me."

"Let Rachel die of that infection on purpose?" Aleta's gaze into the past was as grim as the lowering sky outside. "Only God and Abe himself know that—and I'm thinking Abe would never face that head on. Because that would make him an even greater sinner than his wife, and he's gone his whole life putting her down and raising himself up."

"I can't think about this," Carrie whispered. "It's too horrible. If it's even true."

"It's true she died," Aleta said. "And it's true their marriage was unhappy. And it's true he said those things to me. Draw what conclusions you like." Her tone softened. "That man needs our prayers. Maybe God will bring him to confession—even if God Himself is the only one who can hear."

"I hope she does get away," Emma said suddenly. "Lydia, I mean. Carrie is right. That's no house to bring an innocent child into. I wish she didn't feel there's only one road open to her, but there it is. If she can't take care of her baby, then we need to make it clear to her that Carrie can."

Aleta took a breath, but Carrie forestalled her. "I'll talk to Melvin. We're to go up to Rigby on Thursday, coming back Saturday, so he can talk to this man about cabinets in his RVs. I'll do it then."

They had never discussed adoption before, but she had no reason to believe he wouldn't be open to it. After all, it was a far better option than IVF when it came to the will of God—many Amish families adopted children who had lost their parents to accidents and disasters.

If she had Melvin on her side, and the women of the community, surely it would only be a matter of time before Lydia would be convinced, too.

CHAPTER 19

Carrie had learned how to wait in a rigorous school. She had waited on weather to bring rain and sun for the garden that would sustain them through the winter. She had waited on human nature when it seemed that all that stood between her and hunger was the compassion of her neighbors. And she had waited on God to send her the one thing she prayed for—a child.

So waiting to speak until they'd traveled up to Rigby and Melvin had had his meeting with the RV man was easy by comparison. Brian had provided enough money for supper in the hotel restaurant, which was good, because the last of the cold meat and other supplies she'd brought in the little cooler had gone for their breakfast this morning. But two suppers were paid for, and from the relaxed look on Melvin's face, the talks had gone well.

"He's ninety percent convinced that we should have the work." Melvin settled back in the red leatherlike booth and spread the menu out in front of him. "He'll travel down to Whinburg next week, which will give us time to make a few different prototypes." A wry expression settled around his mouth. "What we really need is an old RV that we can remodel, but what would we do with it afterward?"

"Rent it out to someone's hired man?" Carrie smiled and settled on a Reuben sandwich, her favorite. And fries. She hoped there was a nice pile of fries as big as the sandwich. She was ravenous. "Or use it for a fancy chicken house."

He laughed. "Trust you to say something like that. I'm glad Joshua is able to look after your birds while we're gone."

"They don't need much looking after for just two days. I filled the feeders and the waterers and left them a heap of peelings. But it makes me feel comfortable that someone is looking in on them."

"He'll have the barn loft floor roughed in by the time I get back, and we can finish it together once the snow starts falling."

They gave their orders, and when their meals came, Carrie finished her sandwich before Melvin was halfway through his lasagna. She simply couldn't wait a moment longer.

"Hungry, *Liebschdi*?" He eyed her plate with amusement.

"I was, and it was *gut*. But mostly I wanted to talk to you about something without my mouth being full."

"And what's that? I've hardly let you get a word in edgewise, have I, with all my business talk?"

So she told him. About Abe and Rachel, about Lydia and her plans, and about the idea that she and his mother had been led to through both compassion and conviction.

"My mother?" He laid down his fork. "I think this must be the first time the two of you have agreed on anything."

"Second time," Carrie said, twinkling at him. "Both of us agree her watermelon pickles are far better than mine."

But he did not smile back. "But you're content to go along with this...this plan you've hatched up, you and my mother and all the women, all without asking me?"

"Of course not." Carrie shifted on the booth seat. It was too soft. It swallowed her in a hollow that others had made, and didn't let her sit up straight. "This all may come to nothing anyway if I can't convince Lydia that leaving her baby on the firehouse steps is a bad idea."

"So you come to me with it now."

"*Ja.* We've never really talked about adoption. And now with—with the IVF idea given up, I wondered how you felt about it."

He opened his mouth just as the waitress came and collected their plates. Carrie felt bad that she had not thought to stack them neatly, but the girl didn't seem to mind. She loaded everything on one arm, said, "I'll be back with more coffee," and wound her way out of sight.

"I can't talk about this here," Melvin said. "Too many people listening, too much noise."

Carrie choked back her dissatisfaction that he had not given her an answer while he paid the bill and even as they were walking upstairs to their room. But when the door closed behind her, she couldn't keep it back any longer.

"Do you think we can do this, Melvin? If Lydia agrees? It could take us months to convince her, but in the end I hope she'll—"

"Do you want to know what I think?"

She resisted the urge to say, *Wasn't that what I just asked?* Instead, she merely nodded.

"I think this desire for children has become unhealthy. Carrie, you know my feelings on this. If it is God's will that we become parents, then we will. But all this running after first one idea, then another…it has to stop." He took a breath as though trying to control himself. "You break my heart, *Liebschdi*. One crazy plan after another, when if you'd just find peace in accepting God's will, you would be so much happier."

"I am accepting God's will. He keeps putting opportunities in front of me and I am following them."

"The devil is throwing temptations in front of you, you mean. Eavesdropping on two women in a shop is not an opportunity from God. Witnessing the shame of a girl who can't say no to temptation is not, either. Listening to those who sin is no way to seek God's will. It's just the opposite."

How he twisted her words! "And what is listening to your mother? Is that a sin?"

"Much as I love my mother, I also know her faults. She is a widow who loves to meddle in the lives of her children. All of us know that. And you weren't so slow to see her faults not so long ago."

"We're becoming better friends," Carrie managed around the lump in her throat. "So you will not do this with me, either? Is that it? We can only become parents in the one way—your way—despite my feelings about it?"

"There is only one way to become parents, Carrie."

"Don't treat me like a child. Of course there isn't. Lots of our families adopt—why, look at Young Joe's youngest daughter. She and her husband adopted his sister's children after their parents died in that pileup on the freeway."

"That's different. That's family. Not the random offspring of a child who will never know his father—or his grandfather, for that matter. The child has bad blood, and I don't want it under my roof."

Now we are getting to the truth.

"The child is not responsible for the sins of his parents." She and Melvin never argued, and she never raised her voice to him. Then who was this red-faced virago she could see in the mirror over the desk, whose voice was perilously close to being audible in the next room?

"Maybe not, but his parents can certainly be responsible for him. Lydia must take care of her own mistake, and if she cannot, then it is good that an *Englisch* family will make a home for it, and keep this sin out of the church."

Maybe he would make sense to Daniel Lapp—or Abe Zook—but her own beloved was making no sense to Carrie. "And this is your decision?"

"*Ja*. It is, Fraa. Be content in His will, and God will provide." He tried to take her in his arms, but she shrugged out of them and went into the bathroom.

The water in the gleaming shower was gloriously hot, and never-ending. But it didn't do much to wash away the tears that stung her eyes. She squeezed them shut, closing out the bright electric lights and the glint of the steel faucet and taps.

Behind her lids, the darkness of the orchard stretched on and on in front of her. And everywhere she looked, there were trees.

* * *

Emma had written a piece for *Family Life* not so long ago about back sides—the back sides of people's houses, the back sides of their businesses—the things you saw from the train and not the road. The messes people left where they thought others wouldn't see them.

Carrie had hardly been aware of them on the way up. It was true she hadn't been that excited about the trip in the beginning, but the novelty of traveling so far with Melvin and excitement over how she would broach the adoption plan had overshadowed things like back sides.

Unfortunately, she had no such happy thoughts to occupy her mind on the trip home. Mess after mess slid by the train windows, to the point where she wondered if there was any beauty left along the whole line, from Pittsburgh to New York City.

Melvin spent the two-hour trip sketching and making notes of his conversations with the RV man. She put on a brave face and smiled when it was required, but the only real smile of the whole day was getting home to the chickens. Dinah and the others were glad to see her—she was away from home so rarely that they weren't used to it.

"Did you think I'd been eaten by a coyote?" she said into Dinah's feathers as she cuddled the bird, then put her on her roost. "I'm safe, and so are you."

She had to snap out of it. Was this how her life was going to be now? A roller coaster of highs and lows as hope was kindled and then extinguished? One temptation after another until her strength was exhausted?

Lord, I already put this matter of babies in Your hands. I don't understand. Am I reading too much into the people you send me—reading signs and wonders where none exist? Help me, Lord. I don't think I can do this anymore. Please give me the peace Melvin talks about. Or at the very least, some sleep.

She shouldn't have been so surprised, that night in her own bed, when she slept deeply and woke feeling refreshed. The *gut Gott* answered prayers, she knew that. Little ones and large ones, He heard them all. She just needed to have more faith in His plan for her.

Faith is the substance of things hoped for, the evidence of things not seen.

The Lord knew what she hoped for. She just needed to believe in what was hidden from her right now, that was all.

She read that verse after breakfast, when she and Melvin and Aleta lingered in the kitchen over their coffee. Aleta was seven eighths of the way through her annual reading of *The Martyrs' Mirror*, and Melvin read the German bible with quiet concentration. Carrie loved the off-Sunday mornings... the peace, the knowledge that it was the Lord's Day to rest in and savor, without the bustle of getting ready for church.

Aleta looked up from her reading, removed her glasses, and regarded her son. "Has Carrie spoken with you about Lydia and her baby, Melvin?"

It took him a moment to surface from God's word and bring his mind back to the kitchen table. "*Ja*, she did. And we agreed that this was another crazy plan, and she should seek peace in waiting on the will of God."

"She agreed to that, did she?"

Carrie resisted the urge to take Aleta by the arm and hustle her outside for a quick summary of the situation. "I did," she said quietly instead. "And I feel at peace—I must, because I finally got a good night's sleep."

Aleta made a noise halfway between a snort and a cough. "I don't believe it. *Ja*"—she held up a hand—"I know you're being a good Amish wife and submitting to your husband, but Melvin, you remember there's another side to that verse."

"I remember."

"*Husbands, love your wives as your own flesh.* Is it so easy to make the desire for a child go away in your own body, son?"

Melvin closed the Scripture. "Mamm, this is a matter between Carrie and me. I appreciate that you're supporting her in this adoption scheme, but I've already made up my mind. I don't want the child of some nameless *Englisch* boy growing up in my home, bringing who knows what bad blood with it."

"You make it sound like it would have some kind of disease. He or she would just be a baby. A baby who needs love and food and a warm home."

"And I hope the child finds it." He gazed at her. "But I'll hear no more about it, Mamm. This is one bowl you can't put your spoon into and mix things up. I've said my say, and that's that."

"And you would take away Carrie's dream so easily?"

His cheeks reddened. Oh dear.

"It's my dream, too, Mamm. Don't make me into the villain here."

"You're allowing your imagination to run away with you. You, my boy, are making an innocent child into some kind of juvenile delinquent, ready to poison the well and burn down the house."

"I can't help how I feel."

"No. Well, neither can I. And I feel your wife has the right of it, and you're being a stubborn mule who is letting pride get in the way of giving a needy child a loving home. Maybe the women of this community can't convince that girl to do one good and right thing. Fine. But I would have expected more of you." She pushed away from the table. "Maybe you'd be kind enough to call an *Englisch* taxi."

His mouth fell open. "On Sunday? Are you going somewhere?"

"I am going home."

Carrie finally found her tongue. "But you were staying for Thanksgiving."

Aleta's face softened in a way Carrie had rarely seen before. "I'm finding it difficult to count my blessings right now. I can't stay and not be tempted every single day to bring this matter up until Melvin yields. And that's not right. He is the head of this household, and in order to respect that, I must take myself back to my own."

"Mamm, *nei*," Melvin protested. "I won't have you leaving on such bad terms."

"I'm not." She put a comforting hand on his shoulder on her way past his chair. "But if I stay, I might, and that would be a shame. I'll pack my bags and see if I can get the noon train. If not, I know there's a bus."

And nothing they could say would change her mind. That was the Millers all over. Once they turned all the information over until there was nothing left to examine, they made a decision and stuck with it.

The taxi came and Carrie clutched her shawl tightly around her as Aleta turned in the backseat to wave a final good-bye through the rear window. "I wish she hadn't gone," she said. "It isn't right."

"She's gone plenty of times before, and I've never heard you say that." The angry color had long faded from Melvin's face, and she had a feeling he wished he hadn't spoken so harshly to his mother.

But what was done was done.

"It's true," Carrie admitted. "But I never felt I had a friend in her before. Isn't it strange that it's taken more than ten years for me to see her good qualities?"

"Then at least someone has learned something from this experience." And Melvin turned and walked across the yard. The barn door closed behind him with a hollow sound.

He found his refuge in his horses and his tack and the sweet smell of old summer in the hay.

She found hers in the chickens and their innocent companionship and the simple joys they found in garden and orchard.

Why couldn't they find their refuge in each other?

Carrie was afraid to look at such a question too closely, in case she found the answer.

CHAPTER 20

Thank goodness Tuesday came before Wednesday, which meant Carrie could gather strength and grace from quilting with Amelia and Emma before she met with the women of the community.

With the trip up to Rigby and everything that had happened, sending out another flock of notes to cancel the meeting had not occurred to her even once, and by the time Emma brought it up toward the end of their frolic, it was too late to call it off.

So, on Wednesday at two, Carrie held open the door just long enough for the rain and wind to push women through it, and slammed it behind them. Amelia and Emma came together, bringing Amelia's mother, Ruth Lehman. Carrie's sister Susan picked up Mary Lapp, and then collected Lydia's aunt, Priscilla Bontrager, at the Whinburg bus station on their way in. And to Carrie's surprise, Esther Grohl brought her youngest sister, Sarah—she who had been seeing Alvin Esch.

"She and Lydia used to be friendly, before all this happened," Esther explained as she took off her coat and black away bonnet, both dripping with rain. "She wanted to help."

Carrie slipped an arm around the girl's waist and squeezed her. "I'm sure she can."

She'd been up at five that morning baking, so there was a carrot cake, juicy with canned pineapple and raisins, three kinds of pie, and a blueberry coffee cake with a cinnamon streusel topping. Everyone had brought something—even Sarah opened her navy-and-pink backpack and shyly offered to cut the banana loaf inside if Carrie would lend her a knife.

When everyone had a mug of coffee and a plate of something to enjoy, and had settled on the sofa and various kitchen chairs in the sitting room, Carrie cleared her throat, before everyone got to visiting and forgot the reason they were all there.

"*Denki*, everyone, for coming. I know you're busy and have households and hungry men to get back to before long."

"Aren't you going to wait for Lydia?" Mary Lapp asked.

"And Aleta?" Ruth Lehman angled her head to look down the hall, as though Aleta would step out of the guest room at the sound of her name.

"My mother-in-law went home a few days ago," Carrie said steadily, "and Lydia said she would not be coming."

Mary sat back in her chair. "Well, I wish I'd known that. It's a little hard to make plans for a baby without its mother here."

"Carrie couldn't exactly drive over there and force her into the buggy," Susan pointed out. "Besides, we can help whether she wants us to or not. There are all kinds of things we can do."

Priscilla Bontrager looked from one face to another. Carrie had made sure she knew everyone's names, but the woman hadn't taken much part in the chatter over the plates of sweets. She was maybe thirty-eight or thirty-nine, with dark hair and a sweet, rounded face under her organdy *Kapp*. Her eyes were brown and filled with apprehension. And in the downward tilt of her eyelids, in the crow's-feet at the corners of her eyes, lay sadness—the kind she had lived with a long time. The kind that you don't expect will ever leave, so you just get used to bearing it.

Maybe that was what made Carrie say, "Priscilla, Lydia is your niece. Maybe you could tell us the best way to help her—even if she's adamant that she doesn't want any help."

Priscilla swallowed a mouthful of coffee as though it would give her courage. "I don't know where to start," she said hoarsely, then coughed and went on, "I haven't seen Lydia since she was twelve."

Someone drew a sharp breath.

"I know that sounds terrible, but it's the truth. I only live fifteen miles away, but it might as well be fifteen hundred." She looked out the window at the rain, which was now sheeting sideways with the violence of the wind. The big window shuddered under the fist of it. "Our family is small. My parents were old when they had Rachel and me—we're twins—and they're gone now. So is my older sister. After Rachel's death"—her eyes filled with tears—"well, the doctors say it was pneumonia, but I know full well my dad died of grief, and Mamm wasn't long behind him." She sat straighter, and blinked several times. "I'm sorry. You didn't ask for ancient history."

Aleta would have asked whether the family thought Abe Zook had allowed his wife to die. How many of the women in the room were silently wondering the same thing? But such a question could never be asked—or answered—in public.

"Lydia has told Carrie that she plans to give the baby up

to an *Englisch* family for adoption," Susan said gently. "She says she wants it raised *Englisch*, not Amish. But if she could be convinced not to do that, are you able to take the child? You're her closest relative that we know of."

Carrie drew a breath at the sharpness of the pain that lanced through her. Amelia and Emma both slid concerned glances her way. How could Susan ask such a thing?

But then, in all fairness, Susan didn't know that Carrie wanted the baby. Her question was natural. Right. It had to be asked.

But oh, how it hurt!

"My husband works at a shop in Strasburg, making things out of wood for the tourists. I sell quilts out of our home, and we have eight children in a four-room house. Of course I would take the poor little *Bobbel*, but..." Her voice trailed off while the picture she had painted resonated in the mind's eye of everyone in the room.

Carrie felt a moment's guilt at having three bedrooms for only two people in this big farmhouse when this woman would probably thank God rejoicing if she only had a lean-to out back to put some of the children in.

Then again, if Carrie had eight children to love, she would thank God rejoicing, too.

"Of course you would," Mary Lapp said. "But if perhaps there was a home that had not yet been blessed with children, would you consider allowing them to adopt?"

"Adopt my niece or nephew? My sister's grandchild?" The color faded from Priscilla's cheeks, then flooded back in. "I don't know. Perhaps it won't come to that. Perhaps Lydia will change her mind when her baby is put into her arms."

"And perhaps she won't." Esther Grohl glanced at her teenage sister. "Tell them what she told you, Sarah."

Sarah blushed scarlet at having to speak in front of a roomful of women who were older and had more responsibility than she. "She...she said her baby wasn't going to grow up Amish, and if she had to take the bus into Lancaster to have it at the county hospital, she would."

"Why would she do that when we have a perfectly good hospital right close to Whinburg?" Ruth asked.

"Anonymity," Emma said. "A big, bustling hospital where you could give a false name on the way in and leave with no one being the wiser."

"I think they would be the wiser," Ruth said. "Has that girl ever been in a hospital to have a baby? Have you, for that matter? I don't think that would happen."

"Of course not," Emma said with admirable calm. Ruth didn't mean to be offensive, Carrie was sure. But she, Aleta, and Mary were afflicted with the habit of telling the truth without grace, and you just had to take it into account. "But I can see how a teenager would have these ideas."

"Let's deal with those difficulties when we get to them," Amelia suggested. "How are we going to help Lydia now?"

"She's not taking any vitamins," Carrie offered, "and I can't get her to promise to see the doctor. That seems like the first thing to sort out, I think."

"The baby's not going to thrive on a diet of pizza and potatoes, that's certain." Mary Lapp gave an emphatic nod. "I'll make it my business to get her to Doctor Stewart in town. After she cured Amelia, she can do anything, maybe even get a teenager to take her folic acid."

"She didn't actually cure me," Amelia said gently. "She just gave me the right diagnosis."

"Regardless." Mary Lapp went on with majestic disregard for fine details. "That doctor's young, too, and red-headed.

Maybe Lydia will take to her. On the subject of food, I can organize a group to bring something nutritious for supper several days a week."

"She can cook," Sarah Grohl offered.

"I'm sure she can, but not when she's working at the fabric store or gadding about in the evenings. We'll look after that. What else?"

"I think the bishop should have a word with Abe Zook," Ruth said. "Abe might not be a help, but we don't want him being a hindrance, either. I don't relish the thought of holding a hot casserole and being chased off his porch for my trouble."

"I'd better start writing these down." Mary Lapp fished in her handbag and brought out a pen and a wrinkled envelope.

"The baby will need clothes and blankets," Susan said.

"We're starting a quilt next week," Carrie told her. "Emma's wedding quilt will be finished, and that's next on our list." Amelia and Emma both turned their heads to stare at her, and she smiled brightly. "A pretty watercolor nine-patch will go together quickly, don't you think?"

"It'd better," Ruth Lehman muttered. "At the rate you three sew, the child will be in school before she gets it."

Carrie's smile grew broader, and the twinkle came back to Emma's eyes as she said, "We'll have it done in a month, I promise."

Susan said, "I have lots of baby clothes saved from when the girls were small. Anything that's missing, I can sew. Tiny garments go together quickly."

Mary Lapp looked up from her notes. "Anything else? What about a crib and changing table?"

Amelia said, "I can lend those. I have them in the attic. Diapers, too."

"You saved diapers?" Carrie said curiously.

Amelia shrugged. "You never know when God will open His hand and send another blessing."

The women looked at one another with interest. Clearly Amelia and Eli were thinking of children of their own. Amelia didn't miss it, either. She blushed and concentrated on finishing up her slice of pumpkin pie.

"I would like to give her some baby clothes, too," Priscilla said softly, diverting everyone's attention. "Mamm saved some of Rachel's little things. Maybe Lydia would like to have them."

"If we can convince her to keep the baby," Ruth Lehman reminded them. "We should focus on getting her to take care of herself before the birth. If she really does give it up, then she'll have no use for clothes and changing tables."

In the excitement of planning for a new baby, even Carrie had forgotten the possibility that it might not come home. A cold feeling tiptoed down her back. Surely with all the love and concern in this room, Lydia could be convinced to do the right thing?

And how could Carrie pray for the girl to keep her child, when she herself wanted to give the baby a home so badly it hurt?

* * *

Carrie had been looking forward to a family Thanksgiving, with Aleta accompanying them to the King homestead, which her parents had been farming now for forty years. Her mother, Miriam, loved it when all her chicks were back in the nest, particularly when they brought their children, and other relatives came in from outlying areas of the district. The table just expanded to fit everyone, making a big U-shape between the dining room and sitting room.

For Carrie, this year's family dinner was overshadowed by Aleta's absence—which she would never have imagined in a hundred years. Was it because she had wanted to cultivate that tiny sprig of friendliness between them? Or because it seemed that Aleta was the only one close to Melvin who really saw things from her side?

The temptation to spill out her desire to adopt to her mother and sisters as they worked side by side to cook the dinner was overwhelming, but she hauled it back. If she said anything, negative things about Melvin's refusal to consider it would come out, not to mention the real reason Aleta had gone home. Loyalty prevented it. It was one thing for Amelia and Emma to know. But her family, much as she loved them, never met a secret they didn't set free, most of the time accidentally in conversation about other things.

So there you were. She laughed and dished up mountains of potatoes and cut an unending series of pumpkin and raisin pies, and said not a word about what was really in her heart.

For Christmas they traditionally traveled to Aleta's to spend the holiday with Melvin's family, but the Tuesday after Thanksgiving, a letter came.

Dear Son and Daughter,

I hope this letter finds you well, and your Communion Sunday last week was a blessing. We are having a cold snap down here, and your brother Peter had to come and help me wrap the pipes. I suppose I should have done it when we had that fine stretch over Thanksgiving, but what with everyone here for the meal, and church being here that very same Sunday, the pipes were the last thing on my mind.

They turn into the first thing when no water comes out of them, I'll tell you.

I had been looking forward to welcoming you to the house for Old Christmas, along with the rest of the family, but my cousin Selma (Great-aunt Mollie's oldest girl) wrote to invite me down to Pinecraft for two weeks. All this time that branch of the family has lived there, and I've never been. I'm nearly sixty and if I don't start doing some of these things I've been meaning to do, I won't get them done before the Lord decides my time is up.

So I will be leaving on December 15 and coming back on January 15. Little Ruthie (Simon's fifteen-year-old) is going to stay here to keep an eye on the pipes and make sure the cats don't tear the place up while I'm gone.

You're welcome to come as usual. Your brothers will be glad to see you. Just let Simon know so Ruthie can change the beds. If you don't, I know you will have a fine time at the Kings while we all remember the little Baby Who was born to show us how to live, and died to save and ransom us.

Your mother,
Aleta

"Do you think she's offended?" Carrie handed the letter to Amelia, who smoothed it with one hand on the quilt top as she read. "This is the first time since I've been married that we haven't gone to Melvin's family's home place for Christmas."

Amelia handed the letter to Emma. "It sounds to me like she's had enough of the weather down there and jumped at the chance to go somewhere warm."

"Yes, but we always go, the whole family. It's like Mamm and Daed's place at Thanksgiving—the only time in the whole year that everyone is there at once."

"It's a lot of work." Emma passed the letter to Carrie, who folded it up and put it in her apron pocket. "Maybe a holiday once every ten years isn't so much for her to ask."

"I just can't help but feel she's taking herself out of the picture so the whole baby mess doesn't come up."

"Does Melvin think she's offended?" Amelia picked up her needle and kept stitching.

The quilt was nearly finished. In fact, today's work would probably see it done—they were turning up the backing to the front side to bind it, with Emma and Amelia on the long sides and Carrie taking the two short sides. Today Emma would fold it up and take it home with her, and next week they would turn their minds to designing Lydia's baby quilt.

"He hasn't seen it yet. It just came today."

"Well, he knows his mother best. Let his reaction tell you the truth." Amelia's advice was always sound. Carrie felt a sense of relief and got down to business with needle and thread.

"We saw Lydia Zook yesterday, on our way home from the train station." Emma's words fell into the room's companionable silence like stones onto a pond rimed in ice, and Carrie felt her hard-won composure crack. "She was coming out of the fabric store and didn't wave or even look at us."

Amelia set three end stitches, snipped it off, and re-threaded her needle with a fresh length of green thread. "That baby looks like more than three or four months. More like five. She's not a very big girl to begin with, and she's carrying him all out front. I can't believe none of us noticed long before this."

"Maybe it is more," Emma suggested. "Maybe it's April, not June. Has Mary convinced her to see a doctor yet?"

"If she hasn't, she will." Carrie's voice held all their knowledge of Mary Lapp. She was like a force of nature when she had a mission to accomplish. "And I hope it's soon." Time to turn the subject back to Emma—the whole subject of babies was so sensitive it made her stomach hurt. "How was Thanksgiving in Paradise?"

"Grant's parents are wonderful," Emma said. "They gave us his grandmother's china, which means I don't have to worry if Zachary or the girls break a plate. We'll have a second set as backup. And it was nice to go to church with them, too. Both of his brothers want us to come for another visit before planting starts."

"You'd better go," Amelia said. "You don't want to be traveling if you're pregnant."

"What?" The needle fell from Carrie's nerveless fingers. "Are you—you can't be—" It was too soon. She hadn't even been married a month.

Emma shot a glare at Amelia. "Don't be starting rumors, you. Carrie, don't look like that. Amelia is just teasing." She half rose. "Carrie? Are you all right?"

But she wasn't. Black spots danced in front of her eyes, and the wind seemed to have picked up something awful, roaring around the room as though it meant to get in.

"Amelia, grab her! She's going to fall."

Amelia was a second too late.

CHAPTER 21

Carrie had fainted once or twice before, back in the hungry days, but time had not made it any more pleasant. She tried to sit up, but Amelia pressed her shoulders back.

"Put your head on the pillow, *Liewi*. I have a cold cloth here."

"Did you eat lunch?" Emma asked, worry lines stamped between her brows. "How do you feel?"

"I'm fine. Truly." Then, "That feels good." She took the cloth from Amelia and pressed it to her forehead, then her cheeks and neck. This time, when she sat up, they let her. "And *ja*, I ate a good lunch. I don't know what that was about."

But she did. It was about babies, and about—

"Emma, *bischt du im e Familye weg*?"

"*Nei*, not that I know of." Emma was no slouch. Her gaze met Carrie's and held. "Did that—is that why you fainted? Because you thought I might be?"

"I don't know. Maybe." She got up slowly, half expecting the blood to drain out of her head again. But it didn't. "Or maybe I just need to eat more spinach and broccoli."

"I have broccoli." Amelia watched her carefully, as though she would collapse again at any moment. "It's growing nicely in the bed on the south side of the house. The boys will be delighted to give you their share."

The fact that she could laugh was a good sign.

"I'm sorry I upset you with my teasing," Amelia said more softly, contrition in her voice. "I should know better."

"It would be a shame if you had to put a watch on every word because of me." Carrie gripped her hand and then stood slowly. "Words don't come between us, and I hope they never will."

Even as they settled to their stitching again, her friends kept an eye on her. Not only that, they made sure their conversation touched on anything and everything but babies.

Carrie set the last stitches and snipped her thread. "I'm done."

"I beat you." Emma smiled with satisfaction, her shoulders relaxing when Carrie seemed to be breathing and acting normally again. "And Amelia is bringing up the rear."

Amelia snipped her own thread, and together they shook the quilt out over the guest bed.

"It looks *wunderbaar*," Emma said softly. "I can't wait for Grant to see it." She slipped her arms around their waists, one on either side of her. "*Denki* for giving it to us. Tonight we'll sleep covered in love."

Tears welled in Carrie's eyes. "It belongs to you, and always has."

"Even when I thought it was going to the auction—when I wanted it to go, so that Grant could make his house payment—the thought of giving it up hurt me." She took a long breath. "The Lord always provides. I can keep our quilt, and with the money from my book, we've even been able to pay down the principal a little."

Amelia released her. "Let's fold it up and get you home. It looks like there's going to be another storm."

Emma hesitated. "Should we stay with Carrie until Melvin gets home?"

"No, you should not." Pointedly, Carrie held open Emma's big tote bag and Amelia slid the folded quilt into it. "I'm less likely to faint again than you are to get soaked. And I know how you hate driving in the rain."

"That I do." Emma pulled on her coat and her away bonnet. "Very well, then. Melvin should be home soon, shouldn't he?"

"Within the hour." Carrie hugged them both. "Be safe. It's already getting dark. You'll have to turn on the lamps."

"*Ja, Mamm.*" Emma made a face at her, and she and Amelia ran down the steps to the barn, where the presence of another buggy told Carrie that Joshua was in there. He must have hitched up Emma's horse while he was at it, because they were on their way in minutes, waving from behind the storm front.

Carrie pulled her shawl over her head and, pushed roughly by the wind, dashed across the yard and into the barn.

Joshua, wearing his tool belt, was standing below the loft looking up, hands on his hips.

"Thank you for hitching up for them," she said a little breathlessly. Maybe running so soon after fainting was not the smartest thing to have done.

He turned. "What are you doing out here?"

"It was kind of you."

"It was sensible. I know what time they usually leave, and

I figured if I could save them a few minutes of getting wet, then that would be *gut*."

She gazed at him for a moment. Would he be offended if she said what was on her mind?

"What?" he said. "I know that look. Spit it out."

She smiled ruefully. "I was just thinking that when you first came here, I thought you were so self-centered and *batzich*. And now look at you, doing things for your friends."

His eyebrows rose. "I have the least reason to be proud of anyone in the *Gmee*. But self-centered I probably am. Comes of not having anyone to put before myself."

"Except for Jesus." Her tone was dry. "Everything follows from that, you know."

He kicked at a stray nail in the sawdust that lay in heaps and trails on the barn floor. "Trying out for preacher, are you?"

"No, just telling the truth." Hopefully with more grace than Mary Lapp. But it did lead into something she wanted to know. "You put Lydia before yourself, too, I noticed. Do you happen to know if she's been to the doctor?"

"I thought you women were making a project of her."

"We are. But the first thing to do is to make sure she's taking care of herself. Mary Lapp was going to kidnap her and take her in to Doctor Stewart. I haven't heard if she succeeded."

"You'd better ask Mary Lapp, then." Bitterness flavored his tone the way a bit of mold could spoil a whole mouthful of food. "Lydia doesn't talk to me."

"I thought you were friends. Isn't that what you told me when you were urging me to talk to her?"

"I thought we were, too." He turned abruptly. "I should

just marry the girl and give the *Gmee* what they all want—to be proven right."

Carrie let that go and concentrated on the important part. "I think she's a little young for you." Though she hadn't been too young to find an *Englisch* boyfriend and make a baby with him.

He hefted the hammer out of his belt and whacked a nail in the nearest post as though it were out of line. "Lydia might be young, but she's no child. I know I don't have much, but the hired man's rooms at Hill's are a sight better than what she's got at home."

Carrie couldn't quite put her finger on it, but she could hear a quality in his voice that had never been there before. "Do you love her, Joshua?" she asked softly.

"Love?" Something broke over his face, but whether it was pain or disgust, the light was too poor for her to tell. "Some folks don't expect love to work into their plans, Carrie Miller. Some folks are happy to have a place to live and a good meal once in a while." Still holding the hammer, he walked toward the ladder that led up to the new loft. "I expect that baby'd be happy to have both, no matter who offered it."

Carrie turned when the sound of hammering up above told her that the conversation was done. Outside, the rain fell in skeins past the open barn door. The tears she had not allowed to fall earlier welled up and streaked down her cheeks.

Stubborn, foolish Lydia, taking her own way at the expense of her baby's health and surely its future. What would become of her? What would become of the child?

O Lord, help us, her heart cried silently. *Help Lydia. Help me, and Joshua, and my Melvin, who has hard places in the*

*fields of his heart where no compassion lies. Your will be done,
but O Lord, give me the strength to know it...and to do it.
Somehow. Before it's too late.*

* * *

She should be chopping onions and getting down a jar of
stewed tomatoes from the pantry for spaghetti sauce. But
instead, Carrie spread her songbook on the windowsill and
thought over what had happened upstairs earlier that afternoon.

Amelia had teased Emma about being pregnant, and Carrie had fainted. But in between...for a single moment, she
had felt a wave of jealousy so huge that her heart had felt like
it was going to explode. No wonder all the blood had drained
out of her head.

As she stood there turning pages, her face heated with
shame.

What a horrid, ugly moment. Jealous of her best friend,
simply because of the possibility that she might be blessed
with something Carrie was not. Thank goodness she had
fainted, then. Better that than to blurt out what she felt
and burden Emma with it.

Ah. Here it was.

> *You see your brother walking*
> *Beside you on the road*
> *Your burden feels so heavy*
> *And his a lighter load.*
>
> *You wish someone would switch them*
> *Why should his steps be light,*

When yours have been so heavy
As you struggled through the night?

O brother, be not jealous
Your envy try to quell
For the Hand that lifts his burden
Is lifting yours as well.

She would take a lesson from this song she'd copied down, oh, nearly fifteen years ago. Yes, the green-eyed monster had raised its ugly head and roared. She had been jealous of Emma's side of the road, and had completely forgotten the nearly eleven happy years she had already spent walking beside Melvin while Emma was treading her path all alone.

With prayer, she could overcome this fault.

When the happy day came that Emma actually told them such news, she would actually feel the joy that she'd make good and sure was on her face.

* * *

If the previous winter had been one of the wettest on record, Old Joe Yoder declared that this one was a deep freeze to rival any *Englisch* electrical freezer—in fact, Melvin told her with a laugh one Sunday after church, Old Joe had told them Sarah had put a plucked chicken down on the porch while she opened the kitchen door, and before she could turn around, it had frozen right through.

Old Joe had a tendency to pull people's legs, but Carrie could half believe it. The days seemed frosted together, one very much like another. People stayed inside, their animals warm in sturdy barns. Carrie led the chickens through the snow into a fenced-in area inside the barn next to the horses when word went around that the wind chill was going to drop to thirty below. The coop was not heated, but with thick walls and horses in it, the barn was warm.

And every other week, they went to church, and the *Gmee* was treated to a front-row view of Lydia Zook, getting bigger and bigger as the winter limped on frostbitten feet toward what Carrie imagined was her due date.

Mary Lapp had indeed succeeded in getting her to Dr. Stewart, but whether the girl was taking her vitamins and paying attention to things like iron and folic acid was anybody's guess. Inquiries were met with a shrug and a disappearing act. The only part of their project that seemed to have any success was the food-delivery part, and Carrie suspected that was only because Abe Zook was getting hungrier the more unwieldy and unable to work Lydia became.

On the last Sunday in March, when the thermometer climbed to a balmy thirty-eight degrees and everything from the trees to the sky to people's noses seemed to be dripping all at once, Bishop Daniel called Carrie and Melvin, Joshua Steiner, and Abe Zook and Lydia into one of the spare bedrooms in his house, where church had been that morning.

When they were all inside and the door closed, he didn't waste any time. "There is a matter that concerns Lydia and our brother Joshua Steiner. And Melvin, you and Carrie and Abe are involved too."

Carrie couldn't imagine what subject might concern the five of them, unless it was something to do with the baby. With an adoption. Her heart began to pound. She glanced at Joshua, who stared at the bishop, much the way a rabbit out in the field stares at a stooping hawk, wanting to run but knowing there is absolutely no escape.

Since Lydia would not stand next to her father, that meant Joshua was closest to her. It looked eerily like they were about to take wedding vows...except that she was heavily pregnant and he was as white as his good Sunday shirt.

"I regret that this is necessary," the bishop began, "but the sin of fornication, while performed in secret, must be judged openly. Joshua, it has come to my attention that you and Lydia Zook committed this sin in the hired man's rooms at Hill Farms, and in the barn at Melvin and Carrie's place while they were away in the western part of the state. Is this true?"

Carrie's mouth fell open. She didn't dare look at Melvin.

Joshua's throat worked, and it took a moment for any sound to come out. "*Nei*. She came into my rooms, and to visit one day at Millers', but all we did was talk."

"Lydia, is this true?"

"*Ja*. Someone is making up stories. Maybe that someone should be here in this room instead of Joshua."

Abe shifted, and his hands twitched as though they were itching to smack something. Or someone.

The bishop looked at her over the rims of his spectacles. He was the father of five girls, which was evident in this moment. "You are not in a position to judge your brethren, young lady. Have all these months on that front bench taught you nothing?"

"I'm sorry." Her head was bowed. She had one hand to her back as though it ached. How, then, was she able to inject so much defiance into two words?

The bishop's face settled into lines of sadness. "Joshua, you have behaved foolishly and given the appearance of evil, which has caused distress among your brethren. You are older than Lydia and should have known better. You should have been an example to her."

Abe Zook had been shifting his feet, and Carrie could hear his breathing becoming more agitated from across the room. At the bishop's words, he could no longer contain himself.

"I don't believe him!" He shook a finger in Joshua's face. "No good Amish man lets a young girl into his room—and you're no good. Everyone in Whinburg knows your reputation, Joshua Steiner. Everyone knows you can't be trusted around anything in skirts. How dare you bring shame on my name like this!"

Carrie would have expected Joshua to leap to his own defense with the sarcastic temper she'd seen signs of in her own kitchen. But he merely gazed at Abe as though he were a new species of bull, pawing the ground, but safely behind the fence.

Instead, Melvin spoke up.

"Everyone in Whinburg can believe what they want, but I'll believe what I've seen with my own eyes. Joshua has lent me a hand around my farm and never asked a penny for it. He did it out of friendship and because he saw a need. He's never given us any reason not to trust him."

"I heard a few rumors along that line," Abe snapped.

Carrie swayed as though she'd been slapped.

"Then you need to close your ears and use the brain God gave you," Melvin said quietly. He put a steadying hand on the small of her back.

Carrie had never heard Melvin speak in such a way to anyone, much less a man so much older than he, and in front of the bishop to boot.

"My wife and the bishop's wife have been trying to help Lydia. Maybe you ought to think about that more than these rumors you've been listening to."

"Don't you—" With a glance at Daniel, who was being

admirably silent, Abe reined in his temper. "It don't matter if they're true or not. A godly man would be making an offer to the girl, not letting her be publicly shamed."

How could Lydia stand it? He sounded so holy, as if he'd never committed a sin or had a single fault in his life—or done his share to shame her.

"I have already proposed marriage to Lydia, and she turned me down."

It took a moment for the bishop to regroup. Behind the lenses of his glasses, he blinked rapidly. "In that case, Lydia," he finally said in a tone that was almost gentle, "I beg you to reconsider this decision. Joshua can offer you and your child a home. If he has been willing to make you his wife, do you not think you can accept him?"

"*Nei*," she said. "I told him I was leaving Whinburg and that he was welcome to come with me. He didn't want that, so..." She shrugged.

"I am glad to hear he was not willing to give up his salvation for you." Daniel looked at Joshua, who had no answer. He gazed at his feet, at the quilt on the bed against the wall, at the door. Anywhere but at Lydia. "So you will not marry him."

"*Nei*. This baby will be adopted by an *Englisch* couple, I hope, and I will be leaving."

"Leaving Whinburg, or leaving the church?"

For the first time, Lydia hesitated. "Leaving Whinburg." Carrie couldn't imagine what would happen if she said she was leaving the Amish in public. Would Abe be put under *die Meinding* for raising such a disobedient child? Would they all be told they could no longer give her assistance?

At least Lydia wasn't willing to risk that. Carrie wouldn't put it past Abe Zook to take it out of her hide if she put him in that position—even though his neglect had likely led to it.

What would the bishop do now? He had clearly expected Lydia and Joshua to obey. Had he made a second plan?

"Lydia, what you have said grieves me," he said at last. "I must consult with the ministers and pray on this matter. We do not want you to leave, or your baby either."

The set of her thin shoulders and the purse of her mouth told Carrie that Lydia didn't believe it.

The bishop dismissed them, and Melvin took Carrie's hand and hurried her out of the room. But afterward, a kind of gloom seemed to hang over them as they ate the simple lunch of bread and *Buhnesupp* the women set out. Conversation was hushed. Even if the others didn't know what had been discussed, the simple fact that they had been spoken to privately was enough to cause a waterfall of silent speculation.

Not for the first time, Carrie thanked God that she was a woman and would never have to find the slip of paper in a copy of the *Ausbund* that would point to her as the next preacher, minister, or bishop—a responsibility that ended only with death. She did not have to oversee the affairs of the congregation, both natural and spiritual.

She had enough of a battle to oversee her own.

CHAPTER 22

"So Joshua Steiner has chosen the way of God after all." Melvin shook the reins over Jimsy's back, and they turned onto the wide shoulder of the highway. The township always plowed it all the way across the shoulders to accommodate buggies as well as cars, but with the sudden warm-up, the banks had slumped into slush and the road was running like a river. There would be black ice tonight. "When I hired him to help us out, I have to say, I had my doubts."

"The way he behaved sometimes, it was no wonder." Carrie tucked the buggy blanket more firmly around her legs. "He's like the prodigal, only he came to the end of himself after he came home, not before. I'm glad you stood up for him. We all need someone to stand in the breach for us—especially when it comes to Abe Zook."

"Abe Zook needs to spend less time listening to gossip and more time listening to the Lord. Speaking of coming home, Brian and I are going back up to Rigby tomorrow to sign papers. I'll be back Tuesday by noon. After all this, will you be all right?"

"I'm not going to move a muscle except to go to Amelia's to work on the baby quilt for Lydia—and I'll walk. I don't trust these roads."

"I guess Abe is giving her a pretty hard time. Foolish girl." Melvin shook his head. "The bishop practically hands her a husband on a plate, and she turns him down."

"I hope Joshua has the courage to ask another girl someday."

Melvin huffed a laugh. "*Ja*, though after this, even Esther Grohl wouldn't take him. But Carrie, it gave me peace about this business of her child."

"Peace?" Did he mean he had not had peace up until today?

She wished she could have some peace. Her heart was a whirlwind of shame for Lydia and pity for Joshua. The girl who eventually had the courage to marry him would have to live with the defiant ghost of Lydia Zook for as long as people's memories lasted.

"*Ja*. I know you were disappointed about the baby. But it was the right decision. Think of the child of a girl like that— stubborn, proud, disobedient."

"Children aren't always exactly like their parents," she said quietly, just loud enough for him to hear over the wet clop of Jimsy's hooves and the hiss of the wheels. "You can train those things out of a child."

"Well, no matter. You and I will not have to do it, will we?"

No, they wouldn't. And that night, after they said their prayers together, Carrie lay in the dark and silently prayed what she could not say aloud.

Father, help me to forgive him for taking this chance away from me—and have peace about it. I know that all peace comes from You, but Lord, I beg You for a portion. I wanted the chance to convince her it would be right for the baby to have a home and parents who would love it. Is that so bad? O Father, help

me to submit—to You and to Melvin both. Take this resentment
out of my heart by the time he gets back on Tuesday, so I can kiss
him with lips that don't lie.

It seemed as though the *gut Gott* had answered her prayers
when she hugged Melvin good-bye in the yard and he kissed
her soundly, while Brian Steiner looked out over his horse's
ears and tried not to smile. She waved the buggy out of sight
and then tugged her shawl around her more tightly.

The Lord gave His people work to do to keep their
minds and thoughts out of *Druwwel*, and work she did—
Monday being wash day. Since Melvin was not home to
make a big supper for, Carrie ate leftovers with the appetite
of a woman who has done four loads of laundry by hand
in a wringer washer. She pegged it out on the line Joshua
rigged for her in the new loft, moving around Joshua and
his tools, where the warmth from the animals rose to dry
it. Of course, that meant carrying the heavy baskets up the
ladder, but at least the clothes wouldn't be frozen to planks
in the morning.

"Another cold one tonight," Joshua said as he gathered up
the reins at the end of the day. "I want to get over to Mamm
and Daed's before dark. I heard on the radio at Hill's that
there were six car accidents due to black ice in the county last
night, and tonight is shaping up to be as cold. I hope you
brought lots of firewood in."

"Melvin made sure of it." Their conversation had been like
that all afternoon—just pleasantries and small talk. No mention of what had happened the day before. Maybe that was a
good thing. Carrie patted the buggy door and stepped back,
and his horse started forward.

There might be things in life she didn't have, but the
things she did have were what mattered—a snug, well-

insulated house, a husband who showed his love in the little things he did, and one last slice of the Dutch apple pie she'd made on Saturday.

The only time she got to eat and read simultaneously was when Melvin wasn't there to tell her not to. She'd borrowed a lovely big book on gardens from all over the world at the library, and after she finished her pie, she hung over it, drinking in the beauty of drifts of bluebells in England, of knot gardens made of herbs in Virginia, and of fountains and topiary in Italy.

When footsteps pounded up the steps and someone knocked so hard they could only have been using their fists, she practically screamed in fright at being jerked back to real life.

Good heavens, it was nearly ten o'clock!

She ran to the door and peered through the four glass panes at eye level, but she couldn't see a thing. Someone was in trouble, that was clear.

She yanked it open.

"Oh Carrie." Sarah Grohl stood shivering on the porch, tears running down her face and a knot forming over her eye that would be very ugly by morning. "Help. I need help."

Carrie grabbed her arm to pull her into the warm kitchen and the girl gasped in pain. "I think I broke something."

Carrie released her as though she'd been burned. "I'm so sorry. What happened? Oh Sarah, please come in and sit down before you fall down. I'll—"

"I can't. You have to come. You have to help her."

"Who? Where?"

"Lydia," Sarah gasped. "We were driving back from… from seeing a movie, and the road was so slippery… and some *Englisch* guys went by in a car and honked the horn and it scared the horse and it slipped and, oh Carrie, you have to hurry. I think it made the baby come."

Oh, dear heaven help them all.

Carrie pulled on her heavy boots and wound a thick woolen scarf around her head. She donned Melvin's wool work coat and buttoned it up to her chin. "Where is she?"

"At the cutoff that goes down to the creek. The horse jumped sideways into the ditch, and when she tried to get out of the buggy, it tipped and threw both of us out." Sarah stopped, gasping for breath. "Hurry. She's lying on the ground and it's so cold."

"Sarah, I'll go. You run next door and ask them if you can use the phone. Call nine-one-one and get them to send an ambulance."

The girl gaped at her, teeth chattering.

"Sarah, go!"

"I don't need to." She turned sideways. "In my pocket. I can't move my arm to get it out."

Carrie reached in and pulled out a cell phone. This was no time to ask her why she had one—only a time to be thankful she did. "Call nine-one-one. Tell them where she is, and then tell them where you are. They'll help you with your arm. I'll go down there now."

She dashed into the guest room and snatched up the heaviest quilt she could find, then pushed out the door. Behind her, she heard Sarah's quavering voice explaining to someone who she was, and then the door slammed and the silence of the night surrounded her, huge and unforgiving. The only sound was the crunch of melted and refrozen snow under her feet as she ran.

Not a soul was out on the highway as Carrie crossed it, for which she thanked the *gut Gott*. Her boots had rubber soles with heavy treads, but even so, she skated over half the ice-slicked passing lane before regaining her balance and picking up her pace—half run, half fast walk.

Let her be all right. Let the baby be all right. Please let help get here in time. she chanted, half under her breath, in time with her jogging steps. *Please, Lord. Please don't let them be hurt.*

A horse snorted in the dark and its hooves clattered. She'd startled it, running up on it. "It's all right, boy. It's okay, it's only me."

By some miracle the buggy had righted itself as the horse had pulled it out of the ditch and back onto level ground. But she didn't have time to make sure the animal was all right. It was too dark to see, anyhow.

"Lydia? Lydia, where are you?" If she had been frightened before, the silence terrified her. "Lydia!"

Tracks. Gashes in the snow. Ah, the snow. It had probably cushioned the buggy so it hadn't gone all the way over—just enough to make the girls slide violently against the door and fall out. There were no locks on them, after all, not like *Englisch* cars.

She followed the deep scoring through the bank and down into the ditch. Ten steps away was a patch of darkness deeper than the blue of abused snow.

"Lydia!" Carrie fell to her knees beside her and put a chilled cheek next to her open mouth. Breath fanned against her cold skin.

"Thank You," she whispered. "Oh, thank You." She patted Lydia's face—almost as pale as the snow. Her eyes were open. That was good. "Lydia, can you hear me?"

She groaned—as welcome as a choir of angels singing. Carrie shook out the quilt and tucked it around and under her as best she could. Her instinct was to slip her hands under Lydia's armpits and haul her up to the highway, but she didn't dare. If her back was hurt—or her ribs—or the baby—

Lydia groaned again, and it ended in a shriek. She said a word Carrie had never heard any Amish woman say before, no matter how provoked.

"Lydia?"

"It *hurts*!"

"Where does it hurt?"

"I'm having a *baby*!" She shot Carrie a glare of disgust and stared up at the starry sky. "I got to ninety-two. Where am I?"

"You were thrown out of the buggy. Do you know who I am?"

Her eyes rolled in Carrie's direction, then closed as the contraction—or some other, more terrible pain, Carrie couldn't tell—receded. "Carrie. Where—"

"You're in the ditch on the county highway. Our drive is closest. Sarah came and got me. The ambulance is on its way."

"I don't want this."

"Of course you don't." She kept her tone low, soothing, the way she'd spoken to the edgy horse. "Nobody wants to be in an accident. But it wasn't your fault."

"The baby! I don't want it to come."

"Oh *Liewi*. Wait until you hold him in your arms. We'll get you into the—"

"*Nei!*" Her voice rose to a shriek. "Don't—want—"

In the cold and the misery and the darkness, Carrie's heart broke for the poor little *Bobbel*. Unwanted from the very beginning. Could the baby hear its mother screaming such words? Would they pierce its heart the way they pierced

Carrie's now? Would they go deep, and come up in some awful way in its later years—a memory long buried but waiting to do some terrible damage?

"Breathe, Lydia." She'd been with Susan for her last delivery. Being number four, little Silas had come much faster than any of them had expected. "Little short breaths. Lots of oxygen to help you ride through the pain. Go on. Like this." Carrie panted—no hard task, since she was still half out of breath from running.

In the distance, she heard the wail of an approaching siren. *Thank You, Lord.*

"You breathe, Lydia. Don't stop panting. I'm going to go tell them where you are."

"*Nei!*" Pant, pant. "I don't want it!" Pant, pant, pant.

Good enough. Carrie scrambled up the slope, snow falling into her boots and going up the sleeves of her coat. Flashing lights crested the hill and she waved her arms.

Headlights flooded her and the ambulance tried to stop, skidded on the ice, and began to swing sideways. Carrie screamed as the rear bumper missed the horse by a shin's width, then rocked to a halt on a patch of asphalt that had managed to dry from passing traffic earlier in the day.

The EMTs jumped out, one of them swearing a blue streak and the other hollering at him about the horse.

"Over here!" she shouted. "She's down the bank!"

They yanked a stretcher out of the back and tossed a big red case on it, then followed her, their boots pounding in syncopated time.

What a blessed relief it was to hand over the responsibility to men who knew what they were doing. "She's having a baby," she told the nearest one, who was checking Lydia's pulse. "I don't know how badly she's hurt."

"Never rains but it pours," he said cheerfully, apparently recovered from nearly wiping out the Grohl horse and buggy with his ambulance. "Are you the one who called?"

"No. Sarah—"

"Lydia?" came a call from up the slope. "Carrie?"

"Is that the broken arm?" the other man asked. "Tell her to stay by the truck—we'll take them both in soon as we get mommy here stabilized."

Carrie struggled up the hill and told Sarah what the man had said. "Is she all right?" Sarah's eyes were huge, and her face pale and drawn in the light from the interior of the ambulance.

"She's awake. She talked to me. I have to get back down there. Don't move."

They had worn such a path in the snow that she got down the second time much faster than the first. The EMTs had put a big thick collar around Lydia's neck and were just lifting her onto a hard board. As she watched with a kind of incredulous horror, they pulled big pieces of tape off a roll and ran it across her forehead, then across the collar. She'd lost her *Kapp* somewhere in the snow and Carrie hadn't noticed until now. With a tearing sound, they pulled straps across her chest, her hips under her huge belly, and her legs.

"Ready, honey? We're going to carry you up the hill. Don't worry, you won't fall off. The C-collar's to keep your head still in case your neck is hurt. Here we go." The two of them lifted the board as though she weighed nothing, and, carefully placing their boots in the snow and mud, carried her up the slope.

"Carrie," Lydia called weakly.

"I'm here, *Schatzi*." She fumbled for her hand. How cold it was—cold as the snow itself.

"Don't leave me."

"I won't. I'm right here. Sarah's here, too."

They slid her into the back, where one of them grabbed a blanket and began rolling it up. Shouldn't they be covering her with that? They'd left her quilt in a heap in the snow, so it wouldn't do much good, but—

"I'm going to tilt the backboard a bit, honey, and slide this under it. We don't want the baby cutting off your circulation, okay?" He glanced at Carrie and Sarah. "Josh, do something with that arm while I get her on oxygen."

In moments the second one had Sarah's arm in a temporary sling while the first one slid the prongs of plastic tubing into Lydia's nose. Then the second one ran to the front, and Carrie heard him put the vehicle into gear.

"You ride here, ma'am, if you're going with her. We don't have any time to lose."

Carrie climbed into the back of the ambulance and hung on.

CHAPTER 23

The EMTs wheeled Lydia through the double doors of Whinburg Township Hospital, and Carrie gritted her teeth and ran beside them, hoping no one would grab her, tell her she was out of her place, and send her away.

Someone had obviously called ahead, because a man in green cotton pajamas and a couple of women in shapeless pants and tunics were waiting for Lydia. Carrie fell back against the wall. If she got in the way, they'd send her out. And even though she had no idea what was going on, she couldn't leave.

"BP one-eighteen over sixty-seven," the EMT said to the man in the pajamas, who couldn't have been much older than Brian Steiner. This must be the doctor. "Heart rate one-fifteen, respiration twenty-three."

She's having a baby! Carrie wanted to scream. Why were they worried about a bunch of numbers when Lydia's stomach was the biggest thing in the room?

The EMTs folded up their gurney. "She was conscious and totally ticked off when we got there. The broken arm's in the next room."

"Get the ortho resident paged and have him set it."

And they jogged out, their duty done. Carrie supposed it

would only be a few minutes before a call came and they'd have to go right back out on that highway.

"Now, honey," the doctor said. "I'm going to have a look at you and see what we've got. What's your name?"

Carrie opened her mouth to answer, but Lydia got there first. "Lydia Zook."

"Okay, Lydia, tell me what hurts."

Lydia rolled her eyes.

"Lydia? Do you hurt anywhere?"

"I'm having a baby. *Ja*, it hurts!"

"Okay, clearly there's nothing wrong with your breathing. Airways good. Circulation's not great. Do you remember what happened?"

"*Ja*. The buggy tipped. Sarah landed on me. Or maybe I landed on her. I forget. I couldn't get up. Then Carrie came."

"Neck hurt?"

"*Nei*. The baby—my stomach hurts."

"We'll get to the baby real soon. First we have to make sure you're going to be okay. Tell me what happened before the buggy tipped."

"Those *Englisch* boys honked the horn. Poor Jessie—the Grohls' horse—jumped sideways. It's not her fault."

"I know, honey. And after you landed on the ground? Did you fall asleep?"

"It was too cold. I counted stars until Carrie came. I got to ninety-two."

"Okay. I'm going to take this collar off you." He made short work of the tape and Lydia's head fell back on the pillow.

"Nothing broken," the man said, moving her arms and legs. "That's a miracle. Not concussed. Nurse, get these clothes off her."

Before Carrie could move, the nurse picked up a huge pair of scissors and cut everything off Lydia—dress, apron, and underthings. She hooked her up to a monitor that began to emit beeps at rapid but regular intervals. "We have a fetal heartbeat." She frowned. "Wait—"

"We have some blood here. If she's hurting from more than contractions—nurse!" He turned to the one with the scissors. "Ultrasound."

"Right here." She ran to a machine on a cart and wheeled it over. Carrie couldn't see what they were doing past their backs, but on a screen, a cloud of fog swirled into being in a black field. The doctor made a whooping sound and Carrie started forward as though she'd been pushed. "You heard right, nurse. We've got twins, people. Good news— one's moving, though I don't like the look of—"

Twins!

The doctor's voice faded in and out as Carrie sagged against the wall. Lydia's mother had been Priscilla Bontrager's twin. No wonder Lydia looked so big! Twins! How could she not have suspected? How could they all have been so blind?

"Give me some room. How's that BP?"

"Dropping, Doctor."

This was bad, from the look on the doctor's face. Then he said something that sounded like "abruption" and suddenly the energy level in the room doubled.

"Where's the OB?" he snapped. "Wasn't she here earlier?"

"I think she might have gone home," the nurse ventured.

"Well, get her back here, then! I'm going to need some help. We've got to get these babies out of there." He turned to the second nurse as the first one ran from the room. "Four liters of oxygen and a non-rebreather. And I want four units of packed red blood cells, stat."

"Yes, Doctor. It could take a little while for the blood to—"

"Then get going! And send that resident in. Good grief, did everyone pick tonight to go to the movies? We've got to get those babies delivered before we lose them."

Carrie felt the blood drain out of her head. *Do not faint. If you do, you'll take time and attention away from Lydia and if the babies die, it will be your fault.*

She dragged in as much of the antiseptic-scented air as her lungs could hold, and the black spots dancing on the edges of her vision faded.

Another man, in blue pajamas this time, ran in. The doctor didn't even look up. "Get me two grams of magnesium and a tocolytic. We've got to stop these contractions or the placenta will peel off even more. *Did we find the OB?*"

"She was in the cafeteria. She's scrubbing now."

"Well, thank—look out! She's crashing!" The machine on the wall was blinking frantically, and both doctors bent over Lydia with needles.

A woman ran in wearing a smock and a pair of jeans. "We got an abruption and twins in here?"

"About time," the doctor snapped. "Hope you enjoyed your dinner."

The prayers in Carrie's head no longer even formed sentences as the two doctors sniped at each other and finally got down to business. She wasn't praying anymore—it was more like a gabble of fear that the Holy Spirit was just going to have to translate for the Lord.

"We don't have time to get her up to L and D," the lady doctor said. "We're going to deliver these babies right here, right now. Get her ready for a C-section with anesthesia. *Where's that blood?"*

And suddenly both doctors seemed to be on the same side. Carrie turned from the door to find a nurse reaching for her arm. It was all she could do not to cry out. "Are you with the patient, miss?"

"*Ja*. I came in the ambulance with her."

"Carrie?" Lydia stirred at the sound of her voice. "I want Carrie."

"Is that you?" the nurse asked. When Carrie nodded, she said, "I'm sorry, Carrie, but they're going to put her under to do a Cesarean section." She glanced over her shoulder as though checking how much time she had to talk. "You'll need to wait outside."

"But she wants me."

A new doctor ran in. Carrie watched him set up yet another machine, while the nurse said, "If this were a normal birth, you'd be her breathing coach, but that's the anesthesiologist, so that's our cue to get you outside. Okay? I promise, she'll be fine. I'll let you know when we transfer her to Recovery and you can see her."

That was all she could do to help? Wait outside? She'd known they would make her leave at some point. But there was nothing she could do other than nod and obey.

So she stood outside the door and watched and prayed, like the watchman on the wall.

The blood came, and she prayed it would strengthen Lydia for the fight ahead. Someone inside shouted, "Where's the other warmer? We need two!" and she prayed for the little lives struggling to make their entrance into the world. Toward the end, it was possible she left off praying and opened her heart directly to God, until she heard a sound behind the door that made everything fly straight out of her head.

A baby's cry.

The door banged open while someone rushed past her and Carrie heard someone say, "Apgar five at one minute." She got a glimpse of a nurse standing next to an apparatus that looked like a bubble. The doctor said, "And here's her brother. Aw, man." Both of them, man and woman, swore, and a second nurse said, "Apgar zero at one minute." The woman doctor shouted, "Resuscitate!" and the door banged open again as the second nurse pushed the bubble-shaped apparatus out and ran it into another room.

What did it mean? Why were they taking the baby away? What was Apgar?

Just before the door swung shut, the first nurse said, "Apgar seven at five minutes. She's pinking up just great."

Carrie's throat closed up and her knees finally gave out. She slid down the wall until she was sitting on the cool linoleum, her hands clasped in front of her mouth.

Please let them be all right. Please let all three be all right.

An eternity crawled by on leaden feet, though the clock above the nurses' station down the corridor showed it was only half an hour. Then the nurse who had taken the bubble-thing away came out, followed by two other girls in blue pajamas. The nurse was wiping tears off her cheeks with the palms of her hands.

Tears. That couldn't be good. Carrie pushed herself up the wall so she was standing, and the nurse caught the movement and looked up. "Is the—is—" Carrie couldn't get the words out.

"You're the friend?" Carrie nodded. "I'm sorry to say that

we couldn't save him. We did everything—even CPR on his tiny chest—but—" She drew a shuddering breath and straightened her spine. "We lost him. I'm sorry."

The little boy hadn't survived the trauma of his own birth. A huge lump rose in Carrie's throat and hot tears spilled over and down her cheeks.

Tears of grief. Tears of frustration. Tears of mourning for the little life that would never see the sun or play in the creek with his sister or hit a baseball in the schoolyard with the other children.

"And the other?" Her voice didn't even sound like her own. "The little girl?"

"Let me find out for you. They'll be taking the mother up to Recovery now. Would you like to be with her when she wakes up?"

"Oh, yes, please." And by then maybe God would have given her the words to tell Lydia about her little son, about how sorry she was that she would never get to know him.

And maybe they would let her hold him. Even if it was only to say good-bye.

After another interminable wait during which no one would tell her anything, one of the girls in pajamas of an awful green took her upstairs to a room where Lydia lay in bed, tubes running every which way and monitors blinking in the background.

A nurse stood next to her as her eyelids fluttered open.

"Lydia?" Carrie whispered. "Can you hear me?" She groaned and turned her head. Their gazes caught. "Do you know me?"

"Carrie. My head. It feels like a balloon."

"That's the anesthetic," the nurse said. "It will pass and you'll feel normal soon." She glanced at her stomach. "You'll be sore, though. We've got you on a drip for the pain. You'll be wanting to see your babies, but—"

"*Nei*." Lydia clutched Carrie's fingers. Her hands would be bruised in the morning...if it wasn't morning already. Carrie had no idea what time or even what day it was.

"I'm sorry, honey." The nurse squeezed her other hand. "Your little boy didn't make it. We did our best, but—on behalf of Whinburg Township General, please let me offer my condolences—I'm so sorry—we'll bring him in so you can—"

"Don't want them."

The nurse didn't seem to understand. And Carrie just plain *couldn't* understand. Even that *Englisch* nurse had mourned the little boy...and his own mother didn't care...Carrie swallowed and looked away. How *could* she?

"Your little girl will be up here in a jiffy, as soon as the nurses get her washed and measured and all that good stuff."

"*Nei!*"

The nurse released her hand and met Carrie's eyes. "It's the anesthetic. You should hear some of the things that come out of women's mouths in this room. Their husbands would be shocked."

"I don't think it's the anesthetic." Carrie captured Lydia's hands and clasped them between her own. "It's all right, *Schatzi*. The nurses will take care of the *Bobbel*. Everything will be all right."

"Don't bring them. You do it."

Them? Had she not heard the poor nurse's attempt to break the news to her? "All right. I'll look after them. You just rest, dear. Rest and get well."

The nurse went to the door. "Maybe it's better it hasn't sunk in. She needs to get stronger. You'll stay with her?"

And be the one to tell her again—and be understood this time? *Ach*, God's will could be hard. Carrie nodded. Lydia's fingers were relaxing, and the fretful creases between her brows smoothed out.

The other girl, the one in the green pajamas, came in. "Remember me? I'm Sylvia, the maternity ward nurse. How's she feeling?"

"Not very sensible," Carrie told her. "I'm glad you're giving her something for the pain, though."

"Is Lydia married?" she asked.

"No."

"What about the father? Is he in the picture?"

"No one knows who he is."

"Ah. You'll be her designate, then?"

"Her what?"

"She designated you as a second caretaker for the children." Sylvia held out a form and a pen. "If you can sign here? You'll get a baby bracelet so you can come and go in the NICU just like the mother would."

"Oh. That's *gut*." If "designate" was as close as she'd ever get to motherhood, she'd take it gladly and sign whatever they wanted.

"It's all right," the girl said to her in rapid *Deitch*. "She'll warm up to the baby when she gets to hold her. Sometimes it takes a little while for the bond of love to form—and loving the little girl will help her through the loss of the little boy."

Carrie's face went slack with surprise. This woman had grown up Amish.

But she'd left. And now she was nurse to a girl who was determined to leave as well. Truly God's ways were mysterious.

"I hope so," she answered in English. Somehow it didn't

seem right to speak their mother tongue with someone who had chosen to live outside.

Somehow nothing seemed right. A tiny life had been extinguished despite the efforts of five—six—eight people to save him.

Would anything be right ever again?

Why, Lord? Why did You take him, so small and so innocent?

But the *gut Gott* in his infinite wisdom did not answer.

* * *

Carrie fingered the bracelet that the nurse had told her would give her as many privileges as a mother. It looked like a string of little candies, with a tag that said "ZOOK" and a lot of incomprehensible numbers and letters.

"Don't worry, it isn't jewelry." The ex-Amish nurse, whose full name was Sylvia Hostetler, leaned over the counter at the nurse's station to smile. "Think of it as an ID card you don't have to carry in your purse."

Carrie slipped it on her wrist. "Can I see the baby now?"

"Right this way."

Since Whinburg Township Hospital was small and rural, the nursery wasn't large. At the moment, it only held the baby that had been born earlier that day, and the warmer holding Lydia's little girl.

Her beautiful, healthy, *alive* little girl, whose hair had dried into a blond fluff tinged with red.

"She's so small," Carrie breathed.

"Not really—I've seen them a lot smaller. She's four pounds six ounces and in pretty good shape, considering the way she arrived."

"Can I hold her?"

"You can feed her if you want. Lydia's milk won't come in for a couple of days, so we use a formula until it does."

Carrie looked up in surprise. "She's going to nurse her?"

"So far, she says no, but I'm hoping you can persuade her. It would be better for the baby." The woman hesitated. "Any idea what she wants to call her? I mean, we can't exactly put 'Baby Zook' on the birth certificate, and neither Denise nor I can get a reply out of her."

This should be a string of joyful moments—holding a baby, deciding on a name, nursing for the first time. But Lydia lay in her bed like a fallen gravestone, refusing to have anything to do with her children. An hour ago, Carrie would have said that nothing could be as heartbreaking as the little bundle they had tried to lay in Lydia's arms. Eventually she herself had taken it and said a prayer over it. Had kissed the cold little forehead and allowed the nurse to take it away.

But this tiny girl was still alive, and didn't deserve to be refused a name. Carrie gazed down at her. Her eyes were scrunched up as though she couldn't bring herself to look at her own prospects, and her little hands opened and closed as though looking for something to hold on to.

"Lydia's mother's name was Rachel," she finally said. "I will ask her if we might call her that."

Sylvia nodded. "She looks like a Rachel. The Rachel in the Bible was fair of face, wasn't she? And this little one surely is. We'll wrap her up and you can sit there in the mommy's chair with her. I'll get the bottle for you."

Carrie had held any number of newborns—her own younger brother, her sisters' children—but she had never experienced a moment as sweet as this. She sank into the upholstered chair and took little Rachel in her arms—so small, so vulnerable—and cuddled her to her chest.

Warm. Alive. Moving. What an unspeakable gift, after such a night.

The Bible is right—joy cometh in the morning.

If only she could feed her from her own body. But the bottle would have to do. Once she got the hang of it, Rachel sucked as though she meant business, her cheeks working in and out, her eyes still scrunched shut. When she turned her head away from the nipple, it seemed like the most natural thing in the world for Carrie to lay her on her shoulder and rub the brief length of her spine until she heard a wet burp.

"Oops. You'll want this." Sylvia handed her a piece of flannel to wipe her shoulder with. "You're a natural. How many do you have?"

"None," Carrie whispered. None but this one. For this moment, this morning.

The woman's eyes widened, but to her credit, she said not a word. "When she falls asleep, let me know and I'll put her back in the warmer. Then maybe you and I and Lydia can fill out some paperwork, okay?"

They were the happiest forty-five minutes Carrie could remember in many months. Somewhere in the back of her mind, a little voice warned her not to get too attached, not to open the floodgates of love that were already leaking and bowing outward under the pressure of it.

But for those all-too-brief minutes, she could pretend this child was hers—and no one could deny her.

CHAPTER 24

When she and the nurse took the paperwork for the birth certificate in to Lydia, Carrie prepared herself for a fight. Maybe it was the pain medicine, or maybe it was simply lack of interest, but when Carrie suggested she name her after her mother, Lydia merely nodded and rolled her head to look out the window.

"And the father's name?" Sylvia persisted.

Silence. Then, "I'm not going to say." All the exhaustion and despair of the night hung in her voice. "I don't want to—" Her throat closed. "It doesn't matter."

An hour of questions by Sylvia, her supervisor, and even another doctor produced no results. Carrie had never seen anyone so exhausted and yet so stubborn. Abe Zook might not have been the girl's father, but in some cases nurture obviously was a lot stronger than nature.

Sylvia bought Carrie some yogurt and oatmeal in a plastic cup down in the cafeteria, since her purse was at home where she'd left it and she had not one cent on her. When she'd eaten it, Carrie fell asleep in the mommy's chair after Rachel's second feeding.

When she woke, Melvin was perched on the edge of a plastic chair next to her.

She stared at him, wondering where she was, and what he was doing there.

"*Liebschdi*, do you not know me?" His face paled, as if he were worried she had been admitted as a patient for some illness no one had told him of.

She held out a hand, and his was so warm, so strong, that she nearly wept with relief. "How could I not know my own *Mann*? How did you find me? What time is it? What day is it?"

"It's two o'clock on Tuesday afternoon, and the news met Brian and me when we got off the train. Boyd brought me straight here when he picked us up. And Sadie and Aram Grohl offer you their thanks for seeing to Sarah. They've collected their horse and the buggy, and she has gone home with them already. The whole family will be back for a visit tonight if you are still here."

Carrie took a breath. "Sarah. They shouldn't thank me—oh Melvin, I never gave her a single thought until now. The poor girl had a broken arm, and I left her down there in Emergency all alone."

"I don't think she'll hold it against you. Not when the two of you seem to have saved Lydia's life—and that of her *Bobbel*."

"There were twins." Her lips trembled. "No one could save the little boy. God took him before he was even out of the womb."

"Ah." He looked down as the news settled on his shoulders. "And the other? She is well?"

"I've been holding her and feeding her. She is so beautiful, and sucks so strongly. We've called her Rachel."

"We?"

"Lydia. And me. She—she doesn't want her, Melvin. She

didn't want either of them. Even in the worst of her labor, she kept saying so, as though the labor should stop and the babies just go away."

"Don't cry, Carrie." His face twisted in pain. "I can't bear it."

"Someone has to cry for the little boy—for poor Rachel, beautiful and well favored—" She slid to the floor and buried her face in his lap, sobbing with the pain of loss and injustice. He pulled her onto his knee and held her, and when she finally lifted her head, hunting in her sleeve for a tissue, she saw that a tear had found its way down his cheek, too.

"I was so frightened, *Liebschdi*, at first," he whispered. "They were talking so fast and I thought it was *you* who had gone over in the buggy. I think my heart actually stopped at the thought that anything might have happened to you— that because my work had taken me away from home, God was punishing me."

She put a finger on his lips, her breath hitching. "God was too busy bringing blessing into the world. I just wish Lydia could see it."

"And where is this little blessing?"

"*Kumm mit.*" She slid off his lap and tugged him in the direction of the nursery. "I have a mother's privileges here." She waggled the bracelet and then wiped her nose with the last dry bit of the tissue. "And I decree that you may see her."

He hovered over the baby in her plastic bed just the way she had spent any number of hours doing this morning. And when Rachel woke, the nurse put her into Melvin's big woodworker's hands. "Don't worry. She's fragile, but she won't break."

"It is difficult to believe." He looked around for a place to lay his black wide-brimmed hat, and cautiously adjusted the baby against his chest.

"Sylvia, this is my husband," Carrie told her. "Melvin, Sylvia Hostetler has been a huge help to me."

He nodded at her. "Thank you for looking after my wife."

"You two were made to be parents," Sylvia said.

Melvin stiffened. "That blessing is in God's hands."

Sylvia glanced at the door, in the direction of the room in which Lydia was recovering. "If that girl doesn't come around soon, I hope God has a plan for Rachel. Do you know she actually told the floor nurse she was planning to leave town as soon as she could walk? Without the baby?"

Sooner or later they were going to believe Lydia meant what she said. "After going through an operation like that, getting to the toilet would be a major accomplishment," Carrie said mildly. "She's not going anywhere for a while."

When Sylvia came back with the bottle, Carrie settled into the chair feeling as though she had been doing this half her life. Melvin watched her so intently she might have blushed if ninety-nine percent of her attention hadn't been focused on Rachel—on her breathing, on whether she was warm enough, on the strength of her appetite.

"One thing I will say, you're more of a mother to her than her own mother is," Sylvia said softly. "There are things in this world I will never understand." She left quietly as though she didn't want to disturb them, the only sound the squeak of her crepe soles on the linoleum.

Melvin's gaze rested on little Rachel. "She is a good eater."

"I hope so. She needs to be five pounds before they'll let her leave. We have a couple of ounces left to go, don't we, *Schatzi*?"

"And will Lydia be ready to leave at the same time?"

"They wouldn't let them go separately." She looked up. "I would like to drive her home, Melvin. She'll need someone to help her organize things."

"And someone to help her face her father?" Carrie was silent, but Melvin read the truth in her face. "Has he come to visit?"

She shook her head.

"And she's determined to send the baby away for adoption?"

"She hasn't mentioned that, exactly. All she'll say is that she doesn't want her." Carrie lowered her voice, as if Rachel might hear the ugly truth and be hurt by it.

"We should adopt the little one, Carrie."

The blood seemed to come to a stop in her veins, then lurch into motion again at a gallop. "But I thought—you told me—what about the father and his bad—"

He winced, as though his own words pained him. "In those moments when I thought it was you who was hurt, God pulled the cover off a multitude of my sins. And chief among them was arrogance. Selfishness. And lack of love and compassion." His voice broke on the last syllable. "He made me see what kind of man I am. And I wondered how you could live with such a man."

"Because I love him, faults and all," she said softly. "The way he loves me, with all my shortcomings."

"If Lydia will agree, I want to be a father to this little one. I don't know what we will have to do to make that happen, but if you can go and talk to a doctor about making babies in plastic dishes, then I can go and talk to someone about adopting one."

"*Ach*, Melvin." Tears welled over her lashes and dripped

down her cheek. "You've made me so happy. We'll make Lydia see that this is the right thing to do."

"Seeing you a mother is the right thing." And he slid off his chair to kneel on the floor, and gently took the two of them into his arms.

* * *

It would have been in Carrie's transparent nature to rush down the hall and fling her plans over Lydia in her hospital bed like a crazy quilt. But Melvin held her back.

"Let her see what a good mother you are to the *Bobbel*," he said. "Show her that you would be a better choice than any *Englisch* woman. She may even bring it up herself."

So Carrie bit her tongue as Rachel gained weight, as Lydia's stitches made her itchy and cranky, as they filled out paperwork and finally secured her release.

A nurse's aide pushed Lydia through the main doors in a wheelchair, as Carrie followed with Rachel securely wrapped up against the April breeze. She had bought one of the *Englisch* car seats with a little bolster that ran around the inside of it, and Melvin had rigged a simple strap on the floor of the buggy to attach it to. Rachel was as snug as a chick in a nest—which didn't prevent Carrie glancing over her shoulder twenty times during the trip over to the Zook farm, just to make sure.

As they made the turn onto Camas Creek Road, Carrie glanced at her silent companion. "The women will have put the baby things in your room," she said. "Mary Lapp sent a message by Melvin last night that she'd finished collecting everything—layette, changing table, bassinet—and she and my sister Susan set it all up yesterday."

Lydia chewed her upper lip and said nothing.

"If you're worried about your father," Carrie said gently, "Mary said he was fine about all the things coming in."

"He's not likely to argue with the bishop's wife. He's all about the letter of the law."

"He may have been disappointed in you, and maybe even angry, but once he sees Rachel, he will change his tune. You'll see."

Though Lydia hadn't changed anything since the night of the accident except her dress. She hadn't looked over her shoulder once, either. Rachel could be a pumpkin going to the farmer's market for all the interest she showed in her.

It was on the tip of Carrie's tongue to say, *Please let me adopt this little girl I already love so much*, when they turned down the Zook lane. It was a conversation that would take much longer than the hundred yards of time they had, so Carrie choked it back.

And then they drove into the yard.

Carrie's hands went slack on the reins, and Jimsy came to an obedient halt. Beside her, Lydia seemed to have turned to stone.

Then she dragged in a breath that sounded like a sob. "See? I told you. I knew this would happen."

In front of Jimsy's forefeet lay the bassinet, its mattress and cheery blanket tumbled in the dirt. Tiny baby clothes in pale blue and green and white were scattered across the gravel in front of the walk like so many leaves, and the changing table hung at a drunken angle off the bottom step of the porch, three of its legs digging into the weeds of what had once been a flower border.

"I don't think Daed likes Mary's choices." Lydia's voice

trembled, but whether it was from fear or tears or hysterical laughter, Carrie couldn't tell. Maybe it was all three.

Abe Zook appeared on the porch, wiping his hands on a rag. "And where do you think you're going?"

Lydia sat silently on the passenger side, all the color drained from her face.

"You can pick up all this nonsense and take it somewhere else. And I hope you have a place to sleep, because it won't be here."

With a sense of shock, Carrie realized that the splash of color that lay in the weeds beyond the changing table was not flowers. It was the baby quilt she and Amelia and Emma had made for Lydia—a watercolor nine-patch made of soft colors of flannel to keep her baby warm.

Carrie was not a feisty woman. She lost her temper about once every decade—and never with someone outside her family.

But their quilt, tossed aside as though it meant nothing! Just like little Rachel and Lydia—tossed out as though they meant less than the scraps that went to the hogs. Something snapped like a rubber band, right in the center of her chest.

She jumped out of the buggy and, fists clenched, marched up the steps until she was nose to nose with Abe Zook. Since he was a good six inches taller than she, it might have looked silly. But clean, howling rage made her tower over him in spirit, even if she didn't in body.

"How dare you!" she said in a voice that she could barely control. "How dare you treat your daughter this way—so cruel and so careless and so completely lacking in compassion!"

"She ain't my daughter." Abe took a step back as though he thought Carrie might take a swing at him.

"She grew up in your house and calls you *Daed*," she said, hissing like a furious goose. "And even if she isn't yours by blood, God's Word tells you to have mercy on the widows and orphans. You are a travesty of a man, Abe Zook." She flung out an arm, and he pulled in his chin in surprise. "Your granddaughter is in that buggy. She is five days old and deserves a home and all the love that's left in that dried-up walnut you call a heart!"

"Ain't my granddaughter, either," he pointed out. "None of my blood in that child. I got no obligation to her."

"You have an obligation to your wife," Carrie shouted. "For her sake a real man of God would take these two in, bring in that furniture and those clothes, and do his level best to bring her up in God's family, even if you don't believe she's a part of your natural family!"

"Now, you listen, Carrie Miller." He made up the ground he'd lost in the face of her rage. "You got no call to talk that way to me. However you think I treat them two, you can't say a thing about my service to this church. You don't know nothing about what I've had to put up with for sixteen years. So you take your self-righteous attitude off my porch and go mind your own business!"

Carrie didn't move. If he batted an eyelash, he'd hit her in the face with it, she was crowding him so closely. "Are you seriously telling me you won't give Lydia and Rachel a home? You're going to turn them out in the cold?"

"Give the girl a gold star. *Ja*, that's what I'm telling you. You take 'em home if you want to show some Christian compassion. I showed it for sixteen years, and this is all the thanks I get."

Carrie had a mouthful of things to say about his Christian compassion, but she gritted her teeth and held them back. "I hope that God gives you from His hand exactly what you've given to these two today." She backed off a step. "If you change your mind, they'll be staying with us."

"I won't change my mind. Don't forget your bassinet."

And with that, he went into the house and closed the door in her face.

Carrie snatched up the flannel baby quilt, all the little clothes, as many of Lydia's dresses and aprons as she could hold, and the bassinet, and bundled everything into the back of the buggy around Rachel's car seat.

The horse formerly known as Jamieson's Victory Dance had never come so close to racing again as he did on that trip home.

CHAPTER 25

When Mary Lapp found out what had happened to the baby things she and the other women had so lovingly gathered together, it was a very good thing that Abe Zook's eternal destination was in God's hands and not hers.

"She was fit to be tied," Melvin told them at dinner, after he and Joshua had brought in the furniture and set it up in the room where the quilt frame had been. "Aunt Mary is a force to be reckoned with when she's calm. She got so riled it was all I could do to keep her from marching over there and giving him a good sound spanking."

"Surely not." For Lydia's sake, and with the gravity of the situation, Carrie told herself she must not laugh. But oh, it was good to know that the bishop's wife was firmly on her side in this, at least. It was good to know that she was doing the right thing in the eyes of the community.

"That woman has brought up five girls with a firm hand," Joshua said, shoveling stew and potatoes into his mouth with the appetite of a single man. "Abe Zook would probably benefit from a good spanking."

Carrie glanced at Lydia. It was probably wicked of them to criticize her father in front of her, but she didn't seem to mind. In fact, she didn't seem to be listening at all, and she'd hardly touched her plate.

"Eat some stew, *Schatzi*," she urged her. "You need to get your strength back."

Obediently, the girl spooned stew into her mouth, but her actions were those of someone whose mind was far away. Those stitches weren't going to heal without some nutrition to work with, and once she'd eaten, maybe she could coax her upstairs to lie down and rest.

And then, while Carrie was feeding Rachel, she might speak of the hope that lay on her heart.

"How are you feeling, Lydia?" Joshua ventured when it seemed clear Lydia was not going to eat any more.

She focused on him as though he was a long way away. "All right. Sore. Itchy. Like a popped balloon. Anything else you'd like to know?"

He cradled his hands around his coffee cup. "There's that cranky female I've come to know. You must be feeling better."

"I almost died. It's going to take more than a plate of stew and some whoopie pies to come back from that."

"These are good whoopie pies." He took a second one and bit into it with relish. Her bad temper didn't faze him at all. "If anyone can come back, as you say, from what you've been through, it's you. Nothing keeps you down for long."

She pushed back from the table. "*Denki* for supper, Carrie." Politeness came with an effort. "And for everything you did today, including yelling at Daed."

"You yelled at Abe Zook?" Joshua gawked at her. "*You?*"

Carrie ignored him, taking heart at the way Melvin was hiding his smile behind his coffee cup. "I'll help you upstairs."

Lydia, who had probably taken for granted the ability to

run up a staircase two at a time, moved from one step to the next as slowly as a *Grossmammi*. Carrie managed to help her undress and put her nightie on moments before Rachel woke for her feeding. With a sense of relief, she fetched the bottle of formula she had ready in warm water on the stove, and settled into her own "mommy chair"—the rocker that had been a wedding present from Susan and her husband. With a couple of quilts tossed over the seat and back, it was as comfortable as the one in the hospital—and no one would be coming in to take the baby away.

No one but her mother.

Carrie pushed the thought away and reminded herself she must only speak when the moment was right.

Lydia hadn't gone to bed, as she'd expected. Instead, she shuffled across the hall and leaned on the doorjamb. "You hold her so..." Her voice trailed away. She had to be too tired for speech. This couldn't be the moment. Carrie should bring this up another time, when she was stronger.

But there was that unfinished sentence. "So...?" she prompted softly.

"So...like you love her."

Rachel sucked like she meant business. Such a strong little thing, determined to get ahead in life after her rough beginning. "I do love her. I think I've never loved anything so much."

A smile flickered on Lydia's mouth. "Even Melvin?"

"It's a different kind of love. I love him, and I love my family, and I love Amelia and Emma—all in different ways. And with Rachel, it's different still." She took a breath, more to calm her quickening heartbeat than anything. "If you mean to go through with your plans to leave, I would—I hope—" She swallowed. "I would like to love her tomorrow, too, and the day after that, and all the days of her life. If you do not want to be her mother, *Schatzi*, please let me be."

It was not eloquent. It was not even coherent. But it was the best she could do.

Silence filled the lamplit space between them, the only sound Rachel's fierce attack on the bottle.

"I think you really mean it."

"I do mean it. With all my heart." And every cell in her body—every thought in her mind. But she could not say that. She didn't want to frighten Lydia away by being too effusive.

"I didn't want her to grow up Amish."

"I know, and I can see why." Heaven forbid she should criticize Abe's service to God any more than she already had. "I'm sorry. I'm judging your father, when goodness knows he could judge me for plenty."

Lydia snorted.

"But I think that the home Melvin and I could offer her would not be like the home you grew up in. She would be surrounded by love, and when the time came, she would be free to choose the life she wanted—whatever that might be."

"I don't want to see her, you know. She could grow up calling you or anyone else *Mamm* and I wouldn't mind."

She could. Was that permission? Carrie hardly dared to hope—she tamped down the leap of her heart and considered what she'd said instead. How could she say such things? How could anyone not want to see this beautiful child, to watch her grow, to love her the way she deserved to be loved?

"If you say so," she whispered. "Does that mean...?"

"It means I'll think about it. I need to get some things set up—a place to live, a job. If I decide to go through an *Englisch* adoption agency, I'll let you know. But in the meantime, she can stay here?" She moved slowly into the room across the narrow hall and sat on the bed. She took deep breaths as though all those sentences had exhausted her.

Look after the baby as though she were her mother for a couple of weeks? Knowing at the end of it Rachel might be taken away anyhow? How much pain was she going to be required to bear?

Two weeks of motherhood is better than none. And Rachel will know it. She will know that someone—two someones—in this wide world loved her as their own.

"*Ja,*" Carrie said. "She can stay here with us for as long as you need."

She put the bottle aside and lay Rachel against her shoulder. The baby knew her, knew her smell, knew the soft spot that she fit in as naturally as though it had been made for her. She could not look at Lydia, who didn't seem to realize how much pain she could inflict by her casual words—how the course of her baby's life depended on how she felt on the whim of a moment.

By the time Carrie had mastered her emotions and put Rachel down on the flannel quilt, Lydia had pulled the covers over herself, curled into a ball, and fallen asleep.

That was *gut.* Because there were times when a woman had to put a watch on her tongue, or lose everything she valued just for the satisfaction of saying what she really thought out loud.

* * *

The coffin, Boyd Steiner told Melvin later, was the smallest he had ever made. It was also the most beautiful, with perfect joints and a glossy finish.

Even as they'd driven to the cemetery, Carrie wondered whether the *Gmee* would turn out in memory of a life that had barely begun before being snuffed out. Would they shake their heads, muttering about illegitimacy and sin, and spare a thought for Abe Zook as they declined to come?

As soon as they turned the corner onto Edgeware Road, Carrie had her answer. A long line of buggies moved slowly into the cemetery, and more people, clad in Sunday black even though it was Monday, were walking toward it on the wayside. The river of mourners puddled around the tiny grave site, where a stone paid for by the *Gmee* would rest.

"*Baby Zook*," it would say. And the dates of birth and death would be the same.

Carrie's throat closed up. It had been difficult enough to get a name out of Lydia for Rachel. She had never even acknowledged the death of her little boy, much less spared a moment to name him. In her own mind, Carrie thought of him as Joshua. Though it was tradition to name a child after its grandmother or grandfather, Carrie couldn't do it. The little boy would never, ever carry the name Abe, even in the depths of her imagination. And Joshua Steiner, say what you would about his past, at least had cared enough about Lydia and the children to offer his name to them.

It wasn't his fault the offer had been soundly rejected—twice.

For all the crowd, the service was fairly short, though Bishop Daniel didn't miss the opportunity to give a homily on the wages of sin. But at least he also spoke of the beauty of innocence, and how this tiny soul would be cradled in the hand of God for eternity, sure in His love.

Carrie was the only one who wept. Even Amelia and

Emma, who stood together at her left shoulder as solid as a bulwark, were dry-eyed, though Amelia came pretty close to it when she saw the tear roll down Carrie's cheek.

She must not go to pieces. A wave of heat rolled up from her chest as the bishop announced a hymn, and she swallowed. The black dots flickered at the edge of her field of vision. Oh no. *Deep breaths.* She couldn't faint—she was holding Rachel, all bundled up against the unpredictable April weather. She would sooner die than put her in any danger.

Melvin heard the change in her breathing and looked down, his brown eyes worried. *Are you all right?*

More dots. Oh dear.

She had just enough time to thrust the baby into Melvin's arms before the black dots all rushed together and she slumped to the ground.

Carrie heard the commotion—knew Amelia's voice as she called for her mother, the *Dokterfraa.* She could tell when Ruth Lehman bustled up and took her wrist in one hand to check her pulse, could feel her hands on her cheek. But not for the world could she open her eyes or speak to let them know she was all right.

It wasn't until someone—ah, Erica Steiner, who carried baby wipes in her pockets, she must remember to do the same—moistened her face that she took a deep breath and found she could move. "I'm all right. Really."

"Can you sit up?" Ruth asked. "Goodness, child, it was lucky you gave that baby to Melvin. It could have rolled right into the grave."

Carrie had been standing close to the lip of the tiny hole, in the place where the baby's family would have been. With no Lydia and no Abe Zook to glower at her, Carrie had felt no compunction about stepping up so that Rachel could say farewell to her twin.

"I'm fine." She struggled to her feet. What a strange sensation. She lowered her voice for Ruth alone. "This isn't the first time. Maybe I should see you about a cure for it."

"Nothing good red meat and dark-green vegetables won't cure," Ruth whispered back. "We'll talk later. The bishop is going to give the blessing, if you're all right."

She felt almost normal—well enough, in fact, to go to the tea afterward at the Lapp farm, though Melvin wouldn't let her stay long.

"Are we meeting tomorrow?" Emma asked her at the door, holding Rachel as Carrie put on her coat.

"I sure hope so." Amelia came to join them, glancing over her shoulder at Eli. "My *gut Mann* is taking me to pick up the boys at school, and then we're going to Mamm and Daed's for supper, otherwise I would visit longer." She hugged Carrie in apology, then bent to kiss Rachel. "You little darling, so good as we said good-bye to your tiny *Bruder*. Not a cry did you make."

"Not even when I nearly dropped her," Carrie said ruefully. "Thank goodness you were all with me. And *ja*, we will certainly meet tomorrow. Amelia, I think it's your turn."

"Though with Zachary and Rachel coming with us, we may not get much done but talking," Emma said as the little boy staggered out of his aunt's arms and wrapped himself around Emma's leg.

"Designing a quilt isn't much more than talking," Amelia told her. "I think we should do another baby quilt. The one we made for Rachel was fun."

"For whom?" Emma raised an eyebrow at her. "Don't go getting ideas, you."

"It never hurts to have a baby quilt in reserve for anyone who might need it."

Emma snorted, and Carrie exchanged a smile with Amelia behind Rachel's tiny head. Emma knew perfectly well that the two of them were watching her like a pair of hawks for the first signs of being in a family way. And she never missed an opportunity to laugh at them for it.

Emma had waited twelve years for Grant. Carrie hoped devoutly that she would not need to wait that long for his baby.

When they got home, Carrie took a squirming Rachel into the house for her feeding while Melvin looked after the horse.

"Lydia, we're back," she called as she went into the kitchen and put a pot of water on to heat. "The service was so *uffrichdich*, so fitting for—" She stopped. "Lydia?" The house had that empty feeling—one that Carrie knew all too well. Had she gone for a walk?

"She'll be back soon," she told Rachel as she heated the bottle. The poor girl would have a hard time walking much farther than the mailbox. She was healing, and a young woman healed fast, but still…

Carrying Rachel and the bottle, she headed upstairs to the rocker. It wasn't until she'd finished feeding and burping the baby and had laid her on the changing table that she saw the piece of paper.

Brown paper, cut from a grocery bag, covered in loopy, girlish handwriting.

Dear Carrie and Melvin,
   By the time you read this, I'll be on a bus for Philadelphia. Or maybe Pittsburgh. Or maybe Columbia,

Missouri. I don't know and I don't care, as long as I get away from here.

Don't worry about me. I had some money saved up that I didn't tell the bishop or my dad about, or they would have made me put it all toward the hospital bill. But I'll need it more than those doctors do, so I'm not going to feel bad about that. I have enough to feel bad about.

I'm leaving Rachel with you, like we said. I just can't face finding an *Englisch* family to adopt her right now, so I'm glad you'll take her. Maybe I'll be back to take care of that next week—or maybe I'll get established somewhere and do it then. I don't know.

I just don't have the feelings that a real mother should have, whatever those are. But you do, Carrie. I hope you don't regret it.

I'll try and write. But it might not be for a while. Thank you for everything.

Lydia

CHAPTER 26

Emma's arms went slack around Zachary as Carrie finished telling her tale Tuesday afternoon. "I don't believe it."

"Read for yourself." Carrie pushed the brown paper across the table, and Emma reestablished her grip on the little boy as he reached for the chocolate chip cookie on her plate and she reached for the letter.

Emma scanned it, shook her head, and gave it to Amelia. "There must be something deeply wrong with that girl. How can a person simply walk away from her child?"

"Or take the bus, as the case may be." Amelia folded up the letter and tucked it under the sugar bowl. "In a strange way, I understand. How can a girl who has grown up without love know how to love a child of her own? Abe Zook makes no bones about how much of a nuisance he thinks she is. So when Lydia treats her little girl like a piece of luggage, to be left wherever it's convenient, I can't be all that surprised. Poor thing."

It wasn't clear whether she meant Lydia or the baby. Maybe it was both.

They'd given up any pretense of designing a quilt, though Carrie had brought some scratch paper and a pencil in her own bag in case they got around to it. Today there were much more urgent topics to deal with.

"What are you going to do?" Amelia asked.

"I'm going to love this little *Bobbel* just as hard as I can for however long Lydia lets me keep her." In a whirlwind of uncertainty, that was the one thing Carrie knew for sure.

"But what if that turns out to be years?" Emma asked.

"It would be worse if it were weeks," Carrie told her. "Can you see that girl changing diapers and doing three-o'clock feedings in some youth hostel in Philadelphia?"

"I can't see her changing diapers at all," Emma said frankly. "Has she really not even touched her own daughter?"

"Not once. It's been me, right from the beginning. But she says herself she doesn't have those feelings."

"But the child of her own body!" Amelia burst out. "Even if you hated your baby's father or the circumstances of your life, imagine not loving someone who is part of you."

"How could you not love Rachel just for her very own self?" Carrie nuzzled the baby's neck. She smelled of a fresh bath and baby powder, and Carrie was like to cry from the simple delight of it. "I worry about Lydia. But if it's the Lord's will that she finds happiness in Columbus or Pittsburgh or even California, then I'll accept it gladly and never look back."

"And if it's not?" Emma asked quietly. "If she comes back in two weeks with an *Englisch* family all arranged, and wants to take Rachel away?"

Emma's gift with words had taken Carrie's deepest fear and expressed it with dreadful simplicity. "Then I'll do my best to talk her out of it. And if that fails, then I suppose *Uffgeva* will become something I do, not something I hear about on a Sunday."

"You'll never be able to do it." Amelia shook her head. "I see you with this baby and she is your own. But from a practical standpoint, I think you should prepare. The church sees nothing wrong in you becoming Rachel's mother. But the *Englisch* doctors will have something to say about it when you take her in for her checkups."

Carrie nodded. "I know. She left everything, you know. The birth certificate, the hospital paperwork, the death certificate for little Joshua. Melvin says we are going to apply to be foster parents, and we'll see where that takes us. The *Englisch* have many more rules about these things than we Amish do. All I care about is loving her." And she cuddled Rachel close.

"In the end, that's the important thing." Amelia touched the baby's cheek.

Emma looked from one to the other before she set Zachary down on the floor and took some blocks out of her carry bag to give to him. "We're not getting any sketches done today, are we?"

Carrie had to smile. "*Nei*, I suppose not." She handed Rachel to Amelia, who settled back in the chair, rubbing Rachel's back like the old hand she was. "But I see Amelia has some of her famous beet pickles out on the counter and I'm dying to try them. Did you make them with that new recipe?"

"I did, but if you want some, you'll have to open them yourself. I am most definitely busy and I must not be interrupted."

Carrie got a butter knife from the drawer while Emma chose a jar of pickles. "I don't know how these can be better than your usual ones. I'm almost afraid to try them."

"I wasn't aiming for better. I was aiming for different."

With Emma hovering close by, Carrie popped the lid off

the glass jar of fuchsia-colored beets. The smell of vinegar and sugar and garlic wafted up, and the contents of her stomach did a somersault.

Emma clapped a hand to her mouth.

Carrie broke into a sweat and set the jar down with a clank.

Emma made a sound behind her hand, and both of them dashed to the double sink and were violently sick, one into each side.

"Carrie! Emma!" Baby on her shoulder, Amelia pushed her chair back with such force that it tipped over, frightening Zachary, who burst into a roar.

Startled at the sudden movement, Rachel did the same.

Carrie and Emma wiped their mouths with two ends of the same towel and exchanged one astonished look before seeing to the crying children.

Amelia eyed the two of them. "Either my beet pickles are a terrible failure or something is going on with you two."

Emma's face was still a little green around the edges, and the towel was still in her hand. "Do you think—is it possible? Carrie? And me? At the same time?"

Carrie sat as though frozen in the kitchen chair. The roaring flame of hope in her chest fought with the cold rush of common sense, of hopes that had been denied before, of dread that this flame would be doused the cruel way it had been six years ago.

It could not be. She would have known. After all this time, she knew the signs the way a woman knew the behavior of her own hair. And except for that once, she had not experienced them.

"No," she whispered. "It can't be. I mean—maybe for Emma, but not for me."

"Those fainting spells of yours," Emma said in the tones of someone who had just had a revelation. "It takes some women that way. My sister Karen fainted with Barbara— it frightened poor John to death until the doctor told them what was causing it."

"It can't be true," Carrie whispered. "Not after all this time. Not after Rachel." She looked down at the little bundle in her arms.

Rachel hiccupped, the tears drying on her cheeks. She gazed up at Carrie. And for the first time, she smiled, her soft cheeks bunching up and a dimple denting the center of the right one.

Rachel had a dimple.

Carrie's own eyes filled with tears at the little gift. "Look. She's smiling."

Amelia glanced at Emma. "I won't tell her it's probably gas if you don't."

"It's not gas," Emma said stoutly. "She is as happy at this news as we are. No matter what, Rachel will stay in this family to welcome her little brother or sister. We'll see to it."

"Oh Emma." The tears were running down Carrie's face now. "Will we really have children together?"

"I think we will. Oh girls, I can't wait another moment. I have to go over to Mandy and Kelvin's house and tell Grant. He's finishing the last of the floors there today."

"I can't believe it," Amelia said, wiping tears off her own cheeks with the palms of her hands. "Babies. Blessings. Oh, God has been so good to us."

And suddenly the floodgates burst open inside Carrie, and hope and love poured through in a rush. Yes, there might yet be danger ahead. Yes, Rachel's future was uncertain. But in God's hands there was always hope, and joy, and the certainty that He meant good for them in the end.

"It's just as we thought when we started your quilt," she said to Emma, who had put on her away bonnet back to front while Zachary clung to her leg chanting, "Daed? See Daed?"

"We thought the pattern was about hope in the Cross. But it's more than that, isn't it? It's the little hopes we have day by day that make life so sweet. The little joys. Like sharing this gift with you."

Emma was not normally a demonstrative woman, but her face crumpled and she pulled off her bonnet altogether as she gathered Carrie and Rachel into a hug. And then Amelia put her arms around both of them and Carrie knew the truth.

They had not just been making quilts for all these months. They had been setting the stitches in a friendship—a sisterhood—that would last all the days of their lives. Come what may, they could face it together, as long as the *gut Gott* held them in their hands.

And for Carrie, with a heart full of hope, that was a fair prospect indeed.

EPILOGUE

One year later

The manila envelope lay on the kitchen table with its official-looking printed label from the family-law attorney they'd been referred to by Dr. Shadle, the chiropractor. The attorney had represented folk from the church numerous times in their dealings with the *Englisch*, and even though he frightened Carrie with his fast words and air of brusque authority, there was no denying he got things done.

Carrie expected Melvin in for supper at any second, since he'd driven in fifteen minutes ago, but she could hardly keep her mind on whipping up biscuits when that envelope lay behind her like something alive.

It was alive, in a way. Its contents would tell her which way their lives were going to go. The *gut Gott* had already made up His infinite mind about this, of course, but Carrie wouldn't know what His plans were until they opened it up.

When she heard boots on the porch, she hurried to drop the last of the biscuits on the baking sheet, and met him at the door. "It came," she told him, trying to keep the urgency out of her voice and failing utterly. "I haven't opened it. I wanted to do it together, but Priscilla and Amelia and Emma and their families will be here any minute."

"Let me kiss my *Maedel* and then we'll find out what it says."

She dimpled at him. "This *Maedel* first."

He kissed her soundly and then crossed the kitchen to Rachel, who would celebrate her very first birthday in eight more days. He lifted her out of her high chair and blew kisses into her neck, which made her laugh in delight—a sound that never failed to clutch at Carrie's heart.

"Where is *mein Bobbel*?" he asked when he slid the little girl back into her seat and given her back the teething biscuit she had been gnawing on for ten minutes.

"Asleep. You're not to wake him—it took me half the afternoon to get him down."

"He's a bundle of energy, that one. We did well to name him David—he's just like my *Daed* was. Always busy, always interested in what was going on around him."

"And just like your *Daed* probably did for you—you can take him for the first feeding tonight."

She wrinkled her nose at him and he kissed it. "I won't wake him. But it's only been three months. I just have to look in on him, my little miracle son."

Carrie was still smiling when he came back into the kitchen. She'd actually seen Melvin in the night, hovering over the bassinet like a protective angel—one who couldn't quite believe this tiny soul had been given into his charge so soon after the blessing of the first.

He came back into the kitchen on soft feet. "Now let us see what this letter will tell us."

One thing about Melvin—he wasn't the kind to carefully

unwrap a gift, saving the paper for another occasion and rolling up the ribbon. He was a ripper. He tore open the envelope with a satisfying sound and angled the sheet of paper it contained toward her so they both could read it.

Dear Carrie and Melvin,

This office is in receipt today of the signed Consent to Termination of Parental Rights from Lydia Zook, who is currently residing in Columbus, Missouri. With this surrender of her parental rights, we have accomplished the next step in making Rachel Zook a permanent member of your family.

We are also in receipt of the second report from Child Welfare Services on your foster parenting. You scored high in all categories, so this will look good on your adoption application. With the termination form in hand, we can now go ahead. We work with a reputable adoption agency, so I will contact them on your behalf and get the process started. Be prepared for a home study, more paperwork, and an appearance in family court. You've already been through this for the foster-home designation, but we have to do it again for adoption.

In the end, the results will be worth it, I'm sure you'll agree.

I hope you folks have a merry Christmas, and I look forward to seeing you in the New Year.

Best regards,
Patrick Weimar
Weimar, Benson & Rhodes

It took a moment for Carrie to take it in.

"She signed it. She actually signed the form giving up all her legal rights as Rachel's mother." Even though she had long ago given up wondering what piece was missing from Lydia's heart that she could do such a thing, Carrie still had difficulty believing that a piece of paper could make it so.

The *Englisch* had many, many pieces of paper to put into motion something as simple as taking a baby into your home. First with the foster-care people, then with the attorney, then with the county...Carrie had lost track of all the papers. But the end was in sight. Soon Rachel would belong to them irrevocably, and no one—not even Lydia—could tear her away.

The rattle of buggy wheels outside told them the first of their guests was arriving. Melvin put the drape aside and looked out. "It's the Bontragers. I'm glad they're going to stay tonight—Moses Yoder says his bones say the first snow will fall."

"And Moses Yoder's bones always seem to be right."

Melvin pulled on his rubber boots and coat and went out to look after the horse, while Priscilla and her brood of eight flooded into the kitchen. And then Amelia and Eli arrived, with Emma and Grant on their heels, and suddenly the entire house was full of children and laughter.

The eldest Bontrager girl swooped in on her cousin Rachel and carried her off, biscuit and all, to play in the sitting room, while Katie and Sarah Weaver made themselves comfortable on Rachel's play blanket, holding baby Zeph as carefully as though he were made of spun glass.

Carrie dropped a kiss on the top of his head. "When he falls asleep, you can put him in with David. Our little twins can keep each other company."

She turned to Amelia and Emma and then extended a hand to Priscilla to draw her into their circle. "You must hear this, too. The letter came today. Lydia signed the paper, and now there is nothing to stop us going ahead with the adoption."

Amelia hugged her while Emma beamed. Tears welled in Priscilla's eyes, and Carrie's breath caught. Had the news hurt her?

Since Lydia's departure that cold day last year, Carrie and Priscilla had become close. Priscilla was Rachel's great-aunt, after all, and her children were the baby's cousins. Carrie would no more separate Rachel from this sweet-faced woman than fly away to Missouri.

"Priscilla, *Liewi*, what is it?" She hardly dared ask. What if she and her husband had changed their minds and wanted to adopt Rachel after all?

"I'm just so happy," Priscilla whispered. "Rachel is one step closer to being where she belongs—in a house filled with love, and two families to make sure she knows it. Forgive me. I don't mean to cry."

"Happy tears are the best ones," Emma told her, folding her into a hug.

"I've cried enough of the other kind to last me a lifetime," Carrie said. "I welcome happy ones."

"I saw a quilt pattern the other day called Baby's Tears," Amelia said, apropos of nothing. "Priscilla, maybe you'd like to join us on Tuesday afternoons? It's time to make another baby quilt."

Carrie stared at her. "You're—are you—*are you?*"

"*Ja*, I am. Eli and I are expecting a little blessing in July."

When the men came in, they found all four of them in a laughing, crying knot in the middle of the kitchen.

Melvin looked at Eli. "Women. What do you suppose is going on?"

"I don't know," Eli said, gazing at his wife as though she were the sun in his summer sky. "But I thank our Father in heaven for them."

Little Katie ran up to Grant and wrapped her arms around his waist. "Daed, *Aendi* Amelia says they're going to make a quilt called Baby's Tears. Doesn't that sound funny?"

Grant smiled his quiet smile at Eli Fischer. "I think that depends on who's doing the crying. Maybe Mamm will teach you how to make one, too."

As her friends rolled up their sleeves and got to work putting out the food they had brought, Carrie's eyes met Melvin's.

There would be more children, and more quilts, and more blessings than one woman's heart could hold.

It would take a lifetime to thank the *gut Gott* for them all.

GLOSSARY

Spelling and definitions from Eugene S. Stine, *Pennsylvania German Dictionary* (Birdboro, PA: Pennsylvania German Society, 1996).

Abstellung: review of the rules of the *Ordnung*
Ausbund: the Amish hymnal
Bann: ban, state of being shunned
Batzich: proud
Bischt du im e Familye weg?: Are you in a family way?
Bobbel, Bobblin: baby, babies
Bruder: brother
Buhnesupp: bean soup
Daadi: Granddad
Daadi Haus: grandfather house
Daed: Dad, Father
Deitch: Pennsylvania Dutch language
Denki, denkes: thank you; thanks
Docher: daughter
Dokterfraa: lit. "doctor woman," or home herbalist
Druwwel: trouble
Eck: corner; tables where the bridal party sits

Es wunnert mich: Lit. "It wonders me," or "It makes me wonder."

Flitterwoch: honeymoon visits

Fraa: wife, married woman

Gelassenheit: spirit of humility, of not trying to get ahead of others

Gibts mir: Give it to me.

Gmee: congregation, community

Gott: God

Grossdaadi: Grandfather

Grossmammi: Grandmother

Guder Mariye: Good morning

Guder Owed: Good evening

gut: good

Gut Nacht: Good night

Hatge: good-bye

Haus: house

Hinkel: hens

Hoch Deutsch: high German

Ischt mir: It's me.

ja: yes

Kaffi: coffee

Kapp: woman's prayer covering

Kinner: children

Kumm mit: Come along (lit. come with)

Liebschdi: darling

Lied: song, hymn

Liewi: dear, darling

Maedel: girl

Mamm: Mom, Mother

Mammi: Grandma

Maud: maid

Meinding, die: shunning, the

Meine Freind: my friends

Nei, nix: no

Newesitzern: attendants (lit. "side sitters")

Ordnung: discipline, order

Rumspringe: running around

Schatzi: little treasure

Schnitz: dried fruit; schnitz pie is made of dried apple slices

Uffgeva: giving up (of the will, to another or to God)

uffrichdich: sincere

"...und glaust daß es vom Herren ist und durch dein glauben und gebet so weid gekommen bist?" And do you believe that this is from the Lord and that you have come to be here by your faith and prayers? —Amish wedding vows

vergesslich: forgetful

"Wohlauf, Wohlauf, bu Gottes G'mein": Come, Come, Church of God (a hymn about the church as the bride of Christ)

wunderbaar: wonderful

Youngie: young people

CROSSES AND LOSSES QUILT INSTRUCTIONS

(Part 3 of 3)

In the Amish Quilt trilogy, the characters make a quilt they call "Sunrise Over Green Fields," signifying the hope of the Cross rising over our lives and work. I hope you'll join me in making it as well, so I've divided the instructions into three parts to go with the three books in the series.

In *The Wounded Heart*, we began by piecing the quilt blocks. In *The Hidden Life*, we assembled the blocks together with background blocks and triangles, then sewed the borders. (You can find these instructions on my website, www.adinasenft.com, and also on the FaithWords website, www.FaithWords.com.) Now, in *The Tempted Soul*, we'll choose quilting patterns, mark them on the fabric, and quilt. Lastly we'll bind the edges, and our quilts will be finished! If you're new to quilting, you'll want to read through all of the instructions before you get started.

Batting

Batting comes in a number of different weights, so choose one that will give you warmth without being so thick that you can't get a needle through it. Cut a piece of quilt batting at least 3 inches wider on each side than your pieced top.

Backing

Cut a piece of backing fabric at least 3 inches wider on each side than the dimensions of your quilt top. You may need to stitch a couple of widths together, or you can do as the women in the story did and create a simple piecing design for the backing out of leftover fabric. In any case, remember that the quilting designs will show on the back, so you want any piecing you do there to complement the quilting pattern.

Using safety pins or T-pins, pin together all thicknesses of the piecing, batting, and backing, making sure that right sides of your piecing and backing face out. Start in the middle and pin toward the borders in sections, making sure there are no folds or wrinkles in any of the layers. Some quilters choose to baste the thicknesses together, using long, fast stitches. Use the method most comfortable for you.

Planning Your Quilt Pattern

There are several methods you can use for your quilt pattern.

You may simply want to "stitch in the ditch" (meaning laying your quilting stitches in the seams of the piecing) and make a grid of diamonds or squares to follow the lines in the piecing.

Amelia, Emma, and Carrie chose to make this stitched grid over the pieced blocks, quilt flower patterns using templates in the plain blocks, and quilt a feathered border on the wide border pieces, also using the plastic templates. You can order beautiful "feather" and arabesque-curve templates online, or buy them in a quilting store.

Do what satisfies your creativity the most. Some quilters use a long-arm quilting machine and simply freestyle the entire quilt in a stippled pattern. If you don't own one of these, some quilting stores will let you rent time on theirs. There are many ways to quilt—as long as it results in your top, batting, and backing being permanently and attractively stitched together.

Marking

In most quilt or fabric stores, you will find plastic templates with punched-out quilt designs. Choose patterns that fit the dimensions of your blocks.

Lay the template on the pieced top where you want to quilt the design and, using dressmaker's chalk or the marking pencils made for quilters (never a lead pencil—it won't wash out), mark your designs using firm, quick strokes. They will brush off or wash out afterward.

Quilting

You can choose to quilt by machine or by hand. If you use a machine, you'll need to roll the quilt up so that you can work in one small area at a time. A "walking foot," or a special presser-foot attachment that allows the feed dogs to feed the quilt top at the same time as the bottom, is a good addition to your sewing box.

If you stitch by hand, thread a needle and, instead of doing one stitch at a time along your pattern lines, rock the needle in and out of the layers evenly so that the fabric bunches up on it. This is called "loading the needle." Then pull the thread through. An accomplished quilter can load ten stitches to the inch. The most I ever did was seven, so don't feel bad if you can't manage that many. Your goal is close, even stitches, no matter how many go on the needle at a time.

Or, you can do a combination. Stitch by machine along the long diagonal rows, which not only cuts down the time but also anchors your three layers so they won't travel while you hand-quilt your patterns.

Binding and Finishing

Binding is the last step in making your quilt. There are two different methods you can use. Amish women bring their backing fabric up and over the other two layers, fold over the raw edge, and enclose the raw edges of the batting and pieced top in a "self" binding. So that's what we'll do.

Alternatively, you can use strips of a fabric that contrasts with or is complementary to the binding in order to add a colorful finish to your quilt. I like to double the fabric to make a good, tough edge that will not wear through easily with use.

Self Binding

For this method, you will have already left extra backing fabric around the quilt. The following measurements will create a 1-inch binding:

1. Trim the backing fabric so it extends 2 inches beyond the edge of the quilt on all four sides to create the binding fabric.

2. Trim the batting so it is the same dimension as the quilt top, being careful not to cut the backing fabric.

3. Fold the raw edge of the binding inward 1/2 inch.

4. Press the doubled edge of the binding fabric.

5. Fold the binding inward again so that the doubled edge meets the raw edge of the quilt top and batting.

6. Fold the binding inward a third time, over the raw edges of the quilt, on top of the pieced top of the quilt.

7. Pin the binding to the quilt to hold it in place on all four sides.

8. Sew through the binding and all layers of the quilt ¼ inch from the inner edge of the binding (the edge that is on top of the pieced layer of your quilt).

9. Finally, sew the edge of binding that overlaps at the corners down.

Enjoy your new quilt!

READING GROUP GUIDE

1. In the Amish community, children are viewed as a blessing from God, to be given in God's time. At the same time, there is some social pressure on a woman to have children. Do you see these as mutually exclusive? Does Carrie?

2. Have you ever been in a situation where you were under social pressure to conform to expectations?

3. What were these expectations like? What did you do?

4. Carrie does everything she can to be a mother, including skirting along the edges of the *Ordnung*. Do you feel she was right or wrong to push the boundaries?

5. What might you have done the same or differently as Carrie?

6. Do you think the Bontragers should have taken baby Rachel in, since they were her blood family?

7. What do you think makes a family—is it the blood relationship or something else?

8. What do you think caused Lydia Zook to refuse the role of motherhood?

9. Do you think Lydia was right or wrong to give up her baby?

10. As Carrie, Amelia, and Emma look to the future, what do you see for them?